COURTING MISS ADELAIDE

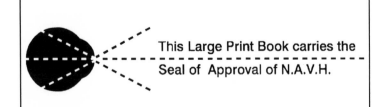

This Large Print Book carries the
Seal of Approval of N.A.V.H.

COURTING MISS ADELAIDE

JANET DEAN

THORNDIKE PRESS

A part of Gale, Cengage Learning

GALE
CENGAGE Learning

Detroit • New York • San Francisco • New Haven, Conn • Waterville, Maine • London

GALE
CENGAGE Learning™

Copyright © 2008 by Janet Dean.
Thorndike Press, a part of Gale, Cengage Learning.

Thorndike Press® Large Print Christian Historical Fiction.
The text of this Large Print edition is unabridged.
Other aspects of the book may vary from the original edition.
Set in 16 pt. Plantin.
Printed on permanent paper.

LIBRARY OF CONGRESS CATALOGING-IN-PUBLICATION DATA

Dean, Janet.
    Courting Miss Adelaide / by Janet Dean.
      p. cm. — (Thorndike Press large print Christian historical fiction)
    ISBN-13: 978-1-4104-1426-7 (hardcover : alk. paper)
    ISBN-10: 1-4104-1426-4 (hardcover : alk. paper)
    1. Single women—Fiction. 2. Journalists—Fiction. 3. Orphans—Fiction. 4. Orphan trains—Fiction. 5. Noblesville (Ind.)—Fiction. 6. Large type books. I. Title.
PS3604.E1516C68 2009
813'.6—dc22   2008054029

Published in 2009 by arrangement with Harlequin Books S.A.

Printed in Mexico
2 3 4 5 6 7 13 12 11 10 09

Bear with each other and forgive
whatever grievances you may have
against one another. Forgive as the Lord
forgave you.

— *Colossians* 3:13

To my critique partner, Shirley Jump —
her slashing red pen,
savvy advice and endless
support helped me
become the writer I am today.
To David Highway, President of the
Hamilton County Historical Society —
a big thanks for his assistance with my
research. To my late parents, who never
stopped believing I'd attain my dream.
To my husband —
a good man, a wonderful
father and the love of my life.

PROLOGUE

From the March 1, 1897, edition of The Noblesville Ledger:

WANTED: HOMES FOR CHILDREN

NOBLESVILLE — A company of homeless children from the East will arrive in Noblesville, Indiana, on Saturday, April 13. These boys and girls of various ages have been thrown friendless upon the world. The citizens of Noblesville are asked to assist the agents of the Children's Aid Society in finding good homes for the children.

Persons requesting these children must first agree to treat the children as members of their family, promising to feed, clothe, send them to school and church and Sunday School until they reach the age of seventeen.

Applications must be made to and approved by the local committee. Interviews will be held on Saturday, March 30, in Judge Willowby's chambers at the Noblesville County courthouse. The following well-respected citizens have agreed to sit on the local committee: C. Graves, J. Sparks, T. Paul and M. Wylie.

Distribution will be made at the Ward schoolhouse on April 13 at 10:30 a.m.

CHAPTER ONE

Noblesville, Indiana, spring of 1897

Adelaide Crum stepped to the open door and peered into the judge's chambers. Her heart hammered beneath her corset. Now that the moment she'd waited for had arrived, her courage faltered. She considered turning tail and scurrying home. But then she remembered the quiet, the emptiness of those rooms. She closed her eyes and sent up a simple prayer. *I don't ask often, Lord, but I'm asking today. Please, let them say yes.*

Squaring her shoulders, she crossed the room, then sat on one of the two chairs and faced the four men who held her future in their hands. To fill the vacant chair with something, she laid her purse on the seat, a seat that mocked her singleness.

Mr. Wylie, a large man who owned a farm north of town, folded his sausagelike fingers on the table. "I've dropped my wife off in front of your shop more times than I can

11

count, Miss Crum." He chuckled. "Usually costs me, too."

She smiled a thank-you for his business.

Beside the farmer sat Mr. Sparks, the town banker. The little tufts of hair fringing his bald head reminded Adelaide of a horned owl. "Perhaps you'd better tell us why you've come, Miss Crum. Do you have recommendations for this committee?"

"I've come for myself." Adelaide laid a calming hand on her midriff to offset the growing urge to deposit her breakfast on the table in front of her. "To ask for a child."

Mr. Paul's nostrils flared, giving him an air of disdain, not a cordial expression for an elder at her church and the town's Superintendent of Schools. "For *yourself*? You're a single woman, are you not?"

"Yes, but —"

"I hope you can appreciate how unfair it would be to place a child in your home, where, if something happened to you, the youngster would be homeless."

"I'm in excellent health, Mr. Paul." She'd take this opening to plead her case. "I have sufficient funds to meet a child's needs. *And* a skill to teach, enabling a girl to make her own way. When I pass on, I'd leave her my worldly assets."

She took a deep breath, pulling into her

lungs the overpowering scent of Mr. Paul's spicy cologne. "I'll see she's educated and brought up in the church. I've lived in Noblesville all my life. You remember seeing me in Sunday school, Mr. Paul. Mr. Sparks, I bank with you. Numerous people in town can vouch for my character." She'd rehearsed the words countless times and they tumbled out in a rush.

One man remained silent. Charles Graves. Her gaze darted to the new editor of *The Noblesville Ledger,* who sat at the far right of the table. Rumor had it he was single. Mr. Graves's generous mouth softened the square line of his jaw. Deep grooves marred his forehead, an indication, perhaps, that a newsman's life wasn't easy. And yet the cleft in the middle of his chin gave him a vulnerable air. Undeniably handsome, broad-shouldered and tall, he overshadowed the other men in the room.

He stared as if scanning the core of her, possibly looking for a flaw that would declare her unfit to rear a child. Their gazes locked and the intensity of his inspection sent a shiver down Adelaide's spine.

Mr. Paul rose and came around the table. "Miss Crum, I believe your character to be without blemish. I'm sure you can do all you say. However, the fact remains you're a

13

maiden lady with no experience dealing with children."

"We have childless couples begging for a baby," Mr. Wylie added. "Couples, with acres of ground and not enough hands to till it, seeking boys. We have tried-and-true parents who've shown their abilities by rearing their own children."

Heat climbed Adelaide's neck. *Fiddlesticks! If I'd had the good fortune to be a tried-and-true parent, I wouldn't be here.*

How frustrating to have men make all the decisions, as they always had in Noblesville. She might be single, but that didn't mean she couldn't bring up a child. She had the capacity, the intelligence, to sit on a committee like this one, to help make important decisions. Why couldn't men see women had a unique perspective with value, married or not?

"Gentlemen, I've proven my abilities by running a successful business while I tended to my sick mother. I can rear a child and do it well."

Her gaze collided with the editor's. Did she see compassion in his warm brown eyes?

Mr. Wylie pointed to the paper in front of him. "We'll only be getting twenty-eight children, mostly boys. We're unable to meet the demand. I hope you understand."

14

She understood all right. They didn't think she could handle the job. *Lord, give me the words to convince them.*

"Gentlemen, please hear me out. The fact I'm unmarried will give me *more* time to devote to a child. I realize boys are needed in the fields. My desire to rear a girl won't interfere with that." She bit her lower lip. "I'd be a good mother, if you'd give me a chance."

Arms folded across his chest, Mr. Paul leaned toward her. "The Children's Aid Society does not seek single parents, except in the rarest of cases. If we weren't overrun with applicants, perhaps we might consider your marital status more leniently."

She searched their faces for help. Mr. Paul's features appeared carved in granite. Mr. Sparks fidgeted in his chair. Mr. Wylie gave her a kind look, but showed no sign of intervening.

Mr. Graves wore a slight frown. He cleared his throat. "Miss Crum made some valid points about her suitability. Any chance, gentlemen, of stretching the rules?"

Adelaide held her breath. *Oh, please, God, change their minds.*

Mr. Paul tapped the edges of the paper-work in his hand. "Charles, we aren't here to make history. Just to make certain these

15

children have good homes. Besides, placing a child in a fatherless home is unscriptural."

Mr. Graves arched a brow. "Would that be Third Timothy Four?"

Adelaide knew her Bible. There was no Third Timothy. Surprised at the jab and pleased he knew the Scriptures, she smiled at the editor. He winked. Warmth spread through Adelaide like honey on a hot biscuit. Could this handsome, successful man be on her side?

Mr. Paul harrumphed. "Perhaps you find that funny, Mr. Graves, but I do not. The Bible makes it clear the man is the head of the family. It isn't right to put a child into a home with no paternal guidance."

Adelaide tightened her hands into fists. Mr. Paul's fifteen-year-old son Jacob perpetually terrorized the town. A few months ago, she'd had to report him to the sheriff after she'd caught him setting fire to Mr. Hudson's shed. The boy had run off and thankfully, she'd been able to douse the flames. Yet, Mr. Paul had the gall to preach paternal guidance. "I had no father growing up. I'm no worse for it."

Mr. Paul leaned forward and patted her shoulder. "I didn't mean to insult you. There are circumstances over which we have no control, but that's not the case here."

16

Adelaide glanced at Mr. Graves. His gaze had narrowed but he said nothing. What had she expected? He didn't know her. None of them really did. They saw a spinster — nothing more.

"I'm sorry we can't help you." Mr. Wylie stood and walked toward the door.

She wanted to scream, but that would only prove her to be a hysterical female unfit to rear a child. She hated being powerless. Hated being at their mercy. Hated being unable to change a thing.

Adelaide grabbed her purse and rose. At the door, she looked back one last time, searching for some sign of softening on their faces, but no miracle came. Tears stung her eyes, but no matter what, she would not let them see her cry.

Mr. Wylie opened the door. "I'm sorry," he murmured again.

Unable to speak, she nodded an acknowledgment. Head high, she strode through the door into the waiting area, past her staring neighbors, and into the courthouse corridor, holding herself together with the strength of a well-honed will.

Every step pounded in her head, reiterating again and again and again. *I failed. I failed. I failed.*

In the hallway, she sidestepped a couple

17

blocking her path.

"Please, Ed, we can't replace our boy. I'd like a girl —"

"A boy is what we agreed on," the man snapped. "I'm trying to put this family back together, and all you do is whine."

The woman's gaze darted to Adelaide, and then dropped to the floor. Frances. Before Adelaide could greet her, Frances followed her husband to the door. Ed turned to open it, giving Adelaide a glimpse of his face. Anger blazed in his eyes. Then, like a shade dropping over a window, he controlled his expression, leaving his countenance smooth and pleasant.

"Miss Crum," he said, giving her a friendly nod.

Adelaide couldn't believe this irate man could be the same person who'd picked her up after a childhood tumble and declared she'd be fine. All these years later, she still remembered his kindness, the gentle way he'd cleaned her scrapes with the red bandanna he'd dampened at a nearby pump.

Losing their son must have changed him. Whatever the cause, if Ed carried that much anger, the Drummonds shouldn't be considered for a child. But they probably would be, since marriage seemed to be the com-

18

mittee's only condition.

The pain of the rejection tore through her. Adelaide bolted for the entrance. She shoved open the heavy door, gulping in air. As she started down the steps, low-slung clouds released their moisture, spattering her face as if nature shed the tears she would not weep. Lightning zigzagged overhead and thunder rumbled, then the sky burst under the weight of its watery load.

In the deluge, her sodden garments grew heavy, but didn't slow her progress. With both hands, she hiked her skirts and hustled across the street. As she trudged to the back of her shop, closed for this momentous day, the mud grabbed at her shoes. Her shoulders heaving with exertion, she pried the dirty shoes from her feet and dropped them outside the door, indifferent she'd ruined their fine leather. Then climbed the stairs to her quarters above the shop.

She removed her soggy skirt, and then wilted onto the bed, dropping her hat on the floor. A curtain of rain veiled the window, darkening the room. Her mother's words echoed in her head. *It's a man's world, Adelaide. If you think otherwise, you're in for a rude awakening.*

Today, four men had found her unworthy to rear a child. She'd built a successful busi-

19

ness, had taken care of herself and her invalid mother, and all without a man's help. But what she wanted most, a child and family, she couldn't have without a man, without a committee of men.

"Why, Lord? Why was the answer no?" No reply came.

There would be no little girl to sew for, no little girl to love. No little girl, period.

A sob ripped through her, then a piercing wail. She burrowed her face in the pillow to muffle the sound, but then remembered she had no one to hear. No one to see. No one to care.

The dam she'd built to hold back her emotions crumbled, releasing a flood of tears. As she wept, spasms shook her body until, long minutes later, exhaustion quieted her. Every part of her echoed with hollowness, emptiness. For the first time in her thirty-one years, she felt old. Old, with the hope squeezed out of her.

But then she remembered Mr. Graves's wink.

Somehow the gesture had united them against the others. He appeared to have confidence in her ability to mother a child. Like butter on a burn, the thought soothed her wounded heart.

But even if no one else did, Adelaide had

faith in herself. And even a stronger faith in God. God would sustain her.

What if the committee's decision wasn't God's final word?

At the thought, Adelaide sat up on the bed. Her chest swelled with hope and her mind wrapped around a fresh determination. The committee's rules weren't etched in stone like the Ten Commandments. She'd never believed all the conventions in her world concurred with God's plan. Until she knew in the core of her being God didn't want her to mother a child, she would not give up hope. She would believe a child waited for her, waited for the comfort of Adelaide's arms.

Charles couldn't get the memory of Miss Crum out of his mind. He wished he hadn't agreed to sit on this committee. He wanted no part in impersonating God. No part in causing the kind of pain he'd read on Miss Crum's face.

If Charles understood anything, he understood pain.

He forced his attention back to the discussion, chagrined to discover everyone looking at him, waiting for him to speak. "I'm sorry. Would you repeat that?"

"We were saying the Drummonds have the

ability to train a boy in farmwork. They lost their only child to a stove fire a few years back. A terrible tragedy."

Charles examined the burly man and his timid wife. From the little he'd listened to, Mr. Drummond had done all the talking. The man seemed affable enough, but during the interview, his wife had avoided eye contact. Perhaps she was merely shy. "Mrs. Drummond, you haven't said. Do you want a boy, too?"

She looked to her husband, hesitating a moment. "I'd be open to a girl." Her voice quavered, but for the first time she met Charles's eyes. He saw a flicker of hope, and something else, something that gnawed at his memory. Before he could identify it, she lowered her gaze.

Mr. Wylie checked a list. "We've been told to expect a brother and sister. Would you be willing to take both of them?"

Mrs. Drummond's gaze darted to her husband.

"How old are they?" Mr. Drummond asked.

"The boy is ten, the girl is, let's see . . ." Wylie scanned a paper in front of him. "Seven."

Mr. Drummond rubbed his chin. "Two pair of hands *would* be a help," he said, considering. Then he smiled. "The missus would like a girl. We'll take them both."

"Excellent. We don't want to split up siblings unless we have no choice."

Mr. Drummond nodded. "Family means everything. Husband, wife . . ." He hesitated, his tone emotional. "Children. Nothing should divide a family."

Mr. Wylie pushed the papers away and looked at Charles. "Any objections, Mr. Graves?"

The couple had the proper references, had said all the right words, but what did that prove? The entire exercise was ludicrous. But perhaps no more so than nature's method of selecting parents guaranteed they'd be adequate for the job.

Yet some kind of sixth sense twisted a lump in his throat, made him hesitate, but just as quickly, he dismissed it. The others knew them, had greeted them warmly.

For the hundredth time he questioned why God, all powerful and all knowing, allowed unsuitable people to have children. He could only be certain about one thing. A child would be better off living in Noblesville than roaming the streets of New York City or living in one of its crowded orphanages. "I have none."

"Good!" Mr. Wylie sent Mr. Drummond

a smile. "I've been meaning to thank you, Ed, for helping fix the church roof."

Ed nodded. "Glad to do it. We can't expect the parson to hold an umbrella over his head while he's preaching."

While Wylie ushered the Drummonds from the room, Charles rose from his chair and crossed to the window. Even in the sudden downpour, the streets crawled with horse-drawn wagons and buggies. A typical Saturday, the day area farmers came to town to transact business or sell produce.

Like most county seats, the courthouse dominated the square, giving a certain dignity to the mishmash of architecture surrounding it. Noblesville was a nice little town. The decision to move here had been a good one. He'd been able to help his brother's family and to bring *The Noblesville Ledger* back to life. That had been his father's plan, but long before that revelation, owning a paper had been Charles's dream, a dream he'd soon achieve.

His hand sought the telegram inside his pocket, notification his father had died peacefully in his sleep. Charles crushed the flimsy paper into a tight ball. Maybe now, he could put his past to rest.

He looked down the block to *The Ledger,* then across the street to Miss Crum's millinery shop. She wanted a child to love, not a worker for her store.

Charles turned from the window. "I'm uncomfortable placing these youngsters to be laborers on farms."

"Work never hurt anyone." Wylie hunched forward, biceps bulging in his ill-fitting coat until Charles expected to hear ripping fabric. "Hard work builds strong bodies, sound minds."

"Some of these 'Street Arabs' have been pickpockets and beggars," Paul spoke up. "We're saving them from a life of crime. If they work hard, they'll make something of themselves."

Charles's thoughts turned to Miss Crum, an easy task. She stuck in a man's mind like taffy on the roof of a tot's mouth. Her eyes had captured him the first moment he saw her. A dazzling blue, they were deep-set under straight, slim brows, gentle, intelligent eyes. Her hair, the color of pale honey, had been smoothed back into a low chignon. Clearly a proper, strait-laced woman, the kind of woman who attended church on Sunday wouldn't abide a man like him.

She'd shown a passel of courage facing the committee, even more strength of will when she'd left with her dignity pulled around her like a cloak. Of all the women

25

he'd met that day, Miss Crum was the only one he felt certain would give a child the kind of home he'd read about in books.

He might have fought more for her, but thoughts of his widowed sister-in-law's struggles had stopped him. Besides, to object further would have been a waste of time. He'd soon discovered folks in Noblesville resisted anyone who challenged their customary way of life.

By noon all the children had been spoken for. The actual selection of the orphans would take place in two weeks on the day of distribution. The four men shook hands, relieved they'd finished their job, at least for now. After the distribution, the committee had agreed to keep an eye on the children and their guardians as best they could.

A fearsome responsibility.

Outside the courthouse the men dispersed. Charles pulled his collar up around his neck and dashed to the paper in the pounding rain, splattering puddles with every footfall. Ducking into the doorway of *The Ledger,* he removed his hat, dumping water on his shoes, his spirits as damp as his feet.

His gaze shifted across the street to the CLOSED sign in the window of Miss Crum's millinery shop. In the months he'd been here, he'd never seen the shop closed on a Saturday.

As he opened the door to the paper, he couldn't help wondering what Adelaide Crum was doing right at this moment, after four men had dashed her hopes as surely as the sudden storm had wiped out the sun.

CHAPTER TWO

Adelaide woke with a start, bolting upright in bed. Something important was to take place today. Then the memory hit and she sank against the pillows. The children would arrive today.

For her, another ordinary day; for twenty-eight couples, this day had blessed them with a child.

The past two weeks, she had relived the meeting with the committee numerous times, trying to see how she could have convinced them. Wasted thoughts. Wasted hopes. Wasted tears.

She'd been certain God approved of her desire to rear a child, yet the committee had turned her down. Could she have been wrong? Didn't God want her to mother an orphan? If not, why?

I'd be a good mother. I'd never be like Mama — crabby, critical, always taking the pleasure out of everything.

After a decade of caring for her mother and running the shop, at first her mother's death had been a relief. The admission put a knot in Adelaide's stomach, and she said a quick prayer of repentance.

Shaking off her dark thoughts, Adelaide held up her left thumb. "I'm thankful, God, for a thriving business." Lifting her index finger, she continued, "I'm thankful for these comfortable rooms that give me shelter." Then, "Thank you, Lord, for good friends." Touching each finger in turn, she found, as always, many things for which to give thanks.

But today, it wasn't enough.

She climbed out of bed and shoved up the window. The clatter of wheels, a barking dog and a vendor's shout brought life into the room. She walked to the dresser mirror and picked up her brush. In her reflection, she found no ravages of age, no sign of crow's-feet. Her nose was clearly too long, but, all in all, a nice enough face.

Nice enough for a handsome man like Mr. Graves to admire?

Adelaide blinked. Where had that thought come from?

She laid down the brush and leaned toward the mirror, then crossed her eyes. *If you don't stop that, Adelaide, your eyes will get stuck there.* Recalling her mother's warning, a smile tugged at the corners of her mouth.

Feeling better, she dressed, then hurried to the kitchen and made coffee. As she sipped the hot brew, her gaze traveled the room, pleased with the soft blue walls above the white wainscoting. Blue-and-white checked curtains, crisp with starch, hung at the window over the sink. This would be a cozy place for a child to have breakfast. The oak pedestal table circled with four pressed-back chairs, plenty of seating for a family.

Neither a crumb littered the floor nor did a speck of dust mar the table. She sighed. All too aware, she lived in the perfect, uncluttered home of a childless woman.

Enough of self-pity. Time to open her shop. Downstairs, she flipped the sign in the window and sat down to mend a torn seam when the bell jingled.

Sally Bender, dressed in drab green with her gray hair stuffed beneath a faded blue bonnet, tromped into the shop. "Land sakes, Adelaide! Are you buried alive under all these hats?" Before Adelaide could answer, Sally went on, "It's high time you got out your frame so we can finish that quilt."

Adelaide's mother's declining health had

30

ended the quilting bees. "Good morning to you, too, Sally," Adelaide said with a teasing grin.

"Oh, good morning." Sally smiled sheepishly, but then parked fisted hands on her hips. "You know I'm right. It's not good to mope like this."

"I'm sewing, not moping."

"You can't fool me, Adelaide Crum. You're hiding out here. The 'Snip and Sew' quilters haven't met in months. Why, the church auction will come and go before we finish that quilt." A spark flared in Sally's eyes. "Is it man trouble?"

"No, just work."

"Then start having some. Ask Horace Smith to the church picnic. Give me something to think about besides this unseasonable heat."

Old enough to be her father, the town's mortician looked barely more alive than his clientele. "If you're relying on me for excitement, you'll expire from a bad case of monotony." She chuckled. "No doubt Horace would thank me for the business."

Sally poked her arm. "Now you sound more like yourself."

Putting aside her sewing, Adelaide rose. "I'll set up the frame. We can start a week from Monday at ten o'clock."

"Good. On the way home, I'll stop and tell the others." She drew Adelaide into a hug. "I've missed you."

"I've missed you, too."

Sally spun out like a whirlwind. Adelaide whispered thanks for a caring friend.

Adelaide kept busy, but the morning dragged. Unable to concentrate, she had to rip out rows of stitches in Mrs. Willowby's bolero jacket and jabbed herself twice with the needle. She laid the garment aside, then stuck the pricked finger in her mouth as she ambled over to the window.

The street was exceptionally busy, even for a Saturday. No doubt twenty-eight of these conveyances held those fortunate couples who'd been given a child.

What if an unexpected child had ridden the train? Maybe I'm supposed to be at the distribution, taking an opportunity God provided.

Adelaide whipped off her apron and raced upstairs for her hat and gloves.

Charles walked the few blocks to *The Ledger,* his stride brisk. Under his hat perspiration already beaded his forehead. He neared Whitehall's Café and the aroma of strong coffee wafted through an open window, tempting him. Up ahead, a group of people huddled, heads bent, talking, unusual for an early Saturday morning. Coffee could wait.

As Charles neared the paper, his reporter came running from the opposite direction, his lanky legs skidding to a halt in front of him. "Mr. Graves, Sarah Hartman hung herself from a rafter in her barn!"

"What can you tell me about her?"

"Nothing except she's an old lady who lived on a farm outside of town. Must've gone daft. Her daughter found her this morning."

"Too bad," Charles said without a trace of feeling. Long ago, journalism had taught him to distance himself from tragedy, to look at events as part of the job, not troubles affecting people's lives. Otherwise, every death would have him bawling like a baby. Though, upon occasion, the sum of all those tragedies circled over his head like buzzards converging on the kill, disturbing his sleep.

"Did the *sheriff* say it looked like suicide, or the town gossips?"

James thrust out his chin, annoyance etching his brow. "The sheriff did. He found a crate kicked over beneath the body."

Charles nodded his approval. "Good work. Get the sheriff's statement. Interview the daughter. While you're at it, ask about funeral arrangements for the obit."

"Mrs. Hartman had one child." James checked his tablet, clearly proud of his reporting skills. "Frances Drummond."

Drummond? Charles had no idea why, but hearing that name left him feeling uneasy.

A crowd gathered as Adelaide slipped into the schoolhouse. Across the front of the room, the orphans sat in two rows of chairs, their young faces etched with uncertainty and a glimmer of hope. Adelaide counted nineteen boys and nine girls. Twenty-eight, the exact number the committee had expected. Her heart plummeted. Still, she couldn't drag herself away.

She studied each child in turn. Some appeared to be in their early teens, others quite young; their small feet dangled above the floor. Though rumpled from travel, all wore proper clothing, with hair combed and faces scrubbed.

They were beautiful, every single one of them.

Across the room she caught the eye of Mr. Graves. His quick smile made her feel less alone in this room of instant families.

Adelaide's gaze returned to a young girl of six or seven. Fair and blond, she leveled aquamarine eyes on the crowd. A brave little thing or maybe merely good at hiding her fear.

"Miss Abigail, what on Earth are *you* doing here?"

With huge proportions and a voice to match, Viola Willowby loomed over her. That a steady customer persisted in calling her Abigail, even though Adelaide's Hats and Sundries hung in bold letters over her shop, set Adelaide's teeth on edge.

She lifted her gaze, forcing up the corners of her mouth into something she hoped resembled a smile. Atop Mrs. Willowby's head perched one of Adelaide's finest creations — a floppy straw hat bedecked with pink cabbage roses.

"Hello, Mrs. Willowby."

"I saw you leave the orphan interviews. Why were you there?"

"For the same reason as you."

Mrs. Willowby gasped. "You can't be serious! It . . . it wouldn't be proper." Mrs. Willowby pulled a lace-edged hanky from its hiding place in the depths of her ample bosom and touched the linen to her nose, as if she feared catching some dire malady that would render her as irrational as she obviously thought Adelaide to be.

Adelaide looked her square in the eye. "And why not?"

"You're a spin —" Mrs. Willowby's face flushed, unable to get the heinous word past her lips. "A maiden lady."

Adelaide wanted to rip the stunning hat off her customer's head and swat her across the face with it. But then she sighed, ashamed of herself. A Christian shouldn't think that way. Besides, Mrs. Willowby represented the thinking of the committee, probably of their church, even the entire town. "You needn't worry. They denied my request."

"Well, I should think so!"

Judge Willowby, an equally large man, tapped his wife on the shoulder. "I'm sure Miss Crum is quite capable of rearing a youngster, Mrs. Willowby." While his wife sputtered like an overflowing teakettle, he motioned to two chairs. "It's time to start." He turned to Adelaide. "Nice to see you, Miss Crum."

Adelaide smiled at the judge. Clearly he found some good in his uncharitable wife.

Adelaide could understand why the Willowbys had been given a child. Years before, they'd lost their two children to diphtheria. Well-heeled, after finding natural gas on their property, they wielded a lot of influence in town.

While she . . . Well, truth be told, she *was*

a spinster. How she disliked the word, but at thirty-one years of age, soon to be thirty-two, Adelaide had to accept it applied to her.

She moved to the back of the room and took a seat, recalling some years back her chance at marriage. She hadn't loved Jack, the man who'd asked. Had her refusal been a mistake? Young at the time, she'd foolishly expected to fall in love. It hadn't happened.

Keeping busy hadn't been a problem. She faithfully attended the First Christian Church, went to prayer meetings on Wednesday nights, where she communed with the Lord, but with not one eligible bachelor. Within the pages of books, she found adventure, but put little stock in the fictitious men who whisked women away to live happily ever after. No, Adelaide lived in the real world, had her feet planted firmly on the ground. Men couldn't be counted on. Her chest constricted. Her mother's life had proved that.

Her gaze returned to Mr. Graves. Light streamed through the window behind him and the rays caught in his thick hair, giving him a halo of sorts. Though with that strong jaw and stern expression, he hardly looked like an angel. But he did, she had to admit, look fine.

Mr. Wylie walked to the front and asked for quiet, then introduced Mr. Fry, an agent of the Children's Aid Society.

A thin fellow with slicked-back hair and a hooked nose walked to the podium, eyeing the crowd over his reading glasses. "Ladies and gentlemen, the Children's Aid Society is grateful for your interest. Many of these children were homeless, sleeping in doorways and privies, selling matches or flowers, working as shoeshine or paperboys. Some begged for food. When they came to us, many wore filthy rags infested with vermin."

The children sat unmoving, staring ahead with somber gazes, showing no reaction to Mr. Fry's words. "You may wonder why New York City has such a vast number of orphans." His hand swept over the children. "Some of these children aren't, in fact, orphans. When John's family —" a thin boy scrambled to his feet "— immigrated to this country, he and his family became forever separated." John sat down.

"Death or desertion of one parent left eight of our twenty-eight children with no one to care for them. Unwed mothers left a few on our doorstep."

Someone murmured, "Poor things."

Tears stung Adelaide's eyes. More than anything, she wanted to take every last one of these children home and try to make up for the deprivation of their young lives with warm hugs and fresh-baked cookies.

"In some cases, family members brought them to us, trusting we could provide them a better life, which, with your help, we're attempting to do."

Adelaide couldn't imagine giving up a child. Nothing could make her do such a thing.

"Mr. Brace, our founder," Mr. Fry continued, "realized we couldn't handle the problem alone. He devised this plan to place the ten thousand orphans we presently have into rural areas and small towns, where they'll receive an education and enjoy the benefits of a healthy environment and family life."

The numbers boggled Adelaide. Surely with that many homeless children, there'd be *one* child for her.

Perhaps if she went to New York —

"Your local committee," he said then consulted his notes, "comprised of Mr. Wylie, Mr. Paul, Mr. Sparks and Mr. Graves, has approved the eligibility of your homes."

Involuntarily, Adelaide's gaze again sought Mr. Graves. Even from this distance, the sight of his determined, serious face shot little pricks of awareness through her limbs.

She forced her attention back to Mr. Fry.

"I've been told more requests were made than we could provide on this trip. Perhaps in the future as more children come to us, we can remedy that situation."

Adelaide caught her breath. If they came again, then, next time she might convince the committee.

Who was she fooling? No one in Noblesville, or New York, would give a single woman a child. If only she could give her world a twist and watch it transform like the bits of colored glass in the kaleidoscope she'd seen at the mercantile. Maybe then, she'd change a few stubborn minds.

"Along with periodic visits by one of our agents, these gentlemen have agreed to oversee the children's welfare. At any time, the agreement to care for a child can be broken, either by the family or by the child."

Perhaps a little girl would be unhappy in her new home and the committee would reconsider their decision.

He cleared his throat. "Now, let's meet the children."

Mr. Fry introduced the bigger boys in the back row. Half listening, Adelaide's eyes remained riveted on the little blond-haired girl. At last, Mr. Fry gave her name. She stood along with an older boy beside her.

"Emma and William Grounds are brother and sister. Emma is seven, her brother, William, ten. Their father deserted his family years ago and their mother recently died. Both youngsters are in good health." Emma and William clutched each other's hands, their eyes conveyed a warning — they were a matched pair, not to be separated.

Mr. Fry continued down the row and the Grounds children sat down. Laying her head on her brother's shoulder, Emma stuck two small fingers in her mouth. Two precious German children, whose father had left them, as hers had done. Adelaide yearned to pull them into her arms until that longing bordered on pain.

Oh, Lord, please bring these children into my life.

Mr. Fry instructed the selected couples to seek out the children and the meeting ended. Almost against her will, Adelaide moved toward the Grounds siblings. She froze when she spotted Frances and Ed Drummond, wearing black out of respect for Mrs. Hartman's untimely death, talking to William and Emma.

As Adelaide watched, Emma tentatively took Frances's hand. William sat silent, his arms hanging limp. A woman who'd ac-

41

companied the orphans on the train joined the couple and spoke to William. Apparently overcoming his hesitation, he took his sister's other hand.

Disappointment slammed into Adelaide's stomach. She swayed and sank onto a nearby chair. *Her* children were going to live with that angry man and his spiritless wife. Helpless to act, she watched the four of them cross to the registration table. The Drummonds signed a paper and left the room before a miracle could bring those children into her arms. Didn't God care about them? About her?

Across the way, Judge and Mrs. Willowby left with a dark-eyed, curly-haired boy in tow. The same process repeated all around the room. Soon all the orphans were spoken for and on their way to new homes.

A heavy stone of misery sparked a sudden, uncustomary anger. Adelaide approached the table where the men who'd denied her application sifted through paperwork. "How could you allow the Drummonds to have the Grounds children?"

Mr. Paul, his face turning a deep shade of crimson, leapt to his feet. "Now see here, Miss Crum, it's not your place to criticize the decisions of this committee!"

Mr. Wylie took Mr. Paul's arm. "No need

to raise your voice, Thaddeus." He turned to Adelaide. "The Drummonds are fine people. Ed sits on the county council, helps his neighbors. You probably heard Mrs. Drummond recently lost her mother." He grimaced. "A few years back, their only child died in a horrible accident. They deserve this new beginning."

Face pinched, Mr. Sparks came around the table. "You're mistaken about the Drummonds. They pay their bills and attend church."

Adelaide wanted to challenge their view, but that meant butting her head into that stone wall of men. Without a doubt, Frances was a good person, but she'd changed into a colorless, weary creature, perhaps downtrodden by her husband.

"Do you have proof they're unsuitable?" Mr. Graves asked.

Adelaide moved forward. "The day of the interviews, Mr. Drummond looked very angry —"

"If that's a crime, we'd all be in trouble." Mr. Wylie chuckled. "I know you've never been married, Miss Crum, but it's not uncommon for husbands and wives to argue."

She tamped down her annoyance. They hadn't seen Ed Drummond's expression.

But they'd already gone back to their paperwork, dismissing her with silence.

All except Mr. Graves, who studied her with dark, somber eyes. But he remained mute.

She turned to leave, then stepped into the bright sunlight, watching wagons and buggies roll away from the schoolhouse. Her gaze lingered on the smiling couples with youngsters.

For a moment, she regretted refusing Jack's offer of marriage.

But then she remembered how he'd gobble dinner, barely speaking a word, and later, hands folded over a premature paunch, would fall asleep in the parlor until he roused enough to go home. No sharing of dreams, no laughter, no connection. His only thank-you for the meal was an odorous belch.

Without a doubt, her main appeal to Jack had been the income from her shop. Adelaide lifted her chin. If marriage offered no more than that, she could manage nicely without a man. But a child . . . A child was different.

Charles watched Miss Crum leave. What had she seen or heard that upset her enough to challenge the committee? With his own misgivings needling him, he followed her. "Miss Crum!"

She pivoted. His heart stuttered in his chest, a warning that when it came to Miss Crum, he was fast losing his objectivity. "I need to ask. What made you say the Drummonds wouldn't make good parents?"

She met his gaze with an icy stare. "I've seen Ed's temper. Frances appears heartbroken, unable to care for two children."

"That's understandable. She lost her mother —"

A light touch on his arm cut off his words.

"Have you ever had a bad feeling about anyone, Mr. Graves?"

"Sure."

"Then you can understand my concern. I have a bad feeling about that man."

As a newsman, he might use intuition to guide him, but he needed tangible evidence, not the insight of one disgruntled woman. "With nothing to base it on —"

"I know the committee's position. They made it clear the day I applied." She gave him a curt nod. "Good day."

Watching her leave, he regretted the committee's decision. No point in getting sappy about it. He wasn't in the business of securing everyone's happiness, even the happiness of a woman with eyes the color of a clear summer sky.

Crossing the street, he slipped between a buckboard hauling sacks of feed and a dray wagon. The image of Adelaide Crum nagged at him with a steadfastness that left him shaken.

Yet, the lady saw things as black and white, right or wrong, while he found areas of gray. Not that it mattered. He had no intention of getting involved with her, with anyone.

He had all he could do running the paper and helping his brother's family. He didn't want another complication in his life, in particular a complication of the female sort.

Yet something about Adelaide Crum made him question his decision.

CHAPTER THREE

Tuesday morning Adelaide sewed pink ribbons on to a child's bonnet, each tiny stitch made with infinite care. On the table beside her, her Bible lay closed. Unread.

As she worked, she pictured Emma Grounds, the little German girl, wearing this hat as they picked daylilies out back. She imagined bending down to gather the girl to her, nuzzling her neck, inhaling the scent of warmed skin, the scent of a child.

Sighing, she pinched the bridge of her nose, fighting tears, then knotted the final thread, snipped off the ends and laid the finished hat on her lap. In reality, a customer would buy this bonnet for her daughter or granddaughter and it would be gone, out of Adelaide's grasp as surely as Emma.

She removed her spectacles and laid the hat on the counter. The bell jingled over the door. The sight of Laura Larson brought a smile to Adelaide's face. Laura's youthful spirit might be encased in a plump, matronly body, but her laughter lit up a room like firecrackers on the Fourth of July. Without her help, Adelaide couldn't have managed the shop during her mother's illness. "Hello!"

Laura strolled toward her, her gaze sweeping the shop. Slicked back into a bun, some of her salt-and-pepper curls escaped to frame her round unwrinkled face. "My, my, haven't you been busy."

Leaning on the counter, Adelaide viewed her surroundings through Laura's eyes. Hats lined every shelf and perched on every stand. Already full when she'd become work-possessed, display cabinets burst at the seams. "I guess I'm overstocked."

Laura giggled, sounding more like a young girl than a grandmother in her fifties. "I'd say so. Do you have some hat-making elves tucked away in the back?"

Adelaide smiled. "No, I made them all."

"Why so many?"

What could Adelaide say? She'd been drowning her sorrow in hats? That for the past two weeks she'd been sewing, rather than praying about her problems? "Would you like some tea?"

"Tea sounds wonderful, if you have the time."

Adelaide headed to the kettle on the tiny potbellied stove in the back. "One thing I have plenty of is time."

"What you have plenty of, dear, is hats," Laura said, following her.

Pouring steaming water into a prepared teapot, Adelaide chuckled. For a moment, the sound stopped her hand. How long had it been since she'd laughed?

Adelaide gathered two cups with saucers and added a teaspoon of sugar in each, the way she and Laura liked their tea. She carried the tray into the showroom.

Laura joined her at the table, a cozy spot where her customers leafed through copies of *Godey's Lady's Book* while enjoying a restorative cup of tea.

"Why not mark them down and run an ad in the paper?" Laura said. "You'll need the space when it's time to display wools and velvets."

Running an ad meant seeing Mr. Graves. She would like to strategically poke a hatpin into every member of the committee, even *The Ledger's* editor. Of course, she'd do no such a thing.

Filling Laura's cup, Adelaide sighed. "I'll run an ad."

Laura took a sip, and then rested her cup in the saucer. "You missed Wednesday night's prayer meeting. Again." Laura touched her hand. "Tell me what's wrong."

Adelaide lifted her head, meeting Laura's gentle and accepting, ready-to-listen eyes. Her gaze skittered away and settled on the bonnet lying on the counter, then over to her unread Bible.

She considered telling Laura about her struggles, but it might sound as if she blamed God. And she didn't. It was her fault she resisted His will for her life. Or was it the committee who refused His will? Her mind had been so full of hurt and discouragement she no longer heard with certainty the quiet, inner voice that had guided and sustained her.

Laura gave her hand a squeeze, but said nothing, simply waited. Tenacious as a bulldog tugging at a trouser leg, Laura wouldn't let go until she got the story.

"A couple weeks ago, I asked to care for one of the orphans coming to town on the train, and the committee turned me down."

"Oh, no."

"Afterward —" She bit her lower lip until she could continue. "To keep busy, I made hats."

Laura turned over Adelaide's hand. "Which explains your rough palms and bloodshot eyes."

"It's been . . . a difficult time."

"Yes, I see —"

"Do you? Do you see this was my last chance —" Adelaide blinked hard and pulled away her hand.

"I'm sorry, dear," Laura said, her heartfelt tone bringing a lump to Adelaide's throat.

"No, I'm the one who's sorry for burdening you with this."

"Don't be silly! I'm your friend." Laura slapped the table. "That committee is made up of nitwits."

"Some nitwits. Only the superintendent of schools, the president of the bank, the editor of our newspaper —"

"Mr. Graves?" Laura scooted to the edge of her seat.

"None other."

"Now *there* is a handsome man," Laura said, with a grin. "Looks like his father."

Adelaide gasped. "You knew Mr. Graves's father?"

Laura nodded, her eyes shining like a brand-new penny. "He grew up in Noblesville. Back then, I had a huge crush on Adam Graves. But he only had eyes for your mother."

"My *mother?*"

"Yes, dear, it might astonish you to hear this, but as a young woman, Constance

51

Gunder reigned as belle of the county."

Her mother had been an attractive woman, but the pained expression she'd worn as long as Adelaide could remember suggested Constance had never known a happy day in her life.

"For a long while, Adam and your mother were inseparable," Laura continued. "Everyone assumed they'd marry."

Adelaide hadn't been told any of this. Why had her mother gone from belle to bitter? "What happened?"

"Constance fell in love with your father. Not a staying kind of man, but he swept your mother off her feet." Laura sighed. "Adam moved away right after that. Landed in Cincinnati, I believe. Your folks got married. As far as I know, Adam never came back, not even to visit his parents before they died."

"That seems callous."

"A broken heart can change a man — and a woman. I've always wondered if that's what damaged your mother."

Adelaide shook her head. "My mother never opened her heart enough to get it broken." She ran her finger around the cup's rim. "Did you know my father?"

"Not really. A fun-loving, charming traveling salesman with dimples — that pretty

52

much describes Calvin Crum."

"Do you know why he left?"

Laura shook her head. "Constance never confided in me." Laura pursed her lips, as if cutting off something she wanted to say, then brightened. "Well, all that's water under the bridge." She waggled her brows. "I understand Adam Graves's son is available."

"For what?"

"For your ad, what else? And you better get over there, before all these hats start gathering dust." Laura returned to her tea, her face the picture of innocence, knowing full well she'd used the exact words that would convince Adelaide to place the ad and put her into the presence of Mr. Graves.

Whether Adelaide wanted to deal with the editor or not, she needed cash to buy supplies. She couldn't afford to dip into her meager savings.

Besides, she had another pressing reason to see him. "I *do* owe Mr. Graves and the entire committee an apology."

"Why?"

"I lost my temper at the distribution of the orphans." Adelaide glanced at her hands.

"I'd have wanted to give them a piece of my mind, too."

"Yes, but you wouldn't have. I've asked

53

God's forgiveness." She swallowed. "But I've put off the next step."

Laura nodded. "You'll be doing the right thing. You can place the ad as an act of repentance *and* good business." Laura smiled, then rose to give Adelaide a quick hug. "I'll be back to quilt on Monday. I'm only blocks away if you need me," Laura said, then left.

Adelaide restored order to the shop and then climbed the stairs, her stomach lurching at the prospect of facing Mr. Graves and the entire committee. If she had more say in what happened, maybe she wouldn't be in this mess. In her world, an unmarried woman couldn't discern anger in a man, couldn't challenge the decisions of men. Couldn't be deemed fit to rear a motherless child, though countless widows raised their own children.

If only I had a way to get through to these men, to let my voice be heard.

Then maybe —

"Oh, why am I even bothering to dream about what can't be undone?" she said to the empty room.

Adelaide whipped off the apron, smoothed her navy skirt and then donned hat and gloves. Mr. Graves would not see how dejected she'd been since the committee's decision.

In fact, she wouldn't let Mr. Graves see her heart at all.

Downstairs, she flipped the sign in the window to CLOSED, left the shop and stood at the edge of the boardwalk, waiting while horses of every description clopped past. The sight of the huge animals always left Adelaide weak in the knees. Would she ever get over her fear of horses?

Seeing an opening, she hustled across the street, holding the hem of her skirt out of the dust. Arriving safely on the other side without being crushed by the temperamental beasts, she heaved a sigh of relief. In front of *The Ledger,* she took a moment to slow her breathing. Grasping the handle of the door, she turned the knob when the door burst open.

A young man slammed into her. The red-faced youth steadied her with his hand. "Excuse me, miss! Are you all right?"

Adelaide fluffed her leg-of-mutton sleeves. "I'm fine."

"I'm sorry, I didn't see you. I'm rushing to get to the courthouse. A horse thief is being arraigned today, and I'm sitting in on the trial." Holding a pad and pencil aloft, he puffed out his chest like a bantam rooster. "I'm a reporter."

"Not apt to be one for long if you knock down a loyal reader, James," warned a deep masculine voice, a familiar voice that sent a wave of heat to Adelaide's cheeks.

The young man's complexion also deepened to the color of beets. The editor smiled, softening the harshness of his words, and gave Adelaide a wink. The second time he'd winked at her. Despite everything, she couldn't help but smile back.

"Don't worry. I'll take care of Miss Crum."

Adelaide's gaze darted to the editor. Heavenly days, no one took care of her. Even hearing the words unsettled and somehow thrilled her, too.

"I'll expect a full report on the proceedings, James."

The young man nodded, then took off at a run across the street, his long legs dodging buggies and wagons on his way to the courthouse.

Adelaide turned back to the editor. "I don't believe his feet touched the ground."

Brown eyes sparkling with good humor, Mr. Graves chuckled. Without a coat, attired in a pin-striped vest and white shirt, he'd rolled his sleeves to the elbow giving her a clear view of muscled forearms. His broad shoulders filled the doorway.

The kind of shoulders one could lean on, tell every trouble to, a luxury Adelaide had never had.

Laura had said Charles looked like his father. Adelaide resembled her mother. Odd, history repeating itself that way.

He gestured for her to enter ahead of him. "Come in."

The instant Adelaide stepped inside, the odor of ink filled her nostrils. With the presses running, the noise level forced her to raise her voice several notches, disconcerting her. But not nearly as much as the man beside her, who looked more male than any man she'd ever met.

"Your reporter seems like a conscientious young man."

"Yes, but a bit out of control."

Exactly how Adelaide felt at the moment.

He led her to a desk the likes of which she'd never seen. Newspapers, books and a jumble of paper littered the surface and spilled over onto the floor. Her gaze surveyed three coffee cups, two tumblers, one filled with water, the other with pencils, an ink well, scissors, a glue bottle, a crumpled rag stained with ink, rubber bands, an apple and, gracious, the remainder of a half-eaten sandwich.

"Oh, my."

Mr. Graves stiffened. "Something wrong?"

"Nothing really." Adelaide clasped her hands together to keep them from organizing the desk and then giving it the dusting — well, more like the good scrubbing — it needed. That Mr. Graves could work amidst such a mess amazed and baffled her.

He motioned to a chair. "Please, have a seat."

She glanced at the chair he'd indicated, only to find it piled with newspapers. With a boyish grin, Mr. Graves removed them, obviously unconcerned with disarray. She started to sit when she spotted the crumbs.

He followed her gaze. "Let me take care of that." He took out a handkerchief and swiped it over the seat, sending crumbs tumbling to the floor.

She cringed. Heavenly days, fodder for bugs, or worse, rodents. But then he bent near and she caught the smell of leather and soap mingled with ink and filled her lungs, reveling in the scent of him. Suddenly woozy, she dropped into the now tidy seat before she did something foolish, like telling him how good he smelled.

The fumes must have made me light-headed.

The editor cleared a space, then perched on the corner of his desk. His dark gray pants and vest hugged a flat midriff with nary a sign of a potbelly. Her gaze lingered on his hands. Ink-stained, the tips of his long fingers fascinated her. Large, capable, strong — a man's hands, not at all like her own.

With great effort, she pulled her gaze away to look into his eyes and caught him studying her, a puzzled look on his face. Heat climbed her neck. What was the matter with her? She was behaving like a schoolgirl, as if she'd never seen a man.

"Miss Crum? You're here because . . . ?"

Her hand fluttered upward, easing her collar from the heat of her neck. "I want to place an advertisement in your paper."

He folded his arms across his chest. "I'd welcome your business, but I believe you already advertise with us."

He'd paid attention, knew she ran a monthly ad, but then that was his job. "Yes, but I need a special advertisement to promote the sale of my latest creations." She worried her lower lip. "I'm overstocked."

"I see. Perhaps a larger, eye-catching ad would bring in those ladies who didn't get a new bonnet for Easter?"

Adelaide smiled. "Exactly."

"Let's check our type selection for a suitable hat."

Adelaide took in a deep breath. "Before we do, there's another reason I've come, a more important reason."

"More important than business?" He gave her a teasing grin.

"Much." She swallowed over the lump in her throat. "I, ah, owe you an apology."

He raised a brow. "For what?"

"For my outburst the day of the distribution. I don't know what got into me." She sighed. "I behaved badly and I'm sorry."

"You surprise me, Miss Crum."

Adelaide glanced at her hands, then met his gaze. "When I've done wrong, the Bible teaches me to apologize."

His eyes searched her face. "Apparently you do more than carry that book on Sunday mornings."

What a strange comment. One he wouldn't have made if he knew how she'd struggled of late with reading the Bible. "The Bible also says you're to forgive me."

"Yes, if need be, seventy times seven." A smile took over his solemn face. "Forgiving you is an easy task, Miss Crum."

Like rainfall after a drought, his words seeped into her thirsty heart. "Thank you." She shot him a grin. "Though, I trust my behavior won't require quite that much clemency."

He leaned toward her. "That's too bad."

Adelaide's mouth went dry. What did he mean? She lurched from the chair. "I'd like to look at your hat selection."

He smiled, and then with a hand on her elbow, led her to an enormous array of type fitted into shallow drawers. The presses pulsated through the wooden floor into the soles of her shoes and up into her limbs. That had to be why she felt shaky on her feet. Not because of Mr. Graves's touch.

The presses came to an abrupt halt.

The editor stopped his search and faced her. "Perhaps I'm out of line, but I feel compelled to say I disagreed with the committee's decision." He took a step closer until she could see the length of his lashes, became aware of the rise and fall of his chest as he breathed. "I saw the logic in the astute arguments you made regarding your suitability."

Compliments on her cooking she'd had, but no man had ever praised her intellect. Still . . . "Then, why didn't you speak up?"

"I thought about the burdens my sister-in-law carries rearing her boys alone. Too late I realized that even with her hardships, Mary is an excellent mother." He stepped closer yet, until she could feel heat from his body, could see gold flecks in his dark eyes.

"I'm sure you'd be a good mother."

Sudden tears filled her eyes and she looked away.

He touched her arm. "I think I know how much the committee's decision has hurt you."

Adelaide noticed his assistant watching the exchange with interest. Teddy Marshall would be telling his wife about this visit at noon and the whole town would know by nightfall. She smoothed her skirt, then her brow. "Whether it hurt me isn't the point. It wasn't fair."

His gaze locked with hers. "Life is often unfair, Miss Crum," he said, and then returned to his search of the boxes.

From his tone, Adelaide suspected he wasn't simply talking about her situation. Did he have a message in there? Some lesson to learn? If so, she wasn't ready for it. Not with her heart burning with want for something she couldn't have.

He held out two blocks for her to examine. "Here you are."

Adelaide pulled her spectacles from her bag to peruse the blocks, glad for the distraction from all the confusing feelings rushing through her. With Mr. Graves standing near, she found it difficult to concentrate. Taking an eternity to make a simple decision wasn't like her. She forced her focus on business, not on the man at her side.

At last, she selected the larger block engraved with a most fetching hat, complete with feathers. "I'd like to use this."

Remembering her mother's words, she removed her wire-rimmed eyeglasses and stuffed them into her purse.

"Your eyes are pretty either way," he said softly.

Is he teasing me? "I've been told spectacles give me the appearance of an old maid schoolmarm."

"They give you an air of intelligence." He met her gaze. "I find intelligent women attractive."

She fingered the ribbed edge of her collar, her mind whirling around the compliment.

A door slammed. Fannie Whitehall crossed the room, her curly red hair poking out from under a big-brimmed straw hat.

Fannie said hello, and then brushed past Adelaide with as much interest as she'd give a fencepost. She held out two jars topped with a thin layer of paraffin and thrust them into Mr. Graves's hands. "I brought some of my preserves like I promised."

Charles looked at the jars like he'd never

seen jam before. "Thank you, Miss White-hall."

"That jam's mighty fine on biscuits."

He gave a lopsided grin. "I'm sure it is, but I'm not much of a cook."

"I'd make you a batch, but you'd have to bake them." Fannie let out a giggle. "I always burn the bottoms."

"Biscuits are my specialty." The words tumbled out of Adelaide's mouth. Had she actually said that? Out loud? Apparently she had, judging by the startled expression on both Mr. Graves and Fannie's faces. "Ah, as a thank-you for the time you spent on my ad."

"That's kind of you, Miss Crum," Mr. Graves said.

Her gaze collided with his and held for several moments, then darted away, then returned. He gazed at her with an intensity that suggested something important was happening, something significant. No man had ever looked at Adelaide like that before. Her hands trembled and she clasped them together, trying to gain control over her traitorous body, especially with Fannie's sharp-eyed scrutiny.

"I . . . I'd best be . . . going," Adelaide stammered. "I need to get back to the shop."

"Let me walk you out." The editor gently

guided her by her elbow to the door and then opened it. "I'll write up the ad and have it ready first thing tomorrow morning."

The huskiness in his voice set her insides humming and brought an odd tightness to her throat. "I'll stop by the paper to look at it before I open the shop."

They said goodbye. Once outside, the sun shone brighter and the sky appeared shades bluer than when she'd walked over to *The Ledger*. Finding a break in the traffic, she scurried across the street and entered her shop, then glanced back.

Mr. Graves remained in the open doorway where she'd left him. He'd complimented her eyes, even said her spectacles gave her an air of intelligence. No one had ever said anything nicer to her in all her days. Joy zinged through her chest, pushing against her lungs until she could barely breathe.

Then Fannie joined Mr. Graves in the doorway, deflating Adelaide's mood faster than a burst balloon.

Charles watched Miss Crum cross the street and enter her shop. As the door closed behind her, he detected a little twinge of disappointment. Silly. The lady was a client, nothing more.

Beside him, Fannie cocked her head. "Promise you won't forget to take the jam home. I put it on your desk."

"How could I forget?"

She giggled, and then jiggling her fingers at him, she flounced down the walk.

Charles let out a gust of air. He needed to help Teddy get the presses running, but he stayed at the door, thinking not about Fannie, but of Miss Crum.

With his office directly across the street from her shop, he'd noticed since the interviews how little she went out. When he worked late, he'd observe her lamp lit well into the night. After seeing her today, he guessed Miss Crum was a workhorse or an insomniac. Under her pretty blue eyes, dark smudges marred her creamy skin. If he was any judge of people, and in this business he made it a point to be, Miss Crum still suffered from the committee's rejection.

"Miss Crum's a looker, though kind of standoffish."

Charles hadn't heard Teddy come up behind him. For a burly man he had a light step. Charles purposely turned a cool eye on his assistant, hoping to stop what was coming.

"Yes, sirree, she's one fine-looking woman. Thinking about courting her?"

Charles scowled. "Where did you get that idea?"

Teddy smiled, putting his whole face into it, annoying Charles. "Oh, I've seen you watching her comings and goings. It's time you quit thinking about asking her and do it."

"My priority is to get this newspaper in shape."

"Which you've done. Since you've taken over, the paper comes out on time and has another section. Why, it looks downright citified." Teddy swept his arm over the room. "You've made this your life. A lonely way of living, that's sure."

The truth slammed into Charles. He *was* lonely. Since he arrived in town, Fannie had come by the paper with one excuse after another. But her giggling and incessant chatter put a knot in his stomach. From what she'd said, she didn't even read the newspaper.

No, he liked the appearance and manner of Miss Crum. "I've considered asking her to dinner," he said before he thought.

"Miss Whitehall or Miss Crum?"

"Miss Crum."

Teddy raised his brows. "So, what's stopping you?"

"A woman who applied for an orphan

would have only one thing on her mind — getting married and having babies of her own. I've no intention of tying that knot."

Teddy scratched the back of his neck, peering at him with mild hazel eyes. "You running away from matrimony, boss?"

Shoving his hands into his pockets, Charles studied the floor, and then raised his gaze. "In my experience, Teddy, if you smile twice at a woman, she starts planning your wedding." His hand left his pocket and pushed through his hair. "What makes women think they know a man better than he knows himself?"

Teddy hooted. "They do, that's a fact." His eyes disappeared in a lopsided grin, a grin fading faster than morning glories at noon. "What's wrong with marrying? My Grace is a good woman, takes care of me just fine. Gave me four sons," Teddy said, his tone laced with pride.

Countless Sunday mornings, Charles had seen Miss Crum set off for church, dressed to the hilt from the shiny tips of her shoes to the top of her elaborate hat, clutching the Good Book. Yes, a fine Christian woman. As different from him as any woman he'd ever known. Exactly why this sense of a connection between them wasn't logical.

If Charles really cared about Miss Crum, he'd stay away.

But he had no intention of sharing that with Teddy. "We'd best get to work or we won't get this edition out."

Teddy gave him a long, hard look before heading inside. Once they had the presses running, Charles strode to his desk. Miss Crum's dismay at the disorder he worked in made him as uncomfortable as having his knuckles rapped by his first-grade teacher. He began organizing the clutter and then stopped.

He wasn't going to let any woman walk in here and, with one disapproving glance, change the way he ran his office. If he did, next thing he knew, she'd be running his life.

Tousling the paperwork, he restored the desk to its original state and for good measure, dumped the cup of pencils. Slumping into his chair, he eyed the mess with grim satisfaction, promising to steer clear of Miss Crum.

Yet loneliness washed over him, leaving him hollow. Empty. Unlike Fannie, unlike any woman he'd known, Miss Crum captivated him. Though he fought it, he craved substance. Biscuits instead of jam. But that meant letting someone get close. Even a woman like Miss Crum, whose guileless blue eyes tugged at the rusty hinges of his heart, needed to be held at arm's length.

For her sake, more than his.

CHAPTER FOUR

That morning, Adelaide awakened with a sense of anticipation. How much did her excitement have to do with seeing Mr. Graves that day? Everything. That realization scared her more than horses, more than tornadoes — her worst fears . . . until now.

No, spending her life alone terrified her more than anything.

With God only a whisper away, shame lapped at her conscience. A Christian could never be alone. Still, hadn't God intended His children to walk two by two?

Forcing her mind away from the editor, she picked up her Bible and opened it to the pink crocheted bookmark, a bookmark she hadn't moved in weeks. She had a lot of catching up to do. "Forgive me, Lord," she whispered, then began to read.

The clock struck nine. Adelaide jumped, then closed her Bible, amazed she'd read for an hour. Within these pages, pages she'd neglected, she found peace and comfort and strength. No matter what happened, she would never again make the mistake of neglecting Scripture.

She donned gloves and her latest hat, harboring butterflies in her stomach instead of the peace her Bible reading had given her, all because of Mr. Graves.

Minutes later Adelaide walked through the door of *The Ledger.* Mr. Graves and Teddy leaned over the boxes of type, selecting and then sliding them into place on narrow racks. When the door shut behind her, Mr. Graves's gaze met hers.

Teddy threw up a hand. Adelaide waved back, excited to be in this fascinating world of words. Until Mr. Graves's friendly smile put a flutter into the rhythm of her heart.

They met at his desk, a desk with less clutter and no stale food or empty coffee mugs. Adelaide bit back a smile.

The editor stuck his hands into his pockets and tipped forward on the toes of his shoes. "You look festive today."

"Thank you."

Amusement warmed his chocolate eyes as he viewed her hat with its nested bird. "Looks like some baby birds are about to hatch in that bonnet of yours."

Laughter bubbled up inside Adelaide. She

pressed her lips together, trying to keep her mirth inside, but a most unbecoming giggle forced its way out. Heavenly days, she sounded like Fannie. "I like birds."

"Hopefully that fruit is *fake* or the birds you so admire might put your hat on the menu."

"I'll have you know my hat is in vogue," she said, the hint of a tease in her voice. "What you need is someone to teach you and your readers style."

He smirked. "I can't see farmers reading it."

"Well, no. But farmers' wives spend money in town —"

"On birds for their heads," he said.

She raised her chin. "Are you poking fun at me, Mr. Graves?"

His gaze sobered, something deep and mysterious replaced the mirth and sent a quiver through Adelaide. "Not at all, Miss Crum. Not at all."

She glanced away from that look and the unspoken words it contained. "Good because I'd like to write a fashion column for the paper." She covered her mouth with her hand, but the half-baked idea she'd been considering had already escaped. Being around this man scrambled her orderly mind.

Considering her proposal, Mr. Graves tapped a finger on his chin, very near the cleft. "I couldn't pay much —"

"One free ad per column will do."

"You're a shrewd businesswoman. A fashion column isn't a bad idea. Could you give me a sample? Say, by Monday?"

She beamed, barely able to keep from hugging him for this opportunity. A column would give her shop publicity. Perhaps increase sales, something she needed badly. An article would also give her a voice — granted one about style, but still a published voice. "It'll be exciting to see my name in print."

"You and I seem to be kindred spirits."

He cleared his throat, pivoted to his desk and grabbed a piece of paper. "I have your ad right here. Have a seat."

Adelaide glanced at the chair across from his desk, pleased to see it cleared of books and crumbs. She shot him a grin. "It appears you've made a few changes."

"Nothing of consequence." His mouth twisted as if he tried not to smile. "It merely made sense to have one chair fit for subscribers."

She cocked her head at him. "That's very astute of you."

"Under that proper demeanor, you have a

feisty side, Miss Crum, a side that keeps a man on his toes."

Adelaide lifted her chin and reached for the ad. "Stay on your toes if you like, but I prefer to be seated."

His laugh told Adelaide the editor had gotten her attempt at humor. How long had it been since she'd made a joke? Felt this alive?

She tamped down her unbusinesslike feelings. After putting on her spectacles, she read the ad, and with an approving nod, returned it to him. "This is perfect."

Mr. Graves sat on the edge of his desk. He leaned toward her, a wide grin spreading across his face.

Something about this man made her feel content, like she did in church, but had never experienced in her home growing up. She hardly knew him, so the thought made no sense. And Adelaide prided herself on being a sensible woman.

"I'll run this in the next edition," Mr. Graves said.

"And I'll deliver my column personally. On Monday. If you print it, the column should take care of the bill."

He nodded. "Are you always this efficient?"

"I take my work seriously."

"Ah, a woman after my own heart."

He'd called them kindred spirits, declared her to be a woman after his own heart. The words ricocheted through her and left a hitch in her breathing and a huge knot in her stomach. Dare she hope for something too important to consider?

On Monday Adelaide once again sat across from the editor, this time with her fashion column clutched in her palm. When she handed it over to Mr. Graves, her heart tripped in her chest. Why had this column become so important?

"Neat, bold strokes, a woman not afraid to share her mind." He grinned, settling behind his desk to read.

Across from him, Adelaide fidgeted like a student waiting outside the principal's office while Mr. Graves bent his head to read. After he finished, he smiled. "Your assessment of women's fashions is written with the wit and flair I'd only expect from a professional journalist. I'll run it in the next edition."

"I loved writing it."

"If you want another article, let me know."

"I'd hoped you'd want a monthly column."

Mr. Graves ran his fingers through his

hair. "Well, perhaps. Let's see how this article is received first."

"Fair enough."

"I'm guessing we'll get positive feedback from the ladies. Who knows? Maybe the men, too." He tapped the paper. "You have a gift for words."

Slowly a smile took over his face. "Would you be my dinner guest Saturday evening?"

Adelaide blinked. Had he asked her to dinner? She gulped. "Dinner? Saturday?"

"If that isn't a good night . . ."

He must think I'm an idiot. "Saturday will be fine."

A strange tightness seized her throat. How long since she'd shared a meal with a man? Years. And never with a man this attractive, this intelligent. A man, who had only to smile in her direction to set her heart hammering.

Evidently from his calm, easy demeanor, Mr. Graves often asked a woman to share a meal. Something she'd best remember, lest she make too much of the invitation.

"I'll call for you at seven," he said.

"Seven," she repeated.

"I thought we might go to the Becker House."

She nodded, recovering her wits and her

manners. "The Becker House would be lovely."

"When I arrived in town, I stayed there, so I speak from experience. The food *is* great."

The door rattled shut. A rotund gentleman dropped the briefcase he carried, then shoved his hat back on his head and mopped his forehead with a handkerchief. "Whooee, it sure is hot for April. Never thought I'd complain about the heat after the winter we had, but this day is an oven, and I'm the hog roasting inside."

Charles crossed to the stranger. "May I help you, sir?"

"You can indeed. I'm looking for Mr. Charles Graves."

"You've found him."

"Excellent! Saves me a trip back into the sun." He stuck out a palm. "I'm Spencer Evans, your father's attorney. My condolences for your loss."

Adam Graves had died? Adelaide's gaze darted to the editor. Mr. Graves gave a curt nod. She hadn't seen anything about it in the paper. Nor did his son act grieved, but from her limited experience, she realized men didn't carry their feelings on their sleeves.

"I'm sorry about your father, Mr. Graves."

Rising, Adelaide tucked her spectacles into her bag. "I'd best be going."

"I'll see you Saturday evening, Miss Crum."

"Did you say Miss *Crum?*" Mr. Evans turned toward her. "Could you be *Adelaide* Crum?" When she nodded, the lawyer slapped his hands together. "It's a piece of luck finding you here. A sure piece of luck."

"I'm afraid I don't understand —"

"Of course you don't. I apologize for being obtuse. This unseasonable heat must be muddling my brain, what there is of it." He chuckled. "As I said, I'm Adam Graves's attorney. If I locate all the heirs before I melt, I'd like to read his will at one o'clock this afternoon. If you both are available, that is."

Adelaide looked at Mr. Graves, then back to Mr. Evans. "There must be some mistake. I didn't know Adam Graves."

The editor frowned. "Are you certain of your facts, Mr. Evans?"

"I make it a point to be certain of my facts." Mr. Evans gave a nod toward the stack of newsprint. "I'm sure in your business, you do the same. Adelaide Crum is one of Adam Graves's heirs, as is one Mary Graves. Do you know where I can find her?"

Mr. Graves nodded. "Mary lives on South Sixth Street between Maple and Conner. If

79

you'd like, I can take you to her place right now."

Filled with unspoken questions, the editor's gaze locked with Adelaide's. Baffled by the turn of events, she looked away.

"I'd appreciate it." The lawyer turned to her. "We'll meet in the private dining room of the Becker House this afternoon at one o'clock, Miss Crum. That way I can take the morning train back to Cincinnati tomorrow." He shoved his hat back in place.

Adelaide looked at the clock on the wall. "In less than an hour, Mary will be coming to my shop to quilt."

"Wonderful. That'll give me time to speak to her before she leaves. Whoo-ee, it is indeed my lucky day!" Mr. Evans turned toward Adelaide. "And yours, too, Miss Crum." He gave her a jaunty wave. "See you this afternoon."

Then he and Mr. Graves were gone, leaving Adelaide with an uncomfortable feeling that this was not her lucky day. Not her lucky day at all.

Adelaide laid out scissors and thread, and then prepared a sandwich for lunch. While thinking about the odd meeting with the lawyer, she layered ham and cheese on two slices of bread. With so much on her mind, she had no interest in food or quilting. But company might take her mind off the one o'clock appointment.

At exactly ten o'clock, the "Snip and Sew" quilting group, carrying lunch pails and sewing baskets, pushed through the shop door, the four women clumped together as if they'd been stitched at the hips. They chattered and laughed, except for Mary, who gave Adelaide an encouraging smile.

Tension eased from between Adelaide's shoulder blades. At least, Mary didn't appear disturbed that she'd be at the reading of Adam Graves's will.

Bringing up the rear came a fifth woman, the one person Adelaide had least expected to be interested in quilting.

Fannie Whitehall.

Sally pulled Fannie forward. "Fannie's joining our group. She's not a quilter, but she can stitch a fine hem."

"How nice of you to help, Fannie," Laura said.

The others greeted Fannie, friendly as birds on a branch.

The news thudded to the bottom of Adelaide's stomach. From seeing Fannie at *The Ledger,* Adelaide knew the girl hankered to play husband archery, and Mr. Graves was the target. Still, money raised from the sale of the quilt would buy supplies for the Sunday school. Only a selfish woman would resent another pair of helping hands. She swallowed her reservations and offered a smile. "Welcome, Fannie."

"Well, shall we get started?" Laura said.

Adelaide led the ladies to where she'd assembled her frame and had attached the Dresden Plate quilt. The pastel petals and yellow centers looked pretty enough to attract bees.

Adelaide grabbed a chair for Fannie, then she and Mary put away the ladies' lunches.

"Charles brought Mr. Evans by," Mary said in a low voice. "He told me you're one of the heirs."

"I can't imagine why."

"We'll find out soon enough."

Adelaide's stomach knotted. Whatever happened at the reading of the will, there'd be consequences.

By the time Mary and Adelaide took their places around the frame and threaded their needles, the chatter had ebbed and all heads bent over their work.

Fannie sewed beside Adelaide, taking each stitch with care, surprising Adelaide, who'd expected the girl's workmanship to be shoddy. At the thought, Adelaide's needle pierced the layers of fabric, pricking both her finger and her conscience.

Pausing in the middle of a stitch, Fannie looked at Mary with big, innocent eyes. "I'm hoping you can help me, Mary."

Mary tied a knot in her thread. "You're doing a fine job."

"I don't mean help with quilting." Fannie sighed. "I mean help with men. Well, not all men, only one. Charles Graves."

Adelaide missed the eye of the needle with her thread.

Mary shrugged. "I can't be much help. My brother-in-law is a mystery, even to me."

"Adelaide, you were talking to Mr. Graves." Fannie whisked her gaze over Adelaide either sizing her up as the competition — or fitting her for a very tight seam. "You —" Fannie hesitated "— don't have designs on him, do you?"

Adelaide's pulse skipped a beat. "Designs?"

Every hand hovered over the quilt, all eyes riveted on her and Fannie. Adelaide shook her head.

"I didn't think you did. I told Mama, 'Adelaide Crum is too levelheaded for a man like Mr. Graves.' I can't imagine you two courting." Fannie's eyes narrowed. "So you were at the paper on business. Nothing else?"

Heat filled Adelaide's veins. "Yes, business for the shop."

Fannie beamed. "Oh, I'm glad. I'm mad about Mr. Graves. Mama says he'd be quite the catch."

With her teeth, Sally broke off a length of thread. "Are you doing a little fishing, Fannie? Over at *The Ledger*?"

The women chuckled.

Fannie sighed. "I'm not sure you noticed, Adelaide, but Mr. Graves didn't seem all that eager to try my b-biscuits." Her voice quavered. "I don't understand what I'm doing wrong."

As much as Adelaide didn't want to, a thread of sympathy tugged between her heart and Fannie's. The girl meant well, even if she didn't see the consequences of her words or actions.

"Maybe your reputation as a cook is scaring him off," Laura said, one brow arched.

"Well, it's hard to get the temperature right in that huge cookstove of Mama's. But how would Mr. Graves know that?"

"You told him," Adelaide reminded her.

"I did?" Fannie thought a second. "Oh, I did!" Her green eyes filled with tears. "I've ruined my chances with him, exactly like I ruin my biscuits."

Adelaide laid down her needle. "That's no

reason to cry."

"I'm sorry." Fannie dashed away the tears slipping down her cheeks. "It's just that I'm getting . . . well, desperate."

Martha harrumphed. "Desperate? How?"

"In three months, I'll be twenty. I've always planned to be engaged by my twentieth birthday. I'm getting old!" she wailed.

Fast losing sympathy for the girl, and with her own birthday looming, Adelaide bit back a retort.

Laura shook her head. "Fannie, dear, I'm sure you don't intend to, but you have a way of making me feel ancient."

Fannie gasped. "Oh, chicken feathers, Laura. I'm sorry."

"Why are you in such a rush anyway?" Martha asked, smoothing her dress over her bulging belly. "If you ask me, men are like flies. You trap yourself one, only to learn he can be a pest."

"Appears to me, yours has been pestering you plenty," Sally said and the room once again filled with laughter.

Fannie took up her needle again. "I'll lose my looks soon."

Sally waved a dismissive hand. "Phooey! You're pretty. I look like a possum and I still managed to get a husband."

Adelaide gasped. "You do not look like a

possum!"

"I do," Sally said, stitching along a rose-sprigged petal. "Small beady eyes, long nose, gray hair. Why, with my sons toting guns everywhere, I rarely venture out after dark."

Chuckles bounced off the high ceiling. "You're making fun, but I'm serious," Fannie moaned. "What am I doing wrong?"

Laura rose and stepped around the frame, then tilted Fannie's face to hers. "You're too eager. Let the man take the lead."

"I'm only being friendly," she said dismissing the comment. "What I need is a new hat, maybe a new way to style my hair. You always look fashionable, Adelaide. Will you help me?"

Adelaide thought of telling Fannie to leave the editor alone, but that wasn't her place. Nor did she care who he courted, though she had questions about the man. Even more about Adam Graves's will.

Sally gave Fannie a wink. "Play possum more, Fannie."

"Play possum?"

Sally nodded. "When you chase the men like a hound dog after a fox, why, you take all the fun out of it. Pretend you don't care. Pretend you wouldn't feed them a biscuit if they were the last to arrive for the fishes and loaves."

Fannie turned to Adelaide. "You're the best possum I know. Would you help me become more . . . ?"

"Demure," Laura provided.

"Demure?" Fannie smiled wide. "I like the sound of that."

Had Fannie compared her to a wild animal that hung from a tree by its tail? Adelaide worked up a smile before she injured Fannie with her needle. As much as Fannie grated on her nerves, if she refused, the ladies might decide she had an interest in Mr. Graves. "It would be my pleasure."

"With your help, Adelaide, Charles Graves will fall in love with me, and I'll soon be a married lady."

As Adelaide listened to Fannie chatter on about his virtues, she realized her help meant trying to get Fannie a husband and children. She had to wonder —

What kind of bargain had she struck? And what would it cost her in the end?

Charles paced the private dining room at the Becker House. His sister-in-law, wearing her best finery, sat watching him, her expression wistful. Could she be thinking Sam should be sitting beside her, instead of lying in Crownland Cemetery?

He'd wanted to rip into Mr. Evans's briefcase to look at the terms of his father's will. When it came to legalities, the gregarious attorney kept a tight rein on his mouth and skillfully sidestepped every question Charles had slung at him, giving no hint why Adam had mentioned the milliner in his will.

At exactly one o'clock Mr. Evans ushered Miss Crum, looking as perplexed as he felt, into the room. She glanced at him, her eyes filling with sympathy, probably for his loss. She couldn't know grief was the last emotion his father's death elicited.

She still wore the bird nest hat. On her, the silly hat looked good. Every hair in place, her clothing spotless, Miss Crum appeared serene. Only a heightened color in her cheeks suggested either the heat or an inner turmoil bothered her.

Well, she wasn't the only one stirred up by the chain of events. His father was no philanthropist. He'd never cared about the financial problems a woman might have either running a business or raising two children alone. He'd never cared about anyone.

Mr. Evans stepped forward. "Miss Crum, I believe you said that you and Mary Graves quilt together."

Miss Crum smiled. "Yes, and we attend the same church. Mary's father is my doctor."

"This is indeed a small town." Mr. Evans grinned, motioning to the table. "Well, since we're all here, let's take seats and get down to business before we roast and find ourselves on the hotel bill of fare." He chuckled, but no one else laughed.

Miss Crum took a chair across from Mary. Charles strode to the other side of the table and sat beside his brother's widow.

After sitting at the head of the table, Mr. Evans unlocked his briefcase and took out a sheaf of papers. "I have here Adam Graves's last will and testament."

Charles shifted in his seat.

" 'I, Adam Graves, being of sound mind, do hereby bequeath to my son, Charles Andrew Graves, and to Mary Lynn Graves, my son Samuel Eugene Graves's widow, my house in Cincinnati and its contents.' "

Apparently his father had kept his boyhood home. Nothing could ever make him step inside that place.

Mr. Evans glanced at him and Mary. "If neither of you want to move in . . ."

Both Mary and Charles shook their heads.

"Then I suggest the house and belongings be sold at auction. My assistant can ship personal items you might want."

"Sell them all," Charles said, his tone filled with bitterness.

"If Mary agrees, I can do that, except for this." He took a silky pouch from his briefcase and removed a gold pocket watch, the fob hanging from a thin chain. "When Adam made out his will, he asked me to give this watch to you personally."

Taking the watch, Charles felt the weight of it in his palm and took in the intricate engraving on the lid. His gaze dropped to the fob. He pictured Grandpa Graves, a large man with a hearty laugh, dangling the fob from callused hands, coaxing Charles and Sam onto his lap. His grandparents' rare visits were peaceful times. He tucked the watch in his pocket.

" 'I bequeath Charles Graves the sum of two thousand dollars,' " Mr. Evan continued, " 'and fifty percent ownership of *The Noblesville Ledger.*' "

Charles's jaw tightened. Leaving half ownership of the paper to him and half to Mary wasn't good business, but at least Charles knew his sister-in-law wouldn't interfere at the paper.

Mr. Evans handed over the bank draft. "In a moment, I'll go over the ownership papers." Evans turned to the will. "I hereby bequeath to Mary Graves the sum of five thousand dollars."

Charles squeezed Mary's hand, pleased his father had realized she needed money more than he. The money would come in handy in the years ahead, raising Sam's boys. And would give Mary the security she lacked since his brother had died. Weeping silent tears, she took the bank draft with trembling fingers.

Mr. Evans focused on the page in front of him. Charles's pulse kicked up a notch.

" 'I hereby bequeath to Adelaide Crum, daughter of Constance Gunder Crum, fifty-percent ownership of *The Noblesville Ledger.*' "

Constance Gunder? Air whooshed out of Charles's mouth and his gaze settled on the woman across from him.

"Me? Why? I don't understand any of this," Miss Crum said. "Why mention my mother?"

Constance Gunder, the name Charles's mother had hurled in his father's face after Adam had accused his wife of flirting in church. Charles had never forgotten the name — or his father's reaction. Adam had backhanded his mother, knocking her to the floor, and then stood over her, shouting she wasn't worthy to wipe Constance Gunder's shoes and if she ever spoke that name again, he'd kill her. Charles had known then that somehow this woman had been at the root of Adam's anger, anger he expelled through his fists.

Constance Gunder, the woman Charles learned to despise — could she really be Miss Crum's *mother?*

How could his father do this? Was this one last ha-ha from the grave?

"Furthermore —" Mr. Evans began.

Charles jumped to his feet. Mary laid a hand on his wrist, but he jerked away from her touch. "What's going on here?" His voice sounded gruff and he cleared his throat. If only he could clear this nightmare his father had concocted as easily.

"It's quite simple," Mr. Evans said, nonplussed by Charles's reaction. "You and Miss Crum are half owners of *The Noblesville Ledger.*"

"That's ridiculous!"

Mr. Evans's gaze returned to the will. "There's more."

"More?" Unable to sit, Charles strode to the fireplace, putting him across from Miss Crum, the woman who'd made a crack in his frozen heart. *What a joke on him.*

Miss Crum's eyes were wide, probably seeing dollar signs. Yet, even as he thought it, he knew the accusation wasn't true. Still, the idea clung to his mind like a burr under a saddle.

Mr. Evans bent over the paperwork. " 'The equal shares of *The Noblesville Ledger* are not to be sold by either Charles Graves or Adelaide Crum for a period of two months. If either heir goes against my wishes, and sells his or her half of *The Noblesville Ledger* before the end of a two-month waiting period, the equipment and building are to be sold, all proceeds going to charity.' "

Charles stalked back to the table. Mary met his gaze with a worried frown. "He promised the paper to me! Why did he leave a perfect stranger half of *my* paper? Then force us to keep this ludicrous arrangement for months?"

Mr. Evans tipped his head between Charles and Miss Crum. "Perhaps she isn't a stranger, at least not to your father."

Color climbed Miss Crum's neck. "I'm not sure what you're suggesting —"

"My father returned to Noblesville only once — four years ago, when he bought *The Ledger.*" Charles turned to Miss Crum. "Did you two arrange this then?"

Miss Crum gasped. "I've never even met your father."

"Adam didn't share his motives with me, but rest assured, knowing your father, he had his reasons. Where there's a will, there's always a reason." Mr. Evans chuckled to himself.

Charles scowled. "Have you considered joining a minstrel show, Mr. Evans?"

The attorney sobered. "I apologize." He handed Mary and Miss Crum a copy of the will, then laid the third copy where Charles had been sitting. "This lawyering can get dry as dust. I can see this is no laughing matter."

"Surely we can make this partnership work for two months," Miss Crum said, as if her ownership was of no consequence. "I won't be underfoot at *The Ledger*. I have my own business to run."

"Charles, sit down," Mary said, tears brimming in her eyes.

But he couldn't sit. Just when Charles had found some measure of control over his life, his father yanked it out of his hands. Even from the grave, Adam managed to control — no, punish — him.

His gaze sought the milliner's. "If you're expecting this business relationship to be pleasurable, Miss Crum, you're mistaken. As soon as I can, I'll buy you out. In the

meantime, I promise, this will be the longest two months of your life."

CHAPTER FIVE

Minutes later Adelaide stormed out of the hotel and strode up the street. How dare Charles Graves act as if she'd robbed him? She'd considered him a friend, but he'd treated her like an enemy. True, he'd been denied half ownership of the paper, a sizable financial loss, but that hadn't been her doing.

Adelaide dodged a woman holding a towheaded boy by one hand. The sight of the child put a catch in her throat. But she wouldn't think about that now, not when her mind couldn't grasp Charles's hatred of her mother, a woman he'd never met.

She'd get to the bottom of this. No more guessing about her mother and father, about her past. But where should she begin?

Before taking sick, once or twice a year her mother had cleaned the attic. Now that Adelaide thought about it, she always gave an excuse why she didn't need help. The last time Adelaide had been up there, she'd stored equipment used to care for an invalid. She'd seen a few pieces of furniture, a couple trunks. Could the trunks hold the answer?

About to turn the corner onto Ninth, she heard a shout.

"Adelaide, wait!" With one hand clamped on her bright green hat and holding her billowing skirts with the other, Mary rushed toward her. Adelaide slowed her steps.

"You're — a fast — walker," Mary said, her words uttered in hitches as she came alongside.

"Only when I'm angry."

Mary sighed. "I'm sorry about Charles's reaction to the will. He'll get used to sharing the paper."

"I doubt that."

"He calls the paper his dream, but really it's his refuge."

Two men strolled past, discussing the rising price of seed. Once out of earshot, Adelaide leaned closer to Mary. "Do you understand why Adam Graves left me half the paper?"

"I have no idea. I never knew Sam's father, only met him once — at Sam's funeral. He came up to the casket, spoke to me and the boys, and then tried to have a word with Charles. That didn't go well, and Adam left immediately, didn't even attend Sam's graveside service. He never contacted me after that, not even to check on his grandsons."

Mary fell in beside Adelaide and they began walking again, but at a slower pace. When they reached the Masonic Lodge with its impressive gables, Mary cleared her throat. "If you never met Adam, then the connection had to have been between your mother and Adam."

"My mother never mentioned him, but a friend said they were childhood sweethearts. I don't understand any of it, but I'm going to search the attic to see what I can find."

Mary laid a hand on Adelaide's arm. "Do you want company?"

At the gesture, Adelaide blinked back sudden tears. "That's a kind offer, but . . . why would you want to?"

"I wouldn't want to poke around in the past alone. Plus, I knew Sam, and I know Charles. Perhaps I can give you insight."

"I'd appreciate it," Adelaide admitted, then led the way to her shop.

Inside, they found Laura helping a shopper try on a hat. "Back already?"

Adelaide took Laura aside. "Thanks for tending the store. Would you mind staying while Mary and I have a visit?"

Laura greeted Mary, and then smiled. "I'd love to stay. I've missed the shop."

Adelaide ushered Mary up to her quarters, then lit the lantern and opened the door to the attic. Adelaide climbed the stairs with Mary close behind. In the dim light, Adelaide didn't see the cobweb until it plastered against her face, a sticky reminder of the attic's neglect.

At the top of the stairs, the scent of lavender permeated everything her mother had touched, now mingled with the musty smell of age. Regret she and her mother hadn't been close laid heavy on her chest. Maybe here she'd find the clue to her mother's aloofness.

Mary looked around the stand-up attic. "This is huge," she said, then sneezed.

"I'm sorry, it needs cleaning."

Mary laughed. "With two boys, I'm used to a little dust."

Along one wall stood makeshift shelves filled with long forgotten fruit jars, crocks, a glass butter churn with a wooden paddle, a jar of buttons. Across the way sat a dressmaker dummy and an elaborate wicker carriage.

Under the window, Adelaide spied the large camelback trunk.

Dropping to her knees, Adelaide blew a layer of dust off the lid, and then raised it carefully. She removed an old rust-stained quilt then pushed aside a stack of linens. Underneath she found a celluloid-covered box. She tugged it out, and then lifted the tiny brass catch to reveal a stack of handkerchiefs. "Granny must have tatted these."

Mary fingered the lace. "They're lovely."

A visit from her grandmother had been an oasis in the desert of her life. She put the box aside to take downstairs.

Still, no hint here to what went before. Adelaide led Mary past a dresser. Tucked behind a hall tree, she found the small trunk. She rolled it out, its metal wheels squeaking, and then opened the latch. Inside she found another quilt, a half-finished pillow slip, a Bible — Granny's.

Had she been foolish to think she'd find anything that would reveal her mother's past in this dirty, stuffy place?

About to give up, her hand brushed against paper, paper that crackled with age. "Oh, it's my parents' marriage license."

The license promised "until death do us part," yet her parents' marriage had ended nearly as quickly as it began. Her gaze swept over the wedding date. She gasped. January

17, 1866, not the October date she'd been told.

"Is something wrong?"

Adelaide's fingers flew to her mouth. "They married six months before my birth. I didn't know."

A spark of insight ignited in Adelaide's heart. Her mother's warnings about men now made sense.

Oh, Mama, did my conception end your hopes and dreams?

The afternoon sun glinted in through the window, sparking off an old mirror in the corner. Adelaide rose and walked to the window facing the street, thinking about her mother's loss of independence and the load of responsibility she'd carried alone.

A woman and small child, their eyes downcast, came into view. Adelaide's pulse tripped. Emma, the orphan girl, held Frances Drummond's hand. Dressed in black from head to foot, a veil covered Frances's face. They stopped in front of *The Ledger,* then disappeared inside. Perhaps Frances had a delivery problem with the paper. Yet, something about the two troubled her.

Adelaide turned back to Mary. "Your boys will be home from school soon. Maybe we should continue the search later."

Mary looked at the watch pinned to her bodice. "Oh, I should be going, but we haven't found what you wanted."

"I'll look another time." She smiled at Mary. "But thanks, I'm grateful for your company."

Closing the lid of the trunk, and gathering the box of hankies and the lantern, they returned below.

Later, Adelaide waved goodbye to Mary and Laura, then stood at the window, waiting for Frances and Emma to leave *The Ledger.*

Charles threw down his pen and shoved aside the copy he'd tried to edit for the past hour. Even with his insides twisted into a pretzel over losing control of the paper, he couldn't put Miss Crum out of his mind. He'd not soon forget her anger-filled eyes tinged with hurt.

The door opened and he lifted his gaze from the paperwork, half expecting, even half hoping to find Miss Crum standing there. It wasn't. A twinge of disappointment settled in his gut.

His visitor wore a black gauze veil attached to her hat, hiding her face, making it difficult to identify her — until Charles spotted a little girl he *did* recognize peeking around the woman's skirts — one of the orphans. Charles rose and went around his desk.

Carrying a satchel, the woman approached with cautious steps. "Mr. Graves, I'm bringing Emma to you."

He leaned closer. "Mrs. Drummond?"

"Yes." Her hand fluttered to the veil. "I'm feeling poorly . . . since Mama died. Not up to caring for Emma right now."

"I see." But he didn't see at all. "What about William?"

"Ed needs William on the farm. But Emma . . ." She hesitated. "Emma needs someone to see she eats right and keeps up with her schoolwork, needs someone to braid her hair." With a gentle touch, she ran work-worn fingers over Emma's silken plaits. "I hope you might know a good place for her until I'm on my feet."

Charles saw Mrs. Drummond's obvious reluctance to let Emma go and her responsibility for Emma shifted to his shoulders.

"I'd be glad to help." This poor woman carried a heavy load. "I'm sorry about your mother's . . . death."

"I can't believe she'd . . ." Her shaky voice trailed off.

Neither spoke the horrifying truth lingering beneath the conversation — suicide. He could imagine Mrs. Drummond's regrets; guilt for not having seen it coming, for not having done more to prevent such a loss. "Can I do anything else?"

"No." She bent close to Emma, emitting a soft moan, and then kissed the little girl's forehead.

Charles took a step closer. "You seem to be in pain."

"I wrenched my back, but I'll be fine." Mrs. Drummond handed Emma the satchel. "Remember what I told you." The little girl bobbed a promise, her face melancholy. Mrs. Drummond's fingers skimmed over Emma's cheeks. "I'll be going, then." With a hurried step, she walked out the door, leaving Emma behind.

Emma stared after her until the door closed, then turned to him with sad eyes. Where was his assistant? "Teddy!"

"Yeah, boss?"

"Run to the bank and then on to the superintendent's office and ask Mr. Sparks and Mr. Paul to come as soon as they can."

"Sure." Unspoken questions packed Teddy's gaze, but he headed out the door.

Charles cleared his throat. "Emma, I'm Mr. Graves."

She looked back at him, her blue eyes swimming with tears, twisting his innards into a knot. He patted her shoulder awkwardly. "Don't worry. Everything is going to be fine."

He had no idea how to keep his promise.

Tears spilled over her pale lower lashes, becoming visible now that they were wet and spiky. If he didn't do something, she'd start bawling. The prospect sent him behind his desk. He jerked open the top drawer and rummaged through it until he found what he sought — a bag of peppermints. "When I was a youngster," he began, "on my way home from school, I'd pass Mrs. Wagner's house. She'd be rocking on her porch, wearing a gray tattered sweater, no matter how hot the day . . ."

Emma stopped crying, but looked far from cheerful.

"She'd call me up on the porch, ask if I was studying and behaving. Then, she'd reach into the pocket of her sweater and pull out a peppermint." Charles took a candy from the bag. Emma's eyes widened. "She'd say, 'You're a smart boy, Charles. Work hard and one day you'll make something of yourself.' And, she'd drop the candy into my palm — like this."

He opened Emma's small hand and let a peppermint fall into her palm. When the corners of her mouth turned up in a smile, a peculiar feeling shot through him. As it had for him all those years ago, the candy once again worked wonders.

His entire adult life, he'd kept a stash of peppermints around to remind him of Mrs. Wagner, the one person who had believed in him, who'd given him a desire to improve his lot. The candy still tasted as sweet as her words. But even while Emma sucked on the treat, worry etched her face. Paul and Sparks better get here fast. He only had so many peppermints.

Twenty minutes later, Thaddeus Paul and John Sparks entered the office.

Sparks's gaze settled on Emma. "What's the emergency?"

Charles bent down to Emma's eye level. "I need to talk to these gentlemen. Will you be all right until I'm back?"

She nodded, though her gaze lingered on the bag of candy. Charles fished out another peppermint and then motioned for the men to accompany him into the back room.

As soon as they followed him in, Charles closed the door. "Grief stricken over her mother's suicide, Mrs. Drummond is unable to care for Emma Grounds. Her husband is looking after the boy. We need someone to take Emma in temporarily."

Thaddeus frowned. "Any idea who?"

Sparks shoved his bowler back on his forehead. "We turned away a few couples from the area, but it'll take a day or so to get her settled." His brow furrowed. "She needs a place now."

Charles had an idea, one that nagged at him. As a member of the committee, finding someone to take care of the child had to be his first consideration, even if that someone owned half the paper. Still, no one would be more conscientious than Adelaide Crum. He had an even stronger conviction she'd be a good mother — even if her own mother had ruined his family.

Is it my fault I'm Adam Graves's son?

The truth zinged through him. No, no more than Adelaide could be held accountable for the hell Charles called home. He took a deep, cleansing breath. "How about asking Miss Crum?"

"Hmm." Sparks pursed his lips in thought. "Well, her recent apology exemplifies her character. What do you think, Thaddeus?"

Paul frowned. "Can't we find a *married* woman?"

"None of us has time to deal with this," Sparks said, his tone exasperated. "Miss Crum is right across the street. The arrangement isn't permanent, so I have no problem with it."

Paul shoved his glasses higher on his nose. "That would be the easiest solution."

"Then it's settled, if she's willing," Sparks said, his gaze sweeping Charles's face, then Paul's. They all nodded.

"Who's going to ask her?" Sparks plopped his hat back in place. "I shouldn't be away from the bank."

Already heading for the door, Paul turned back. "I need to get back to the office, too. Can you see to it, Charles?"

He'd done the least legwork for the committee so it was only fair he ask Miss Crum. His wayward pulse leapt at the prospect of seeing her, giving her this news. Nodding his acceptance, he walked the men into the main room and out the door, both obviously relieved to dump the matter in his lap.

Charles grabbed his coat and shrugged it on. Without a doubt, Miss Crum would take care of Emma. But the more he thought about it, the more he suspected that once she had a taste of mothering, she'd be starved for more when the child left.

What had he been thinking when he suggested her?

He'd been thinking how she'd look when she heard the news, the sparkle his words would put into her clear blue eyes. He'd taken part in hurting her, both with the committee and now over the ownership of the paper, and he wanted to make amends.

Grateful for Teddy's experience with children, Charles said, "Keep an eye on Emma, will you?"

With a grin, Teddy hunkered down beside the little girl. "Sure thing, if she'll share a peppermint with me."

Charles strode to the door, knowing he danced dangerously close to a web of entanglements. Every instinct warned him off, told him to stay clear of Miss Crum, while every muscle and tendon in his body moved him out of the office and across the street.

Adelaide knotted the end of the thread and then snipped it. Earlier, she'd watched Frances leave *The Ledger* without Emma. She'd wanted to call out to Frances, to ask what was going on, but her classmate's slumped posture had kept Adelaide silent. Clearly, something had happened, but what? And what part did Mr. Graves play?

His last words rattled through her mind, . . . *expecting this business relationship to be pleasurable, you're mistaken . . . buy you out . . . longest two months of your life.*

He'd failed to see she couldn't fix the past,

especially a past she hadn't shared. She couldn't even fix her own problems.

He detested the idea of her involvement at the paper, but she didn't have time to run her shop and work at the paper, too. Still, as part owner of *The Ledger,* she *could* have a voice. Express some important ideas. Maybe make a difference for the women in town. That much she could — and would — do. Whether Charles Graves liked it or not.

The bell jingled bringing Adelaide to her feet. Mr. Graves, his expression solemn, walked to the counter where she waited, her pulse tap-dancing in her temples. If he had come here to berate her mother, she wouldn't listen.

He met her gaze. "I'm glad we're alone. We need to talk."

Adelaide hadn't realized she'd been holding her breath until it came out in a gust. "About you hating the sight of me?"

He had the decency to look discomfited. "I don't." He drew in a breath. "I'm sorry about my outburst. I realized a truth earlier. You can't help that you're Constance Gunder's daughter, any more than I can help being Charles Graves's son." He plowed a hand through his thick hair, leaving furrows deep enough to plant seed in. "I've been a bear. Will you forgive me?"

Adelaide saw something wounded and raw in his eyes, telling her Mr. Graves had suffered. "I forgive you." She smiled. "But you're right, you were a bear."

"Maybe you'll be happier with me when you hear the main reason I've come." He took a step closer, his brown eyes filling with light. "Mrs. Drummond isn't well and needs someone to look after Emma Grounds. The committee thought of you."

She pressed a hand to her heart, for surely if she didn't, it would leap from her chest. Never in her wildest dreams had she considered this possibility. "Emma, come *here?* To live with *me?*"

"Yes." The corners of his eyes crinkled with a grin.

Why? Why had the committee given her this chance? Then she knew. *Thank you, God.* "It's an answer to prayer."

He frowned. "It's the committee's doing, not God's."

She shook her head, a smile riding her lips. "Oh, Mr. Graves, you have a lot to learn about the power of prayer." But she wouldn't worry about that now, not when she had a child to love. Oh, maybe two. "What about William?"

"Mr. Drummond is looking after him."

Charles lowered his head and looked her straight in the eye. "You understand this arrangement is *only* until Mrs. Drummond gets back on her feet?"

Adelaide came around the counter. "Of course."

His eyes narrowed. "Do you? Really?"

"Yes, yes!" For however long He willed it, Adelaide was going to treasure this gift from God. The possibilities raced through her mind — sharing meals with Emma, reading her bedtime stories and teaching her to sew. Adelaide's breath came in gulps and her lungs expanded until they felt ready to explode. "When will she arrive?"

"Is now convenient?" A grin curved across his face.

"Yes! Oh, thank you!" In a second of wild abandon, Adelaide threw her arms around him, giving him a fierce hug. His torso felt hard and wide, masculine. A realization struck — she'd never hugged a man before, nor acted so impetuously. Heat climbing her cheeks, she stepped back. "I shouldn't have done that, Mr. Graves."

He moved closer, until the warmth of his breath drifted along her chin. "No need to apologize. And please, after that hug, I think you should call me Charles."

"Charles." She tasted the sound of it on

her tongue. "Will you . . . call me Adelaide?" A forward suggestion, but given the circumstances, it felt right.

His gaze swallowed her up, left her breathless.

"Instead, may I call you Addie?"

"Addie?" No one had ever given her a nickname or a pet name before. It made her feel special. Her hand drifted to her chignon, fussing with it like an old maid. She quickly lowered her hand to her side.

"If you don't like it —"

"Oh, but I do." To her, Adelaide sounded like a hair-up kind of woman, while Addie seemed like a hair-down kind of gal. The kind of woman she'd always wanted to be.

"Then Addie is what I'll call you."

She smiled, feeling feminine, alive and — oh, my — cherished.

To keep her hands from straying to him, she clasped them together. For now, she'd focus on Emma. She, Adelaide Crum, would be taking care of the little girl she'd sensed a kinship with from the first moment she'd seen her.

"Emma's waiting in my office. I'll bring her to you."

"I'd like to get her myself."

He looked around the showroom, empty of customers. "Can you leave the shop?"

In answer to his question, she walked to the door, lowered the shade and flipped the sign in the window to read CLOSED. Dusting her palms together, she grinned. "I'm the boss."

Charles chuckled. Adelaide joined in.

Filled with gratitude to God, she did something totally out of character, something she hadn't done since a little girl. Hiking her skirts to keep them from snaring her feet, she dashed out the door and ran across the street without her hat and gloves.

CHAPTER SIX

Charles caught up with Addie when she stopped in the middle of the street. She glowed with happiness. No doubt about it, the lady was headed for a fall. Especially if she thought this child heaven-sent. When the Drummonds wanted Emma back, how would she cope? How would God answer her prayers then?

She turned to him, a question on her features. "Charles?"

His given name, almost a caress, slipped off her tongue and warmed him. If only he could forget what stood between them. A dozen issues separated him from Addie. Her mother had destroyed his family. She held beliefs he hadn't shared since his childhood prayers had gone unanswered. She had needs he couldn't meet.

And he was his father's son.

A warning shout made Charles jerk to the right in time to see a team of horses barreling down on them. His stomach in his throat, he scooped Addie up in his arms and dashed for the safety of the walk, barely escaping the hooves. The wagon rattled past, kicking up dust; the driver raised his fist at them, shouting obscenities.

But with Addie cradled in his arms, fitting in the niche as if she belonged, Charles barely noticed. He quickly set her on her feet. She tugged at her clothing, her face flushed.

She splayed shaky fingers across her bosom. "Whew, that was close!" She gave him a weak smile. "Thank you, Charles."

He grinned. "The pleasure was mine."

"Before you rescued me, I started to say — the committee didn't suggest me. You did." She laid a hand on his sleeve. "Am I right?"

Charles nodded.

Tears filled her eyes. "Thank you again."

"You're welcome." Those eyes would be his undoing. He pulled his gaze away and cleared his throat, motioning toward the door of the paper. "Before we go in, I want to warn you Emma is upset. Mrs. Drummond's misery may be affecting her."

"Could be. Suicide has to be far worse than any natural death. I went to school and to church with Frances, so I knew her mother well. Sarah Hartman was a good woman."

Charles glanced over at the trim figure beside him, with her straight posture and youthful glow. "Mrs. Drummond looks old, worn down. I can't believe you two are the same age."

"Farm life must have taken a toll on her, or maybe it's that grouchy husband of hers."

He raised a brow. "You're very outspoken."

"Well, it's true, though I doubt her husband is the entire cause. I can't imagine losing a child." She paused, sympathy taking over her gaze. "Eddie's death had to cost Frances more than hard work or a disagreeable spouse ever could."

"I'm sure you're right." He wouldn't gain favor by harping on it, but the mention of Mrs. Drummond's lost child hammered home the need to warn Addie about the brevity of Emma's stay. "I'm concerned about your taking in Emma."

"Are you saying I'm not competent to care for a seven-year-old child, even for a while?"

He heard the irritation in her voice, the underlying pain of what she perceived as doubt. "Of course not, but when Emma returns to the Drummonds, there's a good chance you'll be hurt."

Adelaide pulled her arm from his grasp. "I'm a grown woman, Mr. Graves. Your concern is touching, but unwarranted. Besides, this is part of God's plan. I'm sure of it." She moved toward the door. "If you're finished, I'd like to get Emma settled."

Charles noted her formal address, the sharpness in her tone. She had every right to be annoyed. He'd suggested her, had dashed over to tell her and then had ruined the moment. "Addie."

She turned back, her expression cool.

"Emma's fortunate indeed to have you to look after her."

Her features softened and a smile crept across her face, lighting up her eyes. "Thank you, Charles."

Her grin touched his heart, tempting him to forget all those reasons he shouldn't get involved, but sanity reigned and he walked her to the door of *The Ledger.*

Inside the office, they found Emma rocking in his desk chair. With eyes closed, head lolling against the slats, her wide grin revealed two missing teeth. While he and Addie watched, the chair slowed and Emma's eyes popped open. Her gaze darted from Addie to Charles and the smile faded.

Addie knelt beside her. "I'm Adelaide

Crum. I remember the day you came to town." She motioned to the chair. "Is that fun?"

The little girl's head bobbed.

"Do you suppose I could have a turn?"

Emma hesitated and then scooted to the side, making room.

"I won't fit, but if you sat on my lap, we could both rock."

Charles's jaw fell open when Emma hopped down and climbed into Adelaide's lap. Soon, she and Emma giggled in the swaying chair, with its spring squealing, the awkwardness of their meeting forgotten. Watching them, something tightened in Charles's chest. How long since he'd heard joy like that?

Stored deep in his memory lived shrieks of terror, sobs and groans — the sounds of his childhood. Charles bit the inside of his cheek, fighting for control, mourning the loss of something he'd never had. Happiness. True happiness.

Pain came in many forms. Charles had thought he'd experienced them all. He'd put them behind him — or so he'd thought. Yet, deep inside he knew he hadn't let go of the past. How could he, when the past lived in him still?

He saw the hope — the faith — in Adelaide Crum and wondered how anyone could have such a thing.

Adelaide brought the chair to a halt. Leaning her chin atop Emma's head, she mouthed a thank-you, widening the crack in Charles's heart. Suddenly, he didn't want their time together to end. "Would you ladies like to walk to the livery to see my horse? We can drop Emma's satchel at the shop first."

Emma bounced off Adelaide's lap. "The livery!"

Addie rose and knelt before the little girl. "Let's get you settled in. We can visit the livery another time."

Emma sighed and gave a sad nod.

Addie studied Emma's rag-doll posture, then chucked her under the chin. "Getting settled can wait."

A look of surprise took over Emma's face, and then slid into a smile.

Charles grabbed a handful of sugar cubes from a bowl near the potbellied stove. "Let's take Ranger a treat."

Emma's hand darted out, palm cupped, and Charles dumped the sugar into it.

Emma beamed. "Ranger is a nice name."

Adelaide took Emma's free hand and Charles offered Adelaide his arm. When she slipped her hand into the bend, she looked up at him, her expression happy, grateful and full of optimism. The idea he could have a family ricocheted through him. He quickly dismissed the notion. He resolved to keep things impersonal, as he always had, but something sharp panged in his chest.

As Adelaide stepped inside the dim, cavernous stable, dust motes floated in the sunlight streaming through the open doorway. The pungent odor of manure and hay filled her nostrils. A horse nickered in a nearby stall, raising the fine hair on her nape. With Emma skipping at her side, Adelaide followed Charles to a stall midway down the aisle. He opened the door and led out a huge brown horse. Adelaide took a step back.

"Ladies, meet Ranger," he said, tying the horse to a post.

Emma gazed at Charles, a look of pure awe on her face. "Ranger's your very own horse?"

Charles grinned down at the little girl. "Yes, he is."

Watching them at a distance, tenderness for this child and this man filled her heart. Then the huge creature shook his head and stomped his hooves, rattling the floorboards — and Adelaide.

"I love horses." Emma patted Ranger's wide back.

"Hold out your hand," Charles said, demonstrating, "flat like a board, so he can see what you've got for him."

When Ranger's lips curled around the treats, Emma gasped, then giggled. "That tickles!"

Charles slipped out of his coat, hanging it on a nearby peg. "Would you like to help groom Ranger, Emma?"

In minutes, Emma teetered on a crate, clutching a brush bigger than both her hands. Charles showed her how to hold it, laying his large hand over Emma's much smaller one, helping her move the brush down the animal's coat.

When he stepped away, leaving Emma to do the job, Adelaide reminded herself not to trust this happy scene. Not to trust Charles. Oh, but the pull to do so wrapped its tentacles around her and squeezed.

Emma made long strokes, then shorter ones until the animal's coat gleamed. She looked at Adelaide over her shoulder. "Don't you want to brush Ranger, Miss Crum?"

Charles glanced at her. "Yes, Addie, don't you?"

A lump the size of a melon formed in her

belly. She'd been ten when she'd tumbled from a horse, breaking her leg and nearly getting her head stomped by the hooves. She'd steered clear of horses ever since.

Adelaide looked into two pair of eyes — one pair dancing with excitement, the other issuing a challenge. With God's help, she'd show this man her strength, her ability to overcome her fear, to be an example of courage to this child.

Raising her chin, she approached the horse gingerly, edging her hand closer. The huge animal raised a hoof, slammed it down, stalling Adelaide's hand midair. Ranger's dark brown tail swished at the flies pestering its hindquarters. Sucking in a gulp of air, she again reached a palm. The horse snorted. She withdrew.

Charles took Adelaide's hand and led her closer. "There's nothing to fear."

Oh, but she knew differently. And it wasn't only the four-legged animal in front of her.

Emma handed Adelaide the brush, leaving her little choice. "Here, Miss Adelaide!"

Charles sent her a gentle look of encouragement. "No rush. A big animal like Ranger takes getting used to."

Adelaide lifted her chin. She'd show him Adelaide Crum had courage. She laid the brush against Ranger's side, slowly moving the tool downward, careful not to press hard. Beneath the bristles the flesh on the horse's belly quivered, but Ranger didn't move.

Emma laughed. "Look! He's ticklish!"

Charles patted Emma's shoulder. "So he is. Maybe it's Miss Crum's touch."

Adelaide ran the brush along Ranger's back and once again down his sides, then stood back and cocked her head at Charles.

"This is fun!" Emma's eyes danced with delight. "Let's visit Ranger every day."

"I know Ranger would love seeing two such pretty ladies." He turned back to Adelaide, eyes gleaming with mischief. "Now that wasn't so bad, was it?"

"No, he's a beautiful animal."

Charles ran a hand along Ranger's dark brown mane. "He's alone too much. That's not good for a horse."

"That's not good for anyone," Adelaide said quietly.

Charles, looking eager to put distance between them, hurried to put the brush away, then led Ranger to his stall and secured the door.

Fine, she didn't want to get involved with a man. Not even this one. She knew first-hand the pain a man could cause. Her father had left her mother, hadn't cared enough to see his daughter again, not even once, as if she were unworthy, unlovable. With God's help she'd become strong, able to stand on her own two feet, all without a man.

So why had she accepted Charles's supper invitation? Loneliness. The answer tore through her, forcing her to take a steadying breath. No amount of hard work, praying or sharing with friends could fill the empty spot inside her.

Charles returned and the three of them stepped outside. Emma ran to the hay mound and then sent a questioning glance over her shoulder.

Adelaide nodded approval. "Go on. That looks like fun."

Emma flung an armful of hay into the air, squealing as it showered down on her upturned face. Grabbing more, she tossed it at Charles, the pieces scattering at his feet. Laughing, he scooped up an arsenal and chased after her. Emma raced behind Adelaide's skirts, at the exact moment Charles tossed the hay.

When the itching strands hit her face, Adelaide yelped, the fun, the sheer freedom of it leaping in her chest. "You're going to be sorry!" She ran toward the hay mound for ammunition.

"Oh, no you don't." Charles dove after her, tugging her down on the hay.

Suddenly he stopped, gazing down at her. With his face only inches away, close enough to touch, close enough to kiss, she froze, her breath caught in her throat.

Even she, a woman who knew nothing of men, recognized longing in his eyes, in the tiny specks of gold in their depths.

"Here I come, ready or not!" Emma tumbled down, pelting them with fistfuls of hay.

Charles and Adelaide sprang apart, the mood broken. For a split second, she'd forgotten Emma and exposed her to unseemly behavior. Thankfully, Emma didn't appear to have noticed.

Charles's gaze shifted to Emma. His hand shot out and tickled her.

The little girl shrieked and scrambled out of his reach, tossing more hay their way. "You can't get me!"

"I will. Just wait." Charles jumped to his feet, and then pulled Adelaide up after him. "Are you all right?"

"Yes." Adelaide's world tipped off balance. Since she'd met Charles, her tidy life had turned upside down, inside out. Her inhibitions had crumbled, as well, turning her into someone carefree and full of life — Addie, the hair-down woman.

Charles took off after Emma and scooped her up. "I'm too fast for you, Emma," he teased, swinging her in front of him.

When he turned to Adelaide with a grinning Emma nestled on his arms, both looking more like scarecrows than themselves, Adelaide ached to enfold them in her arms. Maybe then, she would find the sense of family she'd been looking for her entire life. But she had no trust to give.

Emma burst out laughing, pointing first at Adelaide, then at Charles. "You look funny!" she crowed.

Charles bounced her on his arms, sending pieces of straw fluttering to the ground. "No funnier than you, cupcake."

The little girl giggled. "I'm not cupcake. I'm Emma!"

Charles put Emma down, grabbed a pitchfork leaning against the side of the stable and repaired the mound. Adelaide brushed hay from Emma's hair, then from their shoulders and skirts.

"Can I climb on the fence?" Emma said.

Adelaide nodded and Emma raced off. Charles crossed to her side. "You missed some." With gentle fingers, he pulled strands from her hair. She couldn't meet his gaze.

Adelaide's chignon had pulled loose, and

her clothing was in disarray, totally unlike her finicky nature. "Thank you."

Charles tucked a loose curl behind her ear, the movement of his hands sweet and tender. "You're a mess."

Adelaide's hands flew to her hair, but he clasped them in his, stopping her. "I like you that way."

Their gazes locked; her mouth went dry.

What if someone had seen their silliness in the hay? If so, the committee might hear of it and take Emma. Hands shaking, she tugged the hairpins from her hair and pulled it into a knot, securing a proper demeanor right along with it. "I apologize. Our behavior wasn't suitable."

With a curt nod, he took a step back. "We'd best be going."

Adelaide called to the little girl a few feet away. "Emma, Mr. Graves and I need to get back to work."

With Emma chattering between them, they sauntered down the walk. A robin, with a morsel in its beak, swooped into the leafy branches of the tree they passed, silencing frantic chirping coming from an unseen nest. The scent of fresh-mown grass carried on the breeze. The beauty of the day and Emma's contented expression restored Adelaide's serenity.

Until Mrs. Willowby, the feather on her hat bobbing in rhythm with her stride, headed toward them, holding the hand of the little orphan boy. "I'd like you to meet our Ben," Mrs. Willowby said, her tone laced with pride.

Ben ducked behind his mother's skirts, then peeked around.

Adelaide smiled. "Hello, Ben. Do you remember Emma?"

Mrs. Willowby's gaze roamed over them. "My, don't the three of you look like a family?"

Charles took a step over, separating himself from the two of them, from the image.

Adelaide kept walking, tugging Emma along with her. "Have a good day, Mrs. Willowby. You, too, Ben."

Once they were out of hearing distance, Adelaide slowed the pace. Emma was coming home with her. The thought sung through her. Nothing Mrs. Willowby could say could change that fact.

"Ben looked happy." Emma sighed. "I wish we were a family, like that lady said. Then William could come live with us."

Charles squatted down beside Emma. "You have a family, the Drummonds. Don't you like living with them?"

Emma shook her head.

Charles chucked Emma under the chin. "Why not?"

Adelaide held her breath and waited for Emma's answer, hope rising and falling in her chest like the bobber on a fishing line. But Emma shook off Charles's hand and ran off to examine a rock alongside the road.

Charles nodded toward Emma. "She's a great little girl. Everything delights and fascinates her. She gives me a new view on the world, a world I've tended to see through jaded eyes."

"Jaded? Why?"

A shadow passed over his face and he looked away. "Nothing specific, simply some of the things I've seen."

"Saturday's dinner invitation didn't include Emma," she said. "Perhaps we should cancel our plans." At the prospect, disappointment ached inside her and she hoped he would disagree.

His gaze went to her. "No," he said, the word echoing with finality. "I don't want to cancel."

He held out his arm. Adelaide hesitated, and then slipped her hand through the crook. He drew her close, his hand resting lightly on hers. Adelaide's stomach hadn't rolled like this since she'd won the county spelling bee in the eighth grade.

"It'll be fun to take Emma to a restaurant," Charles said.

"A restaurant?" Emma had rejoined them, a small, smooth rock cradled in one hand. "I've never eaten in a restaurant before."

Charles smiled. "Then it's time you did."

Adoration filled Emma's gaze. Did Charles have any idea how much he mattered to Emma?

They parted ways, Emma and Adelaide to the shop and Charles back to the paper. Despite her resolve, Adelaide missed him already. She sighed. If only she could get inside his head, understand his thoughts. Like a locked door, she had hints of what was on the other side, but until the door opened, she couldn't be sure.

She'd have to find the key. No, better to leave that door locked. Opening her heart to a man would only lead to heartbreak.

CHAPTER SEVEN

Inside Charles's office, the noisy newspaper was downright quiet compared to his afternoon with the gregarious seven-year-old girl. Still, he knew Emma's absence hadn't brought this sense of emptiness. He wanted to be with Addie. Too much. He felt split down the middle, with one side, the rational side, telling him to run the opposite direction, while the other side hungered to see Miss Crum, to savor her goodness. But he didn't dare.

Not when a monster crouched inside him.

People said he looked like his father. When he shaved, his father's face looked back at him — the public face his father wore in town. Charles could still remember his father's gentle touch as he'd run his fingers through Charles's hair during church service. When Adam Graves wasn't drinking, he'd been an affectionate man and Charles had loved him with all his being.

But the years passed and his father drank more and more, quoting Scripture and beating his family. Many a Sunday following a thrashing with a razor strap the day before, Charles and Sam had sat cautiously in the pew. Until the time when Adam quit attending church and his family saw only his private face — that of a man filled with hate.

His father appeared in his mind's eye, as plain as if he stood before him. Lips curled in a snarl, eyes bulging with rage, mouth spewing curses, veins bulging in his neck mere seconds before he'd start hitting. The sounds of fists meeting flesh ricocheted through him with such vividness Charles discerned the familiar metallic taste of blood upon his tongue.

Unseen fingers closed around his windpipe, suffocating him until bile rose in Charles's throat. He leapt from his chair and dashed for the privacy of the alley.

Teddy blocked Charles's exit. "You all right, boss?"

"Don't you have enough to do around here besides poking your nose in my business?" Charles growled, sidestepping him.

In the alley, with sweat beading his forehead, Charles leaned against the brick and struggled to slow his breathing. *Inhale. Exhale. Inhale.*

But childhood memories continued to slam into him with the same brutal force his father had used to subdue his family.

Until the worst memory of all exploded in his brain with such power he could no longer resist — the memory of *that* night.

Even all these years later, Charles could not forgive himself.

He'd better get a grip on his life, on his mind. He had a business to run, Sam's family to help.

Yet, his hands balled at his sides. Adam Graves had been the reason his brother drank. If Sam hadn't been in that barroom brawl, he'd be alive today. Sam had inherited the family legacy of bitterness, distrust and booze.

Wiping his brow, Charles took in a gulp of air. He couldn't change the past but he could leave it there, far from the present, far from everything he'd worked hard to gain.

But images from that night popped up again and again, released by the reading of his father's will and the insane hope he could have a normal life.

Blocking thoughts of Addie, thoughts tempting him to indulge in the fantasy of a family, Charles pushed away from the brick and started inside. After dinner on Saturday, he'd make no more plans with Miss Crum. He wouldn't open her to the pain and anguish of his past, wouldn't taint her pretty world.

From the shop window, Adelaide glanced at *The Ledger.* That simple act set her heart humming. She brushed her fingertips across her lips, reliving the almost-kiss in the haystack. Charles Graves had feelings for her, but only a foolish woman would believe those feelings involved a future. He didn't want that any more than she did.

For now, God had given her Emma, bringing joy into her life. She'd be the best mother she could be. And make sure Charles noticed at supper. If Frances couldn't care for Emma, then surely Charles would support her with the committee.

She turned away from the window and watched Emma roam the showroom, examining the array of adorned hats, captivated by the fruit, plumes and flowers.

Adelaide joined her at the display. "Want to try on a hat?"

Emma beamed. "Could I?"

Adelaide lifted a bonnet from the stand, the one she'd visualized Emma wearing that day in the shop, the same day Laura had bullied her into placing an ad, bringing

Charles into her life, and through him, Emma. *I owe Laura a new hat.* With damp eyes, she placed the bonnet on Emma's head. "I designed this especially for a young lady like you."

Checking her reflection in the mirror, Emma's eyes sparkled. "Oh, it's pretty!"

Amazing how the proper hat affected a female's outlook, no matter her age. "It's perfect for you." Adelaide tied the pink ribbons under Emma's chin. "You must have it."

"I don't have any money."

Adelaide cupped Emma's chin in her hand. "It's a present."

Emma's mouth drooped. "It's not my birthday."

"The best presents are given for no reason."

"I can keep it, even when I go back to the Drummonds?"

The reminder tinged the day with a touch of gray but Adelaide shook off the feeling. Emma wasn't going back for days, maybe weeks. God had a plan. "Yes, and I'll make a bonnet for Mrs. Drummond, too. Would you like to help?"

"Yes!"

Adelaide smiled and then checked the clock on the wall. "It's getting late. That will have to wait until another day."

Emma folded her thin arms. "I don't want to wait."

"You can help me fix dinner. Do you like fried chicken?"

The little girl nodded, her petulance gone. "Yum!"

The tension in Adelaide's shoulders eased, relieved Emma's stomach tempered her apparent strong will. She picked up the satchel and with Emma scampering up the stairs beside her, explained the shop hours.

"I can sell lots of hats," Emma predicted with confidence.

"Perhaps, but you'll have homework to do."

Emma wrinkled her nose. "I don't like homework."

Adelaide's stomach clenched. Would this be a daily battle? She'd always loved her lessons. "Is the work hard for you?"

Emma's gaze sought the floor. "Mama got sick and William and I didn't go to school. The girls in my grade can read better than me, but I don't care. Who needs to read anyway?"

Adelaide tilted Emma's chin. "If I couldn't read, I couldn't run the shop. You'll catch up. I'll help."

Taking her hand, Adelaide led Emma to

what had been her mother's room. A resplendent rainbow-hued quilt covered the double bed. White ruffled curtains crisp with starch adorned the window. How had her mother been gloomy, awakening in such a cheerful room?

From the satchel, Emma retrieved a rag doll, mended and clean with a stitched jolly smile and button eyes. After tucking her doll against the pillows, Emma danced around the room, inspecting each nook and cranny. Seeing Emma chasing out the shadows of her mother's illness brought happy tears to Adelaide's eyes.

Adelaide tucked the little girl's things in an empty dresser drawer and then gave a tour of the rest of the rooms, including her own.

"Your room is smaller than mine," Emma said with the candor of a child. "But it's pretty."

"Thank you. My grandmother made the quilts. She knew how to use a needle. Guess I take after her." Adelaide sat on the bed, patting a spot beside her. Emma joined her, sitting up close. "This quilt pattern is called Ocean Wave. See how the blocks look like the sea?" Emma traced a finger around a triangle-shaped snippet of navy fabric.

Adelaide had started sewing doll clothes

when she'd been about Emma's age. She'd teach Emma some basic stitches. Together they'd make a dress for her doll. Adelaide had so many plans.

Taking Emma by the hand, they walked into the parlor. Emma stepped between two chairs to look at the pictures arranged on the marble-topped pedestal table.

Emma pointed to a daguerreotype. "Is this your mother?"

"Yes, and those are my grandparents."

Emma looked around her. "Where's your papa's picture?"

"I . . . I don't have one."

"Did he run away, like my papa?"

"Yes, I guess you could say that."

Emma considered this for a moment, her face sober, as if trying to figure out something Adelaide had never understood.

Emma saw the upright piano and brightened.

"If you'd like, I could teach you some simple songs."

"You know how to do a lot, Miss Adelaide."

After years of criticism, the remark slid into the marrow of Adelaide's bones and she gave the little girl's hand a squeeze. "Why, thank you."

In the kitchen, Adelaide heated leftover

fried chicken and potato cakes while Emma set the table. At dinner, Emma ate heartily, leaving some crumbs under her chair. They established a pattern for their future evenings, however many there might be. While Emma completed her homework at the kitchen table, Adelaide cleaned up the dishes, helping with schoolwork only if asked.

Emma asked for a pencil and paper, then hunched over it, working feverishly. Soon, she folded the paper and smiled up at Adelaide. "I made you something."

Adelaide's eyes stung. "You made something — for me?"

Emma unfolded the paper and smoothed it flat. "A picture!"

Adelaide stepped behind her to get a better view. Four figures drawn with a childish hand stood outside a house. A tree grew alongside. A smiling sun hung in the sky. "Who are they?"

"That's William," she said pointing to the figure dressed in pants. "That's me." She indicated the shortest figure in a skirt. "This is you, and this is Mrs. Drummond."

All the faces sported big smiles. Adelaide couldn't have been more pleased with an original Rembrandt. "That's a lovely picture. Thank you." She patted Emma's hand

and the little girl beamed. "Where's Mr. Drummond?"

Emma's smile turned to a frown. "I don't like him."

"Why?"

"He yells and stuff."

Adelaide knelt in front of Emma. "What do you mean?"

"I wish he'd run away like my papa and your papa," she muttered, smoothing the drawing again and again with her hand.

Though Adelaide tried to find out more, Emma only shrugged, putting up an invisible wall to Adelaide's quest for answers.

"Can I play the piano?" Emma asked.

Adelaide led the little girl to the parlor. They sat side by side on the bench as Adelaide guided Emma's fingers to play "Mary Had a Little Lamb."

The clock struck half past nine. "Oh, my! Time for bed."

Emma pounded the keys. "Mama let me stay up really late."

"That's probably because you weren't going to school."

"I don't want to go to school." Emma's gaze sparked defiance. "You can't make me."

Adelaide sucked in a gulp of air, unsure how to handle Emma's challenge. But then the Bible's admonition for children to obey their parents stiffened her backbone. "I like having you here," Adelaide said, "but while you're in my house, you'll do as I ask." Then she gave Emma a bright smile. "Let's get you ready for bed."

Though Emma's chin hung to her chest, she followed Adelaide to the bedroom. Later, the conflict forgotten, Emma nestled under the covers, embracing her doll as Adelaide read from her childhood Bible storybook, then listened to her prayers.

"Good night, Miss Adelaide," Emma said, yawning.

Looking at Emma's sweet face, a coil of warmth slid through Adelaide and she kissed her cheek. "Sleep tight," she said, slipping out of the room.

Adelaide had never been part of a real family and now it was within her grasp. She would give Emma attention, hugs and kisses, things she'd never had growing up, for as long as God granted her this gift.

Her mind flitted to Charles. If only —

She didn't dare finish the thought. She'd always been careful what she hoped for, the only way to avoid heartache.

She would savor this moment, not looking forward or back, because she was the happiest she'd ever been in her life, right now, in the present. God had given her this precious girl, and she'd be forever grateful. Forever changed. In a matter of hours, Emma had become firmly entrenched in her heart.

In the middle of the night, something jolted Adelaide awake. She heard Emma crying. She leapt out of bed and raced down the hall to find the little girl thrashing about in bed. Adelaide sank to the mattress beside her and laid a gentle hand on Emma's forehead. No fever. Probably a bad dream.

Adelaide stroked her palm across Emma's temples, offering comfort, until the little girl's breathing slowed and her body relaxed. She remained several minutes longer to ensure Emma would not awaken, and then tiptoed back to her bed.

But sleep eluded her. Could Emma be missing her real mother or William? Or were there other nightmares an orphaned seven-year-old might have, agonizing dreams Adelaide couldn't even begin to imagine? A nagging sense of doubt planted itself in her midsection. What if she couldn't give Emma comfort and security?

Scrunching her pillow, Adelaide recalled years of craving the simplest touch and a kind word. She'd give Emma what she'd missed growing up. After all, she had hugs in abundance and limitless love to share. She prayed that would be enough.

The next morning motherhood required every ounce of Adelaide's patience. Emma dawdled at breakfast and dressed with the slowness of a tortoise. Thankfully, they reached Second Ward School, a few blocks away, right as the bell rang. Adelaide explained the situation to the teacher and then hurried home, vowing tomorrow would go more smoothly.

Adelaide made Emma's bed, then walked to the kitchen and poured steaming water from the teakettle into a dishpan. As she scrubbed the dishes, she remembered where she'd seen this kind of disarray. She'd been eight, when her mother, sick with influenza, sent Adelaide to stay with Winifred Cook's family. Disorder reigned in the Cook household, but Winnie's parents tucked the children into bed with a prayer and a kiss. What a revelation to discover not all children lived in a neat but silent house.

For weeks after returning home, Adelaide's skin ached to be touched. She'd tried to keep the warm feeling by stroking her arms and hugging herself, but it hadn't been the same. Cleanliness was next to godliness, or so her mother said, but neatness wasn't important to children.

Maybe Adelaide needed a little disorder in her very tidy life, too. Hadn't Charles hinted at that yesterday?

The clock struck ten. Adelaide jumped. *Fiddlesticks, I'm late.* She finished wiping the dishes and then raced downstairs. As the clock struck a quarter after the hour, she grabbed the broom, flipped over the sign in the window and opened the door.

She'd no more than stepped onto the boardwalk when Charles appeared at her elbow in shirtsleeves and vest. "Is everything all right, Addie?"

At the sight of him, delicious warmth spread through her and the morning's tension vanished. "Why would you think it wasn't?"

"Why?" He lowered his face to hers, brown eyes dark under knitted brows. "In the three months I've been at the paper, I could set my watch by when you came outside toting that broom. Exactly five minutes before ten, every morning." He stuck his pocket watch in front of her. "It's now twenty minutes after ten, Addie. *Twenty minutes.* That tells me something's wrong."

Gracious, Charles knows exactly when I make my appearance on the walk every morning. He's been fretting about me.

145

As far as she knew, no man had ever worried about her. Speechless, her hand splayed across her bosom.

Charles dropped the watch into his pocket. "Is it Emma?"

"Is what Emma?"

"Adelaide Crum, you can be the most exasperating woman. Is something wrong with Emma?"

"She's fine and in school. We were running late." She gripped the handle of the broom, smiling up at him. "I had no idea you're such a worrier, Charles."

He harrumphed. "I'm not, but this *was* your first day with Emma. Naturally I'd wonder how you two were managing. Then you're late, ridiculously late —"

"Twenty minutes is not ridiculously late. Why, I've seen you darting into the newspaper at half past eight."

A sheepish look came over his face. "Here, let me do that," he said, taking the broom from her hands. "You probably have things to do to open the shop."

"Well, thank you." Adelaide walked inside, but didn't dust the counter, didn't wash the windowpane. Instead, she stood transfixed, watching Charles's muscles as he pushed that broom like a madman.

A desirable, intelligent man cared enough

about her to worry, to take a burden from her shoulders.

Like a husband would.

The thought took her breath away, zinging a feeling of hope through her, hope for a husband, and hope for children. She shoved it down. She had no claim to Charles, no need of a man. She took care of herself. And if God willed, she could take care of a child, too.

But oh, for a moment, she wanted to believe in the fantasy.

Charles appeared in her doorway and held out the broom. As she took it, their fingertips brushed. He yanked his hand away as if he'd been burned. "I'd, ah, better get back to the paper."

"Thank you for . . ." But she couldn't go on. She dared not voice the thoughts filling her heart. *Thank you for noticing, for caring, for making me feel like a woman.*

He turned to leave, then swung back to face her. Adelaide wanted to lean against his broad chest, to feel those strong arms around her, but she looked away, lest he read the longing in her eyes.

"Well, good day, then," he said.

He crossed the street, moving out of her reach, leaving her standing there, heart pumping wildly.

147

What had gotten into her? She couldn't trust these fierce feelings. Even her parents must have had attraction . . . for a while. Her mother constantly drilled fear of abandonment into her, honing her skill at keeping her emotions locked inside.

Until she met Charles.

She hurried to the window and caught a glimpse of his retreating back. Optimism rose up within her. Could Charles be part of God's plan for her?

CHAPTER EIGHT

On Saturday night, precisely at six, Charles stood in Adelaide's shop, basking in her smile, a smile that told him the ownership of the paper hadn't built an insurmountable barrier between them. Emma smiled at him, too, looking confident and happy. Not at all the weepy little girl Mrs. Drummond had brought to him.

He knelt in front of her. "My, don't you look pretty."

"See my new hat?" The little girl twirled, sending the pink ribbons under her chin flying.

"Very attractive." He rose and turned to Addie. Her dazzling indigo eyes sparkled.

Bending down, Addie gave Emma a kiss on the cheek. "You look prettier than irises in springtime, sweetie."

Emma rose on tiptoe and kissed Addie's cheek. With a palm, Addie caressed the spot. Her damp eyes met Charles's and her wordless thanks clutched at his heart.

Planting a fist on her hip, Emma eyed him. "You think Miss Adelaide looks pretty?"

Color dotted Addie's cheeks. "That's not polite, Emma."

The little girl looked baffled. "Why not?"

Addie laid a gentle hand on Emma's cheek. "It's fishing for a compliment and puts Mr. Graves in an awkward position."

Pretty hardly described Addie's softly flushed cheeks, her full lips and the regal tilt to her chin. "Actually, I don't feel the least bit awkward, Emma. Miss Crum looks lovely."

Taking a cue from Addie, Emma took an arm, looking pleased at being treated like a lady. Addie locked the door and took Charles's free arm. As they left the shop, something inside him bubbled like mineral springs in Florida. Something so new, he barely recognized the sensation, but thought it might be akin to joy.

When curious passersby stared at the threesome, greeting them with a questioning air, the feeling ebbed, replaced with a twist of uneasiness. In small towns, people poked their noses in other people's business. He hoped rumors wouldn't take wing and plant the idea he'd be part of a family.

But then he glanced down at Addie, took in her smile and radiant eyes and suddenly it didn't matter what anyone thought. Tonight he'd give her the evening she deserved. He'd let nothing spoil it, not even his disquiet at getting too close.

Charles pushed open the door of the hotel and ushered the ladies inside. The mahogany registration desk gleamed, colorful carpets covered the plank floor and a gas-lit chandelier twinkled overhead. Emma stood openmouthed.

The rotund waiter barreled over. "Mr. Graves, may I seat you by the window?"

"Thank you, Arthur."

Arthur grabbed a stack of menus. "This way, please," he said, leading the way into the dining room.

Charles steered Addie past a few tables occupied by no one he knew. At the window, he pulled out a chair first for her, then for Emma, before taking a seat between them. Arthur handed out huge menus, so large, Emma's hid her from view.

Arthur returned with a water pitcher and filled their glasses. Charles leaned toward the little girl. "That menu is bigger than you are. Here, let me take it before —"

The heavy volume slipped from Emma's fingers, knocking over her glass of water.

Charles rose to wipe up the spill with his napkin. Emma cringed, shrinking into her chair.

An instinct flared. Charles *knew* that reflex. "It's all right, accidents happen," he said, his voice soft, without a hint of reprimand.

Surveying the mess, tears filled Emma's eyes.

Addie patted her hand. "No damage done, sweetie."

Arthur mopped off Emma's menu and tucked it under his arm. "It's my fault, miss. The menu is too large for you to manage. I'll get more napkins." He walked toward the kitchen.

Who had punished this child for making a mistake? Had the Drummonds mistreated her, or her own family in New York, or possibly someone at the orphanage? He recognized the signs — the shrinking away, the fear. Or could he be overreacting because of his past? Seeing abuse where none existed?

Adelaide picked up her menu and helped Emma make a selection. Arthur returned and took their order and they all noticeably relaxed.

Adelaide put on a bright smile. "Emma, tell Mr. Graves about our day at the store."

"Miss Crum sold five hats!" Emma

boasted. "And . . ."

But Charles didn't hear what the child said. He couldn't take his eyes from Addie, the glow of her creamy skin and her shimmering eyes reflecting the light from the chandelier overhead.

"Mr. Graves, did you hear?" Emma's impatient voice cut into his thoughts. "Miss Crum sold five hats."

Charles swallowed, struggling to get back into the conversation. "That's good news. I'm, ah, glad the ad helped."

Arthur appeared with a glass of milk for Emma. Soon, the waiter set plates of steaming food before them.

Adelaide bowed her head and whispered a prayer for them all, then took a bite of chicken. "Delicious."

Obviously determined nothing else would go wrong, Emma ate with exaggerated care, wiping her mouth with her napkin whenever Adelaide did. She took small bites and steered clear of her milk; evidently considering the large glass too risky.

But, not nearly as risky as Charles felt it was to spend an evening with Addie. He'd better watch out or he'd start to care about this woman.

Adelaide had trouble keeping her mind on

eating and her eyes off her dinner companion, who looked distinguished in a dark suit and crisp white shirt. Even the movements of his hands fascinated her.

Reaching for the salt, their hands brushed each other. She clutched the fork so tightly the tines scraped across the plate.

"Sorry," she said, putting down the fork and laying her trembling hands in her lap. "I finished another fashion column, Charles."

"Good, bring it by."

Then silence as they stared into each other's eyes. She groped for a topic of conversation. "Where did you live before moving here?" she asked, her voice unsteady.

He cut a bite of steak. "In Cincinnati."

"Oh, of course." Feeling foolish to have forgotten, Adelaide took a sip of water to ease the unaccustomed dryness of her mouth. "So you moved here because of *The Ledger*?"

Charles laid down his utensils. "My father asked me to get the paper on solid footing. Owning my own paper has been a dream of mine so I jumped at the chance."

An awkward silence followed. Best to change the subject and seize the opportunity to show him how competent she would be as a mom. Adelaide said, "The shop is my

154

dream. In fact, I plan on teaching Emma how to sew and make hats. Who knows, one day that might lead to some dreams of her own."

"Just watching you run the shop should be an education. Your success is a terrific example for her."

"Thank you," she said, pleased Charles had seen what she could offer Emma.

In companionable silence, they concentrated on their food, but she didn't have much of an appetite. "Compared to Cincinnati, Noblesville is small."

"True, but since my brother's family lives here, I already knew something about the town. And with the state capitol only a few miles away, I had no concern about missing the city." He toyed with his fork. "Not that I've had the time. There's always too much to do at the paper. I suppose it's the same for you."

She nodded. "The shop ties me down. I order supplies through the mail or purchase them from salesmen."

"I'm helping Miss Adelaide make a hat for Mrs. Drummond," Emma piped up, her smile wide.

"That's great, Emma." He turned to Adelaide. "You ought to get a clerk to help out. All work and no play . . ."

"When my mother was ill, at the last, I hired Laura as a part-time clerk, but after Mama passed, I had no reason to keep her on."

Charles's gaze locked with hers. "Perhaps you need to rethink that."

Was he suggesting they spend more time together?

"Miss Adelaide, don't you like your food?" Emma said, breaking the link between them. "Remember 'waste not, want not' like your mama always said?"

Noticing Charles's clean plate, Adelaide flushed. Charles pushed back from the table and laid an ankle across his knee, looking more at ease than she'd felt in her entire life. Horrified this man could turn her into a stammering mass of nerves when she intended to show him she could take care of herself and a child, she fought his charm.

"The food's delicious." Though, she could barely remember what she'd eaten. "I'm taking my time, enjoying every bite."

"No hurry." Charles patted his torso. "We need to digest our food so we have room for dessert."

"Do they have chocolate cake?" Emma asked.

"Yes. Pie, too. The hotel's cream pies melt in your mouth."

With the promise of dessert, Emma got to work on her meal.

Charles turned back to Adelaide. "Tell me something about you. You don't have any living family?"

"No, no one." Adelaide took a sip of water. "How about you?"

He straightened and dropped his foot to the floor. "You probably know Sam died two years ago," he said his tone subdued.

Adelaide nodded.

"My mother died when I was sixteen. So all I have is Mary and her two boys."

"I got a brother," Emma chimed in. "William and me slept on the floor. He told me stories." She sighed. "Papa left us and then Mama died. . . ." Tears welled up in the little girl's eyes.

Adelaide's gaze collided with Charles's look of dismay. "Before you know it, you'll be back with William," Adelaide assured her, dreading the prospect.

"Why can't William live with us?"

Adelaide's heart went out to the loneliness in the girl's voice. "Rules, sweetie." She hated those rules herself, rules preventing her from having Emma permanently.

"How about ordering that cake?" Charles said, his words putting a smile on Emma's face.

Charles summoned the waiter and ordered dessert. Emma clanked her fork and spoon together a few times, then rose from her seat, almost tipping her chair.

"Sit down, honey," Adelaide said.

"I'm tired of sitting," Emma whined.

"I know, but you want that chocolate cake, don't you?"

Emma nodded and returned to her seat. Soon Emma swung her feet against the rungs of her chair, the sound echoing through the quiet, high-ceilinged room. Adelaide bit her lip, trying to hide her disquiet. She'd hoped to show Charles her mothering skills, not to look inept.

Across from her, Charles reached into his coat pocket and brought out a pad of paper and pencil. "As a boy, I had a dog I called Rusty. Part Irish Setter. He had long ears like this."

Emma's feet stilled as Charles began sketching the dog, his hand moving quickly across the paper. She slid from her chair to stand beside him, watching him draw one animal after another.

His delightful little drawings charmed Adelaide as much as they did Emma. "I didn't know you were artistic. Do you draw the political cartoons on the editorial page?"

Charles glanced up. "Yes, I do."

"I'm impressed."

He gave her a small pleased smile. "Thank you."

The man had many layers. Each time she saw him, Adelaide discovered something that added to her appraisal. He'd been able to calm Emma when she had not, yet she doubted he'd lowered his opinion of her as a mother.

Still, he remained a man. Even as she thought it, she knew this mistrust of men came from her mother. She needed to evaluate things on her own.

The waiter arrived, carrying a tray with Emma's dessert and two cups of coffee. Emma scrambled back into her chair, Charles's drawings forgotten. In minutes, Emma's unrest vanished as quickly as her dessert.

Eager to know the details that made up Charles's past, Adelaide said, "Tell me more about your dog."

"We had lots of dogs, not only Rusty, sometimes two or three at a time. They lived out back in a pen." Charles took a sip of his coffee. "Did you have a dog, Addie?"

"No, I wanted a cat, but Mama couldn't abide cat hair on her furniture. I found a toad once and kept it in a box in my room.

159

Until Mama found it and said it'd give me warts."

"Me and William had a kitty," Emma said. "Mama called Felicia the best mouser in the building. Will you draw my cat?"

"Sure, what did she look like?"

A smile spread across Emma's chocolate-speckled face. "Like a gray-and-white striped tiger with white patches on her front feet and here." Emma pointed to her forehead and then her torso. "Mama said Felicia wore a bib so when she ate, she wouldn't get dirty."

Charles smiled. "She sounds like a beauty."

Emma twisted her napkin. "We gave Felicia to a neighbor, 'cause we couldn't take a cat to the orphanage. I miss her."

Adelaide's throat tightened for Emma's many losses.

"I can see why." Charles reached over and patted Emma's hand, then drew a curve that quickly turned into the body of a cat, sitting on a stool. On the face, he added two triangular ears and an upside down triangle for a nose.

Watching them, Adelaide marveled at how Charles related to children. Emma had taken a liking to him right away. Charles Graves was a kind man. Adelaide could think of no higher compliment.

With Emma in the middle, they walked home in the dark, their way lit by gaslights along the street. The soft night air between her and Charles crackled, leaving Adelaide shaky but feeling alive.

"Here we are," Charles said, reaching the door of her shop.

She dug into her bag and retrieved the key. All thumbs, she dropped it, and then bent to retrieve it, just as Charles reached to snatch up the key. The two of them almost collided and both let out a little shaky laugh. In the dim light, they stood facing each other, close enough to touch, to reach out. . . .

Adelaide's stomach dropped like it had when she'd swung out on a rope over Phillip's Creek. But she wasn't a child now. Dangling from anyone's rope posed a risk she would not take.

He reached past her, his arm brushing hers, turned the key and opened the door.

"The meal was delicious," she said, though she didn't remember eating a bite.

"I'm glad you enjoyed it."

"Well . . . thank you for a lovely evening."

"I should be thanking you," he said softly, "both of you," he added, his gaze taking in Emma, too.

She and Emma stepped inside the shop. Adelaide chanced one last glance back at Charles. Having a man in her life didn't mean she wouldn't be lonely — Jack had proven that. He'd claimed he wanted to marry her but never exhibited an interest in anything about her, except her cooking and the profits from her shop. Besides, she couldn't be involved with a man who had issues with his faith.

"Would you accompany us to church tomorrow?"

His gaze dropped to his feet. "Mary's expecting me for dinner."

"Mary and the boys will be at church. I'm sure they'd love to have you join them."

He tightened his jaw. "Church and I aren't a good mix."

Hope she hadn't realized she held tumbled from its lofty perch. "Well, if you change your mind —"

"I won't. Good night, Addie." He turned and walked away in the direction of his house.

Charles had used his sister-in-law as an excuse. Why did he avoid church? Perhaps, God had placed her in his life so she could help him find his way back. If so, how?

CHAPTER NINE

The morning of Decoration Day, most of the shopkeepers in town had locked their doors. Nobleville's citizens headed first to Riverside Cemetery and then on to Crownland Cemetery to listen to the speeches and honor the country's fallen heroes. A cool breeze fluttered the flags.

Charles waved at James across the way as he scribbled notes for the paper, and then slipped in beside Addie and Emma. Addie's welcoming smile dazzled him. On this beautiful, celebratory Monday, he wanted to throw caution to the wind, to pretend he'd have tomorrow with Addie and every day after that. He tucked her gloved hand into the crook of his arm and watched the Union soldiers honor their dead.

Emma tugged at his sleeve. "Who are they?"

"Those men fought in the Civil War," he said, bending down to speak into her ear.

163

"See their uniforms? They . . ."

But, Emma's attention had latched on to a dog that joined the parade. Charles returned his gaze to Addie. In the misty depths of her eyes, he saw an understanding of the sacrifices these men had made for their country, along with the countless thousands on both sides who'd died during that hideous war.

The more he knew Addie, the more he perceived the depth of their connection. As much as he knew Addie deserved a better man, she'd taken residence in his mind. And, could it be, even in his heart? No. He'd only bring her trouble. In the end, he'd draw the joy from her life.

After the last speech, men in faded overalls, women wearing sun-bleached bonnets and children itching to shuck high-top shoes flowed across the street or stopped to chat with friends.

As they strolled toward Addie's shop, Charles pulled a lollipop from his coat pocket and handed it to Emma. She rewarded him with a huge smile.

Addie whispered in Emma's ear and the little girl pulled the treat out of her mouth. "Thank you, Mr. Graves," Emma said, then popped the sucker back in.

Charles smiled. "You're welcome. Are you

enjoying your day out of school?"

"Yes!" The little girl twirled in front of them. "I don't have to do math or read or *anything.*" Emma said between licks. "And Miss Adelaide's shop is closed all day."

"Aren't you the lucky ladies?"

Emma's eyes sparkled. "And guess what? Miss Adelaide is going to buy me a doll that gots a china head!"

Addie smiled. "Mr. Hudson offered to open the store."

"With all the farmers in town, Mr. Nickels decided to keep the feed store open, too. Not sure our veterans would approve."

"Well, Emma's glad." Adelaide smiled down at her. "Every girl needs a special doll."

"And you want to make sure she has one." Addie laid a gentle hand on Emma's shoulder. "Yes."

Charles dropped them at the door of the shop "I best get back to the paper," he said, sorry to see the morning end.

Addie cocked her head at him. He assumed a few well-placed hatpins kept the wide-brimmed straw hat from swaying on her head. "I'm sorry you have to be inside on such a pretty day," she said.

Wish I could spend it with you. Instead he said, "Me, too."

165

He walked to his office and while Teddy set type, he tackled his editorial, glad to focus on work instead of the lady across the street. As he finished, the door opened.

Charles greeted Roscoe Sullivan, the previous editor of *The Ledger*. Roscoe pulled at the suspenders that held up his pants. "Too bad you're cooped up on such an afternoon, Mr. Editor."

Charles grinned and stretched his muscles, glad for the company. "I managed to take in the parade this morning."

Roscoe removed his straw hat, the band stained with sweat, and dropped into the chair across from him. "I've been keeping tabs on the paper." He tapped a nearby issue. "I like how you've used the editorial page to instigate reform, like cleaning up our streets and getting support for building the new school."

"I appreciate that," Charles said. "Say, how's retirement?"

"Not sure I like it much, though I hear the fishing is good up on White River." Roscoe flipped a wrist, throwing out an imaginary line. "The main reason I came by is to say thanks for seeing that my nephew got those orphans."

"I didn't do anything special. The decision was unanimous."

"Ed's all the family I've got. When little Eddie died, it about killed Carrie and me." Roscoe shook his head. "Then Frances's mother commits suicide. Life's given Frances one too many kicks in the stomach, but she'll get back on her feet."

"I think you're right." He wished Mrs. Drummond well, but when she recovered, she'd want Emma. The thought cooled his mood faster than a winter dip in the Ohio River.

Roscoe slapped his hat on his head. "Best get a move on."

The two men walked to the door. As if he'd conjured her up, Adelaide left her shop with Emma chattering alongside, probably on their way to buy Emma's doll. They saw him in the open doorway and waved. Charles waved back.

"Ed told me Emma's staying with Miss Crum for now," Roscoe said. "It appears she's doing a right good job."

"Yes, she is."

"Heard tell you were spending time with the lady. Keeping an eye on Emma, huh?" Roscoe thumped him playfully in the arm. "Unless there's another reason for your attention?"

Charles opened his mouth to protest, but thought better of it. There wasn't much he could say to stop the talk; protesting only increased the gossip.

"She's a fine woman," Roscoe continued. "Always wondered why some swain hadn't snapped her up. Maybe you're the one."

Charles put up his hands. "Not me. I'm too set in my ways."

"A woman has a way of changing that." Roscoe chuckled. "Marriage can bring a lot into your life — good cooking, companion-ship. Not a day goes by I don't miss my Carrie." Roscoe's eyes misted and he made a production out of adjusting his hat, then shoved away from the door. "I'm off."

Charles cleared the sudden lump in his throat and returned to his desk and the pile of work awaiting him. By the look of things, he'd be here for hours. And at the end of the day, all that would greet him would be some poor excuse for a supper.

For a moment, he tried to imagine what it would be like to have a wife to come home to, welcoming him with a smile, and a home-cooked meal on the table — a table surrounded by the freshly scrubbed faces of their children.

His life had left him cynical about mar-riage. Apparently, a few — Teddy and Roscoe, if he could believe what they said — had enjoyed domesticity. But without a framework for such a life, Charles could barely imagine it.

At the memory of his boyhood home, tension crept into his shoulders and up his neck muscles. No, having a wife and children gathered around a table didn't ensure a happy home.

Until he had an idea what did, he had no business picturing a future with Addie. She deserved a better man, a man who could give her happily ever after.

Adelaide detected a tug on her hand, but deep in thought about Charles, she ignored it.

"Look! It's William." Emma dropped Adelaide's hand and ran toward her brother. "William!"

Toting a sack of feed big enough to topple him, the boy's face broke into a lopsided grin.

Emma huddled close to her brother. "Is Mrs. Drummond better?" she asked, her voice almost a whisper.

William juggled the sack of feed and shrugged. "I dunno."

"Oh." Emma tucked her hands behind her back. "I miss you."

With the toe of his boot, William rubbed a

line in the dirt. "Me, too. Is living in town fun?"

Emma's head bobbed. "Miss Adelaide's gonna buy me a doll. See my new hat!" Emma pivoted in front of her brother, sending the ribbons flying, almost losing the bonnet. "Isn't it pretty?"

"Yep." William's gaze drifted from Emma's hat to Adelaide and the longing in his eyes turned to envy.

Adelaide smiled. "Hello, William."

He gave a slow smile. She wanted to scoop him up and take him home, but William wasn't hers and neither was Emma, really.

Ed Drummond, wearing a scowl, came stomping up behind the boy. Adelaide's heart leapt in her chest.

William didn't see him. "Thanks for taking care of —"

A rough hand shoved William, almost causing him to drop the feed sack. "I told you to stow that in the wagon. Obey me, boy!"

"Yes, sir." Head down, William scampered for the wagon.

Adelaide bit her tongue to keep from giving Ed the good lashing he deserved. She didn't dare antagonize the man who held Emma's fate in his hands.

Ed climbed onto the seat, never turning

around, leaving William to wrestle with the heavy sack alone. Adelaide hurried to the boy's side and helped him heft the feed onto the back of the wagon. William scrambled up beside it and dragged the sack toward the front when Ed slapped the reins across the horses' backs. The team jerked forward. Losing his balance, William tumbled to the rear of the open wagon.

Emma shrieked.

"Stop!" Adelaide shouted. William grabbed a wooden slat and managed to keep from falling out. As the horses gathered speed, he pulled himself to a sitting position, and held on.

Adelaide released a shaky breath. Though William hadn't been hurt, he could have been — and seriously. Ed had treated him more like a slave than a son and hadn't acknowledged Emma.

Emma returned to Adelaide's side. "He was mean to William."

Adelaide laid a hand on her shoulder. "I know."

Emma's soft blue eyes glistened with tears. "Why?"

Adelaide watched the wagon disappear around the bend. "I don't know." *But I intend to find out.*

"I'm glad he didn't see me." Emma peered

up at Adelaide, her eyes luminous. "Do I have to go back there?"

Adelaide bent down and put her arms around Emma. "Don't worry. I'll keep you safe." She held her until Emma noticed a robin on the walk.

"Wait here a minute," Adelaide said, then marched into the feed store and almost bumped into the proprietor standing in the shadows of the doorway. He had to have seen Ed's treatment of the boy. "Excuse me, Mr. Nickels. The man who left here —"

The feed store owner spat a load of tobacco toward a spittoon, hitting the target with ease. "Name's Ed Drummond."

"Did you see how he treated the boy?"

"Nope. Been too busy."

Adelaide only saw one customer inside. She suspected Mr. Nickels of lying and shot him a look she hoped made that clear.

"Mr. Drummond's a good customer, pays promptly," he said, his gaze pinning her. Then he picked up a broom and swept out the entrance, ignoring her.

Adelaide left the store, then reached for Emma's hand and resumed their walk. The way Ed Drummond had talked to Frances that day in the courthouse corridor and his treatment of William now convinced her that the man shouldn't have a child in his care, never mind two. She would see to it Emma and William were safe. But how? *Lord, send me an answer.*

Suddenly she knew what to do. She would go to Charles.

Their shopping finished, Adelaide settled Emma on a bench outside the newspaper office. Her new doll with its open-and-close eyes — a wonder to Emma — would keep her occupied while Adelaide talked to Charles.

Inside the office, Charles's face broke into a wide grin. He closed the distance between them in a rush, as if . . . *she* mattered.

When have I ever mattered to any man?

"Addie, this is a pleasant surprise." He took her hands in his and gave them a squeeze.

Her concern about Ed Drummond fell away, melted into something warm and soft. She struggled to gather her wits about her, to stick with her reason for coming. Pulling her hands from his grasp, she walked to the window to check on Emma. The little girl's lips moved in a make-believe conversation with her doll.

Adelaide trailed a finger down the glass, then turned to Charles. "I'm concerned about William Grounds's safety."

Charles's brow furrowed. "Why?"

Adelaide took a deep breath, trying to keep anger out of her voice. "I'm alarmed by how Ed treated the boy at the feed store earlier. First, he shoved him, then, while William was stowing a sack in the wagon, Ed drove off, almost causing the boy to tumble out the back."

Charles rubbed his chin. "Perhaps William is causing trouble and Ed is frustrated. Or isn't it possible Ed didn't realize he put the boy in jeopardy?" He smiled. "Not everyone is good with children like you are."

Emma had rebelled a few times. Perhaps William had, too, but that didn't warrant a shove. "There's something else, Charles. Ed completely ignored Emma, like he didn't even see her."

"Maybe he didn't."

"I don't see how he couldn't. He didn't greet me, either."

"Bad manners aren't against the law, Addie."

Why couldn't Charles understand something was amiss? "The boy's afraid of him. I could see it in his eyes."

"Did you see bruises?"

She sighed. "No."

"Was William hobbling?"

"No." She fisted her hands on her hips.

"But in my heart, I know Ed Drummond is a cruel man."

"All right, I'll run the incident past the committee. See what they make of it."

Adelaide frowned. "Couldn't you check with someone else in town? Except for you, everyone on that committee is biased."

"They merely followed the Children's Aid Society rules." He exhaled a burst of air. "I'll look into it."

"Thank you." She laid a hand on his forearm, strong and firm, feeling oddly comforted. "Let me know what you find out."

He gave her a reassuring smile. "Of course."

Charles stepped to his desk and sat on the edge. A book clattered to the floor from the teetering pile. While he stooped to retrieve it, Adelaide gathered the pencils scattered on the desk, organizing them in the cup with points down. It wouldn't do for Charles to get graphite embedded in his palm.

She glanced at Charles. A telltale crease marked the middle of his brow, a sure sign of his irritation. Her hands fell away.

"My, but you're a busy bee."

He touched her hand and tugged her to him.

"The incident upset Emma. Something

175

seemed to be going on, something unspoken between the children."

He appeared to focus more on her mouth than the words coming out of it, tempting her to forget what mattered — the children and the issues between them. "Where's Emma now?"

"She's sitting on the bench outside, talking to her new doll. I didn't want her to overhear our conversation."

"So I have you all to myself." Charles raised a brow and motioned toward the pencils. "Since you're determined to fix things, how about fixing dinner tonight?" He had a twinkle in his eye, daring her to agree.

If he came to supper, she could work on convincing him to investigate Ed Drummond. "All right."

Charles's smile broadened. "Say six-thirty? That gives me time to finish here and still go home to clean up."

"Six-thirty is fine." She walked toward the door. "Do you like pot roast?"

Charles blocked her way by leaning against the frame. "It's my favorite."

She smiled, enjoying the tease. "I can't make it if I don't get home."

With a grin, he stepped aside, giving her room to pass.

"Why, hello, Charles. Oh, hi, Adelaide."

Adelaide turned and almost bumped into Fannie Whitehall, who'd appeared out of nowhere. Or perhaps Adelaide was so besotted she'd failed to notice her. "Hello, Fannie."

Fannie beamed at Charles. "Will you be my guest at our church picnic? It's the second Saturday in June." She clapped her gloved hands together. "Please say yes."

Apparently Fannie had decided not to play possum, her lessons in demureness forgotten. Why hadn't Adelaide thought to ask Charles herself? Because finding an escort for the church picnic was the least of her priorities. At such gatherings, she felt out of place, a solitary oak at the edge of an evergreen forest.

Without children. Without a husband. A woman alone.

Still, knowing Charles could be going with Fannie poked like a misdirected hatpin. Well, he deserved a woman whose mind didn't keep up with her mouth. "Goodbye," Adelaide said.

Fannie took Adelaide by the elbow and walked out a few steps with her. "Was I demure?"

"You were fine." No need to point out that ladies, when issuing an invitation, didn't

177

usually clap. She'd best remember Jesus's command to love her neighbor, instead of having such uncharitable thoughts about Fannie.

Beaming, Fannie rushed back inside, no doubt for Charles's answer. Adelaide gathered up Emma and her doll and left. He might be coming to supper tonight, but she had no claim on the man. Over the meal, they'd share a conversation about William, about her ideas for future columns. Nothing else.

Before they'd crossed the street, Adelaide had started wading through the menu in her mind. She'd add red-skinned potatoes, carrots and onions to the meat. Applesauce she'd canned last fall would be tasty. This simple meal would give her time to make a pie. Oh, she almost forgot. After bragging to Fannie and Charles, she'd have to serve biscuits, careful not to burn the bottoms.

While Emma played with her doll, Adelaide prepared the meal, then mixed the biscuit dough, vowing that with God's help and Charles as her ally, she'd get both children out of the Drummond household permanently.

When she'd finished, Adelaide oversaw Emma's bath, then brushed her hair until it shone and helped her into the new dress

178

she'd made. "You look pretty, sweetheart."

"That's 'cause I look like you."

In the mirror, two blondes with fair skin and blue eyes peered back at them. Heart full, Adelaide hugged Emma. "Thank you. Why don't you read while I get ready?"

After Adelaide bathed, she donned her finest dress, a rose gown with a tight fitting bodice and enormous puffed sleeves that narrowed to hug her forearms. Pulling her hair up into a chignon, she didn't have a single, solitary thought in her brain except soon Charles would be in her home, sitting at her table.

In the kitchen, her belly roiling in anticipation, she set the table. Then she walked into the parlor and fluffed the pillows, picked a piece of lint off the love seat and checked the clock on the shelf.

Below, the bell jingled. "He's here!" Emma called.

"I'll let him in." Adelaide hurried to the top of the stairs and to the door. Seeing Charles through the glass, her mouth went dry. Wearing a dark gray suit and crisp white shirt, he was a beautiful sight. She opened the door and stepped back.

"Evening, Addie." He gave her a dazzling smile, then lifted his nose in the air and sniffed. "Hmm, smells good in here." His gaze skimmed over her. "Looks good, too. That's a pretty dress."

"Thank you." The admiration in his voice warmed her, but what she wanted to know — and dared not ask — was if he had accepted Fannie's invitation to the picnic.

They stood gazing at one another, neither saying a word. The way he studied her, a way no man had ever looked at her before, Adelaide forgot all about Fannie's invitation.

She pivoted on her heel. "If you'll follow me . . ."

"Gladly," he said.

She heard the shop door close and glanced back. He wore a lazy grin. A thrill snaked through Adelaide, making her glad Emma waited upstairs. Instead of being all soft and starry-eyed, she should remember why she'd agreed to this invitation. It had nothing to do with her and Charles, everything to do with Emma and William's future.

Adelaide led him through the shop. The aroma of pot roast hauled them up the stairs by their noses. "Supper will be ready soon."

Charles smiled. "I'm starved."

Could he see her hands shaking? Why couldn't she feel comfortable entertaining a man?

Emma bounded to them. "Hi, Mr.

Graves."

"Hello, Emma."

Adelaide motioned to the love seat in the parlor. "Please, make yourself at home."

He lowered his lanky body onto the dainty furniture, dwarfing the delicate piece. He surely couldn't feel comfortable, yet he looked at home, self-assured, as if he didn't have a care in the world.

He crossed an ankle over his knee, and patted the seat beside him. "Can't you join me, Addie, even for a minute?"

"I . . . I have things to do. Emma, show Mr. Graves your new doll." The little girl raced to her room. Adelaide fled almost as fast as Emma.

In the kitchen, Adelaide put her hands to her burning cheeks and glanced around, trying to get her bearings. Her gaze fell on the pan next to the stove. Oh, yes, she needed to bake the biscuits. Having Charles here had taken every rational thought from her mind. She popped the pan in the hot oven and then lifted the lid on the roaster. Perfect. Everything would be ready as soon as the biscuits finished baking.

She returned to the parlor and found Charles sitting beside Emma. He held the new doll, looking about as comfortable as a trapeze artist without a net. Adelaide bit her lip to keep from laughing and perched on the chair across from them.

Emma pointed at Charles. "He's the daddy."

"We're just pretending," Charles cut in quickly. If the tone of his words hadn't, the look on his face made it clear Charles had no wish to ever be the daddy.

Adelaide's smile faded until she realized there wasn't a bachelor alive who'd want to be caught playing with dolls. Why did she always look for trouble behind Charles's every word or action? She reminded herself of a hedgehog rolling into a ball to protect its vulnerable underbelly. Not an attractive image.

She could take a lesson from Fannie and gain some of her boldness. As long as she didn't end up with Fannie's giggle.

Or end up hurt like her mother.

CHAPTER TEN

Adelaide's parlor wasn't overdone with bric-a-brac like most Charles had been in. Her collection of photographs, books and well-placed items made the room cozy and welcoming.

Emma carried her doll to the piano and fiddled with the keys. She chattered while she did, telling her doll about her made-up tune. Dear, sweet Emma, without a care in the world, so unlike Charles at that age.

"I never realized the furniture in here was so small," Addie said, taking a chair across from him. "Maybe that's because Jack wasn't much taller than I."

"Jack?" Charles straightened. "Who's Jack?"

Adelaide waved a hand of dismissal, as if the name meant nothing. "Oh, Jack was a guy who had the notion we should marry."

It bothered Charles to think Adelaide had once had someone in her life. But why wouldn't she? Pretty, industrious, smart and apparently a good cook, if the enticing aromas permeating her home were any indication, Addie would snare a man's attention. "Why didn't you marry Jack?"

She shrugged. "I didn't love him."

Charles leaned forward. "How could you be sure?"

"How much time do you have?"

Charles chortled. "That bad? So what topped the list?"

"Let's see his conversation was limited to the weather and . . . well, the weather. He dozed off right after supper. He . . ." She averted her gaze. "I don't mean to be unkind. Jack wasn't a bad person."

Just then, Emma tried to play "Three Blind Mice" and hit so many wrong notes Charles suspected she'd left off a mouse or two.

Addie winced, but shot Emma an encouraging smile, then turned back to him.

"Is that all you had on your list?" he said.

She lowered her voice and leaned a little closer, even though Emma's playing threatened to drown out her words. "He . . . well, he gave me the willies."

Ridiculously glad, Charles chuckled. "Hmm, the willies. That's definitely *not* a good basis for marriage."

"That's what I thought," Adelaide said. "Mama insisted I had no one to compare him to, and should just grit my teeth and ignore the effect he had on me."

"That could get mighty hard on a woman's teeth."

"What? Oh!" Addie laughed.

Charles thought the sound enchanting. A desire to pull her into his arms crashed through him, but he didn't dare.

Addie jumped to her feet. "Oh, no!"

Charles caught a whiff of something burning. He followed Addie to the kitchen where she lifted a smoking pan from the oven. She tossed it onto the breadboard, dismay written all over her face. "This is terrible."

Turning Addie toward the table, he gently pushed her into a chair then removed his coat. "You sit. I'll handle the rest."

"No, you're my guest."

"This guest knows his way around a kitchen." He removed the biscuits from the pan and cut off the blackened bottoms, biting back an urge to tease her. No need to make her feel worse. Burnt or not, he'd rather be eating Addie's biscuits than Fannie's. Even gladder she hadn't married Jack.

He snuffed the thought. Being around Addie made him question everything upon which he'd carefully built his life.

She made him rethink his doubts about church, his anger at God . . . questions too painful to examine.

Yet despite all that, he still wanted to be with her.

"At least let me serve before the food gets cold."

He gave her a salute. "Yes, ma'am."

She rose and grabbed a towel to pull the roast from the oven, then began cutting up the meat. She ladled vegetables around the platter and set the dish on the table.

Emma ran into the kitchen. "Is dinner ready? I'm starving!"

"Yes, it is. Go wash up," Adelaide said.

Soon, they assembled at the table, an odd put-together group, not a family, exactly, but still, too close to one for comfort. A bouquet of lilacs in the center teased at his nostrils. Addie's warm, full table held a charm for him he hadn't found at the Becker House or at his own cheerless table.

Addie and Emma folded their hands and bowed their heads. Charles blinked, then did the same. Addie said a simple prayer.

As they ate, his gaze kept returning to Addie's, but Emma's endless chatter kept conversation between them at a minimum.

At last, Emma asked to be excused. Soon the notes of "Mary Had a Little Lamb" —

well most of them — drifted through the air.

"The pot roast was delicious, Addie. Everything was. You're an excellent cook."

"Thank you. My mother taught me."

"Well, you know the old saying — the way to a man's heart is through his stomach." Charles patted his. "You've created quite a path tonight."

Addie stacked her silverware on top of her plate. "I'm not sure there's any truth to that old adage."

"Why?"

Addie ran her thumb down the handle of her spoon. "My father left when I was a baby. Clearly my mother's cooking skills didn't keep him home."

"Maybe his leaving had more to do with who *he* was, than with her cooking."

She nodded, then removed the napkin from her lap, laid it on the table and folded it neatly, smoothing it with her fingers until it looked like it had never been used.

"What's on your mind?" he asked.

She raised her gaze to his. "I feel terrible that my mother jilted your father and caused trouble for you."

"Well, if she hadn't, we'd be brother and sister." He chuckled, and then took her hand. "My father is the one to blame, not

187

your mother. I'm sorry I didn't see that at first."

"I can understand why you'd resent my mother, and then me. Especially after hearing the contents of your father's will."

"I don't resent you or your mother." Charles joined her at the sink. "My family isn't a topic for good digestion."

His brow furrowed. He didn't want to discuss his past.

Charles touched her hand. "It's hard to talk about."

"You don't have to tell me."

"I couldn't talk about this with anyone but you." He gave her a weak smile. "Unlike your father, mine stayed — all the while beating the tar out of us."

Pain ripped through him, and he flinched.

She touched his arm, tears spilling down her cheeks. "I'm sorry."

He smiled and for a moment, covered her hand with his own. "You and I had rough beginnings, but we survived and our pasts brought us together, in an odd way, with the will."

Charles cleared his throat. He didn't want to think about his father. "Let's not talk about any of that." Just for a moment, he'd wanted to pretend he wasn't a product of his past. "Let's talk about you instead."

■ ■ ■ ■

"Would you care for coffee?" Adelaide asked, avoiding Charles's probing gaze.

"Please."

She quickly cleared the dishes and then poured two cups from the pot on the stove.

"Your father never contacted you in all those years?" Charles asked.

"My only contact came through his attorney after he died. He left me his money, the little he had."

She wouldn't tell him the reason her parents had married. Still, Adelaide knew she should stop talking so much, but his warm gentle eyes made her want to share her past. "I can't blame my father entirely. Mama was a critical, aloof woman."

Charles's brows knitted. "My father put her on a pedestal."

"She must have changed. I could never please her. I wasn't pretty enough, smart enough. I suspect she resented me." Her lower lip trembled. No one had loved her. And now Charles knew that, too. She covered her mouth with her hand, dropping her gaze to the contents of her cup.

"Aw, Addie, something must have been wrong with your mother's eyesight." He

189

took her chin in his hand, lifting her gaze to his. "You're a talented, intelligent, caring woman."

She soaked up his words, leaning in to the comfort of that hand. "I wasn't asking for a compliment."

"I mean every word." He studied her, his gaze tender. "After your childhood, I'm amazed you want a child."

"Why? I'm not like my mother."

"How can you be sure?" He grew remote, pulling inward.

The question pestered at her. If she ended up alone without a husband, without a child to love, would the disappointment turn her bitter?

Aside from the faraway sound of a barking dog drifting through the open window and the muted one-sided conversation between Emma and her doll, the kitchen grew silent.

Adelaide shook her head. "I could never be like my mother."

Charles raised a skeptical brow. "If pushed far enough, you can't tell what a person will do."

She folded her arms across her chest. "I'm offended you think I could treat a child unkindly."

"I didn't mean to insult you. I'm merely

saying we don't know ourselves until we're trapped and desperate." His mouth thinned. "I'm a newspaperman. I've seen mankind's depravity."

"Then you should understand my concern about Ed Drummond."

"You could be reading things that aren't there."

She sighed, refusing to argue with him. "I want to protect those children. *And* hopefully initiate some change, so Emma can grow up in a world where her opinions matter."

"Those are lofty goals." He rolled up his sleeves. "Here, let me do this. You did the cooking. I'll do the cleaning."

She swished around some soap in the pan of hot water, then handed him the dishrag. He scrubbed a plate and sloshed it through the rinse water, handing it to her to dry. For a second, their fingertips touched and the plate almost fell to the floor.

"That was a close one," Charles said with a laugh. "Don't want to break the dishes. I may not be invited back."

Adelaide's heart thumped in her chest. *He wants to spend more time with me.* But wouldn't that risk everything she'd worked to build — a life dependent upon no one but God.

Besides, if God had brought a man into her life, wouldn't he be a church-going man? Or did God want her to bring Charles to worship? If so, she'd failed.

With all these confusing feelings, she knew one thing for certain. If she let herself, she could care about this man.

She excused herself to look in on Emma and found the little girl with her doll in her arms curled on the settee, asleep. Gratitude brought sudden tears to her eyes, but she blinked them away and returned to the kitchen.

Soon side by side, she and Charles chatted about nothing, about everything. Keenly aware of his every move, the rise and fall of his broad chest as he breathed, his large hands slipping over the surface of her plates, the hair on his forearms wet and curling from the water, she couldn't tear her gaze away.

Even wearing a dishtowel tucked into his waistband, every inch of Charles looked male. The evening was a fantasy of what married life could be. Yet he distanced himself every time she got close. Charles didn't want permanence, nor did she.

They scrubbed and dried all the dishes. Charles removed the towel and laid it on the counter. Without thinking, Adelaide picked it up and hung it on a knob to dry.

"Cleaning up after the cleanup man?" He chuckled and she smiled, unperturbed by his teasing. But then his expression grew sober and he put his hands around her waist. "We're a good fit, you and I."

He lifted a hand to her hair. "You're a beautiful woman." He took a step back and rested his forehead on hers. "I'd best be going," he said in a husky voice.

The thought of Charles leaving made her feel lonelier than she'd ever felt in her life. "You can't go," she said, smiling. "I made a cream pie."

He shook his head. "Sounds delicious. But —"

"It's one of my grandmother's recipes," she cut in before he could decline. "Sweet and yummy."

"Ah, Addie, I can't stay." He cupped her face in his palm and kissed her lightly on the temple.

Before she could say anything, he snatched his jacket off the chair. "Thank you again for dinner," he said, and then walked out of the room. She heard his footfalls on the stairs and a second later, the bell echoed his goodbye.

Charles had no interest in a future with her. Had she been thinking she could trust a man? If she was ever going to take a chance on love, it would have to be with a special man who shared her beliefs, shared her trust in God.

A man who wanted to do more than give a child a legal name, the only thing her father had given her.

In the meantime, there would be no trusting these wild feelings. She descended the stairs to lock the door to the shop, locking Charles and all those head-spinning thoughts outside.

The next morning, Adelaide woke with the memory of Charles's presence at her table. She knew the Scripture about being unevenly yoked. Charles had told her he believed in God. Perhaps he refused to go to church because he blamed God for his childhood.

Yawning from a restless night, Adelaide trudged to Emma's room. For once, Emma got out of bed on Adelaide's first call, chock-full of questions about the evening with Charles.

In the kitchen, Adelaide cut Emma a piece of pie for breakfast, hoping the treat would distract her from the subject.

Emma scrambled into her chair. "Did you have fun?"

Adelaide set the plate in front of her. "Yes." *More fun than I care to admit.*

Emma took a bite of pie. "He didn't like the food?"

Adelaide rubbed her temples. "Why do you say that?"

Her gaze darted to the pie, with only one piece cut out of the circle. " 'Cause he didn't eat pie."

"Guess he was full." Adelaide took another sip of coffee, wondering why Emma couldn't be a sleepyhead today.

Emma licked her fork clean. "Did you play games?"

"Uh, no."

Emma rested her chin on a palm. "Then what *did* you do?"

Adelaide met her earnest, perplexed eyes. "We talked."

"That's *all?* That sounds boring."

"Grown-ups like to talk." Adelaide rose from her chair and took her cup to the stove. "Better hurry or you'll be late."

After scraping the last bite of pie from the plate and downing her glass of milk, Emma ran to her room, leaving Adelaide alone with the memory of what *had* transpired between her and Charles last night.

They'd shared their pasts and that had forged a deeper bond between them. But then, he hightailed out of here as if the kitchen had caught fire.

Since they'd met, her life had been turned upside down. Now she desired things — a voice, family. Things she couldn't have. Within minutes, she and Charles went from connection to conflict to connection. She'd never felt more alive, nor more miserable. She wouldn't let him keep her off-kilter. Nothing good could come from this silliness, nothing except trouble.

She wouldn't give up trying to have a voice in the community. He'd said good cooking made a path to his heart. Maybe food would forge a path to his brain, too. If she took him a piece of pie from dinner, in between bites she could talk to him about writing a column on an issue important to her. And take back the reins of her life.

Charles took the slice of sugar cream pie from Addie and laid the plate on his desk. The way he'd taken off last night, he'd expected her to be mad, not to be bringing homemade goodies. He admitted he was glad to see her. "Thanks. I'll have that with lunch."

"You're welcome."

"And thanks for dinner, too."

"Even with burned biscuits?" She laughed.

"That's my comeuppance for bragging."

"Anytime you want to give those biscuits another try, I'm available."

She smiled and he drank it in like a thirsty man. "You're a glutton for punishment," she said.

"No, I'm merely a glutton." Why was he asking for another invitation? Hadn't he already vowed to stay away? He eyed the pie. "I may have to eat a bite to see if the crust is burned."

"The pie is perfect, as are all of my bribes."

Ah, there was more to this visit than his stomach. "Why are you trying to bribe me?"

"I'm hoping the pie might sweeten your reaction to a proposal." She took a deep breath. "I'd like to express some of my views in the paper."

"On topics besides fashion?"

The lines around her mouth tightened. He'd known her long enough to recognize her annoyance.

"I do hold opinions that have nothing to do with hats."

Addie had a great deal of opinions and many conflicted with his. "I expected as much. You're an intelligent woman."

"I'm not here for a compliment. I want you to take me and my views seriously."

He shoved back from the desk. "What views do you wish to express exactly?"

Eyes shining with the light of an evangelist, she smiled. "I want to write about issues important to women."

He folded his arms across his chest. "Like what?"

She lifted her chin. "Getting the vote, for one."

When Addie tackled a topic, she picked a mountain not a molehill. Thus far, even he'd steered clear of women's suffrage, the kind of subject that lit tempers and canceled papers.

"I don't see how you can work women getting the vote into a fashion column."

Her brow furrowed. "Did I say I wanted to combine the two? I want two spaces in the paper. What I want is a voice."

Why must she get involved with the paper? Wasn't it enough to run her shop and let him handle what was rightfully his? "A voice? *Two* columns?"

"Unless you'd prefer I express my views in editorials."

He parked his arms across his chest. "You can express your views in letters to the editor, like any citizen of Noblesville. But I'm the editor. I write the editorials."

"I own half of the paper. That gives me a

right to the editorial page. Along with anything else I'd like half of. Like this desk." She cast a dismayed glance at the towering mess. "At least then there would be a few cleared inches of space."

She'd gone too far. Addie might have integrity, but she wanted too much from him. This was *his* paper. *His* desk.

Well, it might not be totally his, but once the two months were up, it would be. Until then he didn't need her "voice" in his paper or anywhere else. He knew what his readers liked.

"Stick with things you know, Addie."

"What? Birds and fruit on hats?" She glared at him. "Is that all you believe I think about?"

He reached out a hand to her, to still the rough waters between them. "As a business-woman, you know more than the average wife and mother. Still, with your shop, you have enough to deal with. No reason to waste your time in politics."

She looked as if he'd slapped her. Though he'd only meant to compliment her, too late he realized his wife and mother comment had cut her to the quick. He couldn't take it back without making it worse.

Addie's blue eyes flashed. "No reason? No *reason,* Charles? The selection committee you sat on, a committee comprised of men, denied me a child."

"We were merely following Children's Aid Society rules."

She stood.

"Yes, but who comprises that group? *Men* are making the decisions in the Children's Aid Society, in the entire country."

He put his elbows on the desk and made a steeple with his fingers. Addie's delicate appearance seemed incompatible to her tough-minded opinions. He'd remain calm and she'd see reason. "Men have the best interests of their womenfolk at heart. They aren't trying to harm you."

"Perhaps not. But why must a woman rely on a man to fight for her? Why can't I speak up for what matters to me?" She strode to the window, pivoting back to him. "The committee turned me down. You don't want my editorial input. Well, here's a news story for you, Charles Graves. I am the only one, besides God, who knows what's best for me. I should have the right to make those decisions. So should every woman."

"I'm not trying to —"

She pointed at him, cutting him off. "Do you want to know what's ironic? *Your father* is the first man in my life who opened a door for me. Now you're standing in the middle of that door, arms spread wide, trying to keep me out. Well, I own half of this paper, and I won't be denied a voice in this town."

Charles jerked to his feet, sending his wheeled desk chair rolling into the wall. "My father wasn't opening a door for *you*. He was slamming one in *my* face! This paper is my life. Having the freedom to run it, to see it grow and prosper are all I have. I don't appreciate you trying to take that from me."

Her blue eyes turned stormy. "I'm sorry my ownership of the paper is such a burden, but you're stuck with me. Be glad I have a shop to run so I don't have time to work here, but I won't be an owner in name only. That's not how I'm made."

"Relinquishing control of the paper isn't how I'm made."

"This is my chance to help women, to change their lives for the better, to change this town for the better."

Were her motives as pure as she believed? "Or grind an ax?"

She fisted her hands on her hips. "That's insulting."

He sighed. "I know you have good intentions. But have you thought about how your editorials will affect the paper's circulation and the harmony of this town? You'll be stirring up trouble between men and their wives. You might end up hurting, not helping women."

"That's ridiculous." She held out a hand to him. "Why can't you understand how much I want this?"

Charles strode to her side, determined to make her see the risk she'd be taking. "I've been in this business a long time. I know a thing or two. The town fathers won't take kindly to a rabble-rouser in skirts."

"I don't need a warning, Charles. I need your support."

Why must she borrow trouble the paper couldn't afford? "I can't give it."

"You don't want me to have that voice, do you? You'd prefer a woman to cook and clean, bear children and keep her opinions to herself." She shook her head. "I've always felt like an outsider. My life doesn't fit the dutiful wife and motherhood mold of my friends. You're like every other man I've met. You'd say anything to keep the paper to yourself. Well, I insist, Charles! I need this chance."

"I'm only trying to protect you."

"From what? A paper cut? A spelling error?"

"From yourself." He looked her in the

eyes. "Don't you know what this could cost you?"

"You're worried about losing a few subscribers. I'll —"

"Emma."

The name stopped her cold. She looked away, considering his words, and then met his gaze. "I'd rather Emma saw me as a woman who fought for what she believed in, not as a woman too scared to speak her mind."

Charles stepped away, disquiet lying heavy in his soul. He hadn't convinced Addie of anything. "Write the column. I suppose I can't stop you. I hope you're prepared for the consequences."

She met his gaze, her eyes the color of a wind-tossed sea. "All my life I've been paying for the consequences of my mother's actions. It's about time I started earning my own."

Red hair frizzing around her peaches and cream complexion, Fannie gazed across the table at Adelaide with puppy-like eagerness. If only she could toss a bone out the door, maybe her protégée would chase after it. Then Adelaide could go back to her orderly life and run her shop in peace.

That being unlikely, she might as well get

on with it. Maybe she could have an impact on Fannie, however small, that would help the girl to be more . . . well, proper in her pursuit of men. And that help might lead to what Fannie wanted more than a career, more than a voice, more than an identity of her own.

A husband.

Though Adelaide hadn't met with success in that area, she would teach Fannie about fashion and etiquette. When it came to looking for a mate, she'd let the girl fend for herself.

"Let's start with decorum," Adelaide said.

"Decorum, does that mean how I dress?"

"Decorum means proper behavior, the same as demure. *Godey's* says a woman's demeanor is to be reserved. Sedate. Shy." Not the terms she'd use to describe Fannie, but after Adelaide's recent confrontation with Charles, the words didn't fit her, either.

Wrinkling her nose, Fannie rested her chin in her hands. "Demure sounds boring."

Adelaide tended to agree. She'd learned she didn't care much for keeping her mouth shut when a good deal needed to be said. Still, Fannie carried friendliness to an extreme. "Perhaps at first," Adelaide said carefully, "but as a woman gets to know the man, she shares more of her thoughts."

She'd certainly given Charles a piece of her mind. They'd reached the point where they disagreed about everything. Perhaps she needed a few lessons in demureness. Maybe then she could live in the confines of her gender and still be her own woman.

"Carriage is important. A woman of breeding doesn't take a room by storm. She walks with grace and dignity." Adelaide strolled across the room, posture erect, chin level with the floor, eyes straight ahead. She turned to Fannie. "You try."

Fannie lurched to her feet, almost knocking over her chair, then shook in a fit of giggling. She leaned against the table until her laughter subsided, then followed in Adelaide's tracks, her skirts swaying provocatively. "Like this?"

"Ah, a little less movement of the hips."

Fannie's brow puckered. "I thought men liked that."

They did indeed. "You don't want to give the wrong impression."

Fannie stared at her blankly.

"That you're . . . well . . . unchaste."

"Oh!" Fannie's mouth gaped open, releasing a nervous laugh.

"Now, try again."

This time Fannie carried herself with a modicum of dignity.

"Much better."

Fannie guffawed.

"You know, Fannie, frequent giggling detracts from a woman's demeanor, especially if she giggles for no reason."

"So I should just smile? You know — the kind of smile that doesn't show my teeth?" Fannie attempted the serene smile, which triggered yet another bout of giggling. "Oh, mercy me, I can't."

Muscles knotted at the base of Adelaide's neck. She'd once possessed patience in abundance, but Fannie's first lesson in deportment had only begun, and already Adelaide struggled to relax her jaw.

Part of the problem stemmed from Adelaide's recent doubt that a woman should have to conform. A man never worried about how he walked or smiled.

Fannie sniggered. "I'm glad I'm not one of those people who giggle so much they get on people's nerves."

By now, Adelaide was grinding her teeth, but Fannie didn't notice.

Instead, she practiced her smile, keeping her lips together. "How's this?" she said, then giggled raucously.

Adelaide rubbed a hand over her eyes. "Fine. Perfect."

Inwardly, she admitted her first attempt

to help one of the women of Noblesville had failed miserably. Effecting townwide change with words had to be easier than helping Fannie learn to walk across a room without swishing her backside like a busy broom.

CHAPTER ELEVEN

A week later with the first of her suffrage articles in print Adelaide passed the dry goods store and almost bumped into Lizzie Augsburger coming out with her arms full of packages. Lizzie's green eyes twinkled, as if she had a funny story to tell. "I'm glad I ran into you. Since you've started writing articles, reading the paper is exciting."

Her words warmed Adelaide clear to her toes. "Thank you."

"I don't miss an issue. Your fashion column's such fun. I totally agree with your thoughts on suffrage, too," she said, using a low confidential tone. "Women should have the vote."

"How did your husband react?"

"Your column caused quite a stir." She waved her free hand. "Got George's sap flowing. Why, he threatened to cancel the paper, told me to buy my hats somewhere else, like there's anyplace else to buy quality hats in this town." She chuckled and shifted the bags in her arms. "I kind of enjoyed the show. It's been ages since we've discussed more than, 'Pass the potatoes.' " Lizzie smiled. "You've brought exactly what we need into our house — a touch of controversy."

"Glad I could help. I think."

"Don't worry. We made up. And that was fun, too." She cocked her head. "Maybe next, you should tackle those nasty spittoons. The men in this town miss half the time. A lady has to watch her step."

They said goodbye and Adelaide headed to the bank, suddenly weary. George Augsburger, the most even-keeled man in town, had threatened to cancel the paper. Everywhere she went she got a reaction to her columns. Her words may have enlivened the Augsburger marriage, but they weren't doing much for *her* life.

She'd made no inroads in her quest to become Emma's mother. She'd wired Mr. Fry. In his reply he suggested she leave the matter in the committee's hands. William's teacher told her he was missing school but Superintendent Paul told Charles many of the boys stayed home during spring planting.

Inside the bank, footsteps clicking on the

tiled lobby floor and echoing off the pressed-tin ceiling overhead, she walked toward the teller's window to deposit her meager receipts. Business in the shop had slowed. If this continued —

"Miss Crum!"

John Sparks stood at the door to his office, motioning for her. What did the president of the bank need with her? From the expression on his face, she didn't want to know.

She crossed the lobby to meet him.

In the shaft of sunlight filtering in from his office window, Mr. Sparks's bald head gleamed. "This stand you're taking on women's suffrage — can't imagine what you're thinking." Behind his thick glasses, Mr. Sparks blinked in rapid succession. "Well, aren't you going to explain?"

She prayed her answer wouldn't hurt her chances of keeping Emma. "Women are citizens of this country, but without the vote, they can't influence the policies that affect them."

"They have husbands to do that for them."

Did everything come down to a woman's marital status? Adelaide counted to ten. "Not every woman is married."

Mr. Sparks shifted his gaze to the floor. "True." He crossed his arms and rejoined her gaze. "But men study the issues and vote for the good of the entire community, for women and children. No need to clutter ladies' minds with government."

Decked out in her Sunday best, Mildred Rogers, the sheriff's wife, entered the bank, paused a moment, then inched closer. Customers who had finished their business and were leaving the bank, slowed as they passed, then stopped to listen.

Adelaide had come to make a deposit, not stand on a soapbox, but she said, "Women have good minds and are capable of studying issues." A murmur of agreement left Mildred's lips. Adelaide cocked her head. "How does *Mrs.* Sparks feel about it?"

Mr. Sparks's brows rose into what had once been his hairline. "Why, I never asked her."

No surprise there. "Maybe you should." Adelaide smiled. "It never hurts to get a woman's opinion."

A couple men stood listening to the exchange. "Are you that troublemaker from the paper?" the tall one asked.

"Yes, that's her," Mr. Sparks said, wagging his finger. "If women get the vote, the next thing you know, they'll be telling their husbands what to do."

Ah, the core of the controversy. How

could she make them understand she upheld the Biblical example of marriage? "Having the right to express their opinions at the polls will merely give women a right to be heard, not a right to silence men."

Mrs. Rogers waved a hand as if asking for permission to speak. "I agree with you there, Adelaide." Mildred shot Mr. Sparks a glare, then moved a step closer. A group of onlookers now circled them, arguing among themselves.

"See all the trouble you're causing? All this talk about women voting puts a knot in my belly." Mr. Sparks rubbed his stomach as if to prove it. "Change. That's what it is. And once that's the law, no telling where it'll lead."

A thin man shot a wad into a nearby spittoon. "Next thing you know, women will be wearing the breeches in the family!"

Adelaide shook her head. "Getting the vote will give women the *same* rights as men. Not more."

"Miss Crum, you're turning this bank into a sideshow." Mr. Sparks shooed the growing group of listeners toward the counter. "The tellers are waiting, folks."

People inched away, looking as if they'd like to leave their ears behind. A few didn't budge, including Mildred, but Mr. Sparks stared them down and they finally left.

Mr. Sparks moved closer to Adelaide, within inches. "With your involvement at the paper, I wonder how you have time to care for Emma," the banker said, his tone sinister.

The threat stomped on Adelaide's lungs and she inhaled sharply. "I write my columns while Emma is in school."

He shook his head. "The controversy's got to affect the little girl. You're molding an impressionable young mind. Classmates are probably teasing her as we speak."

"Are you suggesting the committee would move Emma to spite me? Hasn't she been through enough?"

"I see it as removing Emma before you confuse her." He leaned closer. "If I were you, I'd stick to fashion columns."

Mr. Sparks stepped to his office, giving her one last warning scowl before closing the door with a click.

Motionless, blood pounding in her temples, Adelaide recalled Charles' swarning about this very thing. But she'd felt compelled to speak out, to explain the importance of women getting the vote.

Mr. Paul and Mr. Wylie would undoubtedly share Mr. Sparks's view. Would her words cost her Emma? Had she stepped out of God's will for her life?

God, please show me the way.

To get a better view, Charles pushed through the crowd. Only a smoldering shell remained of the Anderson house.

He found owner Matthew Anderson and jotted down names and ages of the family and the cause of the fire — a knocked-over kerosene lamp. Then Charles walked over to speak to Sheriff Rogers. He'd run a story, explaining the Andersons' plight, which should generate donations for the family of six.

Charles's gaze swept the scene one last time. Mrs. Anderson, holding her baby son in her arms, and two young daughters huddled in a circle of sympathetic ladies. Mr. Anderson and his older boy stood apart, staring at the ruins, when Ed Drummond, of all people, approached. Curious, Charles edged closer.

Anderson laid his hand on his young son's shoulder. "I'm mighty grateful we all got out," he said to Drummond.

A shadow crossed Ed's face. "That's all that matters."

"Reckon you know that better than anyone, Ed."

Drummond nodded, cleared his throat

and then directed his attention to the boy. "A fire's pretty scary, hey, Tad?"

"Yes, sir." The boy heaved a sigh that seemed to weigh more than his small frame. "My straw-stuffed kitty burned up."

Ed ruffled the young boy's hair. "Soon as I heard about the fire, I started gathering things from the neighbors. I've got clothing and blankets in my wagon." He directed his words to Anderson, but his eyes remained on Tad's soot-stained cheeks. "I remember seeing some toys. Wanna go look?"

A grin spread across the boy's face. "Sure!"

Charles couldn't believe he'd suspected Drummond, a man this kind, even tender-hearted toward a child, of abuse.

At the wagon, Ed turned back to Matthew Anderson. "If your family needs a place to stay, the Phillips family has offered their home."

"The missus and kids are going to her sister's. With chores to do twice a day, I'll stay and sleep in the loft."

Charles's gaze turned to the imposing barn and the livestock now turned out to pasture.

As if on cue, Drummond and Anderson swiveled their heads to the ruins. "The fire department couldn't save the house, but I'm grateful they kept it from spreading to the barn."

Ed clapped a hand on Anderson's shoulder. "As soon as it cools down, fourteen men from church will be out and start raising a new house on that foundation. With that many able-bodied men at work, before you know it, you'll be moving in."

Anderson bowed his head and swiped a hand across his wet eyes. "I appreciate it. More than I can say."

"I'll never forget you did my chores after . . . Eddie."

"It was the least I could do." Anderson tugged his son to his side. "When I think how close —" He stopped, shook his head.

Charles walked to the lane, mounted Ranger and rode to town, thinking about Drummond. Ed had gathered what the burned-out family needed and would help rebuild the house along with thirteen others from his church. He'd realized a frightened boy needed a stuffed animal to cuddle. The man didn't fit the description of any child beater he'd ever seen.

But then, Charles's father had been a caring man in the community, always joking, likable — and yet, a fraud.

Could Ed be a fake, too? Charles shifted in the saddle. He flicked the reins, refusing to think about Adam Graves.

His mind turned to Addie. To mention Ed's philanthropy would start a disagreement. Were her suspicions the product of her unconscious hope she'd somehow end up with Emma?

He couldn't take the chance on a hunch. If he did anything that led to Ed and Frances losing those children, and he was wrong, he'd hurt an innocent family *and* ruin his credibility.

Still, he wanted Addie to have Emma. She was a different woman than the one he'd first met at the interview. *That* Addie held her emotions inside. This new Addie stood up for what she believed in, laughed easily, but most importantly loved Emma.

When Emma returned to the Drummonds, Addie's heart would break. At the prospect, his stomach clenched.

Adelaide clung to a thread of emotional conclusions, not to the strong rope of cold facts. For her sake, he either had to disprove her theory — or if abuse existed, uncover the truth.

With the paper out this morning, he had some time and would drive out to talk to Tulley. Maybe Ed's neighbor would give new insight. He'd ask Addie to ride along.

Even with the turmoil between them,

picturing Adelaide's face in his mind, he longed to have her near.

At the livery, Charles left Ranger in the care of the freckle-faced stable hand, and then loped toward the center of town and crossed the street to Adelaide's shop.

As he entered, two ladies toting hatboxes walked past. He held open the door and they gave him a friendly nod.

"Ladies," he said smiling, and then closed the door after them. He crossed to where Addie stood and soaked up some of the radiance from her face. Was it the sales or could he be the reason for that glow?

"Charles." His name sounded gentler, more refined coming from her lips. "This is a surprise." She fingered a garment on the counter. "I figured you were still angry with me."

How could he ever be mad at anyone with eyes that blue? "And you with me. Considering our dual ownership of the paper, it's bound to happen. As a newsman, I've learned not to take a dispute personally."

"As a woman, I've learned a man can be wrong — without taking it personally." She shot him a triumphant smile.

He chuckled. "I kind of enjoy that temper of yours."

Her eyes widened. "Me? What about you?

You —"

"See how easy it is to raise your hackles?"

She let out a laugh. "So you came to pester me?"

"No, ma'am." He stepped closer. "I came to look at you." Her face colored, pretty as a pink rose in bloom. He liked tipping her poise with a few words. "And to hear about Jack."

On the counter, she began ironing the garment's folds with her hands. "I shouldn't have said those things about Jack."

"Oh, but I'm glad you did."

Her chin went up and she shot him a look that would have squelched a weaker man, but Charles merely laughed.

"Don't think you're perfect. You have faults, too."

"Name them."

She examined her nails. "I can't waste my day listing them. You're a smart man. Surely, you can figure them out yourself."

He chuckled, then let his gaze roam her face, memorizing every contour. The high cheek bones, pert nose, slim straight brows. He couldn't let her down. "You looked busy when I came in."

"Those ladies were my first paying customers since my column came out." She sighed. "Still, I've got to start on fall hats.

I've decided to ask Laura Larson to help in the shop two days a week so I'll have more time with Emma."

Charles laid a hand on hers and gave it a squeeze. "And for me, I hope."

"All I can concentrate on is keeping that precious little girl." Adelaide pulled her hand from under his.

"That's why I'm here. I have to see Joe Tulley, one of our county commissioners, for an article. His farm edges the Drummond place. If you want to ride along, we'll ask his opinion of Ed."

"I'd love to." Adelaide gave him a dazzling smile. "What do you want to see the commissioner about?"

He blinked. His mind suddenly blank as a new chalkboard. "What?"

"Why are you interviewing Mr. Tulley?"

He cleared his throat. "Ah, Tulley is pushing for upgrading the county roads."

He was reacting as if she were a magnet and he was a pile of iron filings, losing every coherent thought, except ones of her. He rose and walked to the counter to put some distance between them. "I spoke to the committee. They had nothing new to say about Ed, though they all mentioned the tragedy of his son's death."

"Sympathy for the Drummonds' loss

colors the committee's judgment. And it doesn't help that Ed's uncle, Roscoe Sullivan, is a respected member of the community."

Maybe she had valid points. Still, he suspected Addie of overreacting, not maliciously, but because she cared.

Deep down, Charles knew Addie would never have permitted a child of hers to be beaten, by anyone, even the child's father. Unlike his mother or hers, Addie had an inner strength, a strength he supposed came from her deep faith in and obedience to God.

For her sake, he'd gather information and see where the facts led, hoping they would point to Ed's unsuitability. But after what he'd seen out at the fire, the gentle way Drummond had treated the Anderson boy, he doubted it. "So far, we have no reason to suspect Ed of abusing William."

He saw disappointment in Addie's eyes, knew how much she counted on discrediting the Drummonds, counted on having Emma permanently.

She returned to her work, but her shoulders drooped.

"A ride in the country will do you good. When can you leave?"

"Emma went home with a friend after

school, and she's staying for supper. I can leave at closing time."

He stepped near and caught the scent of her. Crisp and clean, with the faintest hint of honeysuckle. His gaze drifted to those rosy lips. He bent his head . . . Then realized kissing wasn't appropriate in a place of business. He straightened. "Five-thirty, then."

"Thanks for inviting me," she said a little breathlessly.

He strode to the door, then paused and turned back. "Uh, when, ah, did I say?"

She smiled. "Five-thirty."

"Oh, yeah. I knew that."

Charles said goodbye and then dashed across the street, back to the world he could control. One where he didn't make a fool of himself because of the way a woman breathed. One where he didn't lose track of what he'd said all because of a woman's smile. Or didn't lose the objectivity he'd prided himself on.

At five-twenty-five, Charles had hitched Ranger to the buggy and pulled up to her shop, a smile of anticipation curved at his mouth. Evidently she'd been watching for him because she immediately stepped onto the walk.

He jumped to the ground, his gaze resting

on her face. "Hello again."

"Hello," she answered back.

He stood a moment, merely looking at her. She'd donned a wide-brimmed straw hat with blue ribbons that tied under her chin. Whenever she went out, she wore a different hat. Her stock-in-trade, like the tablet he carried.

Inside that pretty head lived a keen, determined mind, which both fascinated and annoyed him. "You're beautiful."

A blush tinged her cheeks and put a glow on her face even the wide-brimmed hat couldn't hide. "Thank you."

He offered his hand to her, giving it a squeeze. When she returned the pressure, the contact filled him with contentment. Is this how other men felt with the women who cared about them?

He handed her into the buggy, then walked to the other side. She pulled aside her skirts, making room. He climbed in, took the reins and then glanced her way. When he caught her gaze, she lowered her lashes, looking feminine and oh, so alluring.

Seeing her smile, touching her hand, these simple things brought him joy and optimism. He wanted to protect her, to see her have Emma. But no matter how much he longed to be with her, he couldn't marry her.

Not with the blackness inside him.

Flicking the reins over Ranger's back, he forced his gaze to the road, away from Adelaide Crum. He couldn't have her, except for moments like this.

The reminder tamped down his emotions and he resolved to keep the day impersonal. He would focus on *The Ledger* and the state of the county roads. And distance Addie, with her controversial column and her distracting blue eyes, from his mind.

Adelaide laid a gloved hand on his arm and his good intentions faltered. "Thanks for this chance to ask about Ed."

"I want what's best for Emma, too."

They drove out of town, passing a field with shoots of corn cracking the dry soil, then another with winter wheat dancing in the breeze. In an evergreen alongside the road, a cardinal whistled a greeting. Open land pushed to the horizon. Except for the beat of hooves on the road, quiet reigned and a sense of peace settled over him.

Adelaide leaned against the seat and sighed. "I can't remember the last time I went for a ride. I'd forgotten how lovely it is to see nothing but fields."

Empathy rippled through him. Addie had

been cooped up much of her adult life, while he'd been free to come and go, riding Ranger into the country whenever he found time.

She removed her hat and held it on her lap. Wisps of hair escaped the knot at her neck and drifted about her face. She pointed to a black horse galloping in the nearby pasture. "Oh, look at him run."

Charles leaned past Adelaide to peek at the sleek stallion. "He's probably tired of those fences and wants to flex his muscles." He found his face very close to hers. Captured by those blue eyes, he couldn't look away.

"It's too bad he's fenced in." She sighed.

He slowed the buggy and with a gentle touch, turned her face toward his. "Do you feel that way sometimes? Boxed in, not by rails but by people's expectations?"

Her eyes widened. "I do," she said softly. "That's why I want a voice at the paper. Do you understand?"

"Why must you work for change? You have nothing to prove."

"I may have nothing to prove, but there are lots of things to *improve* — not just for me, but for all women. With your family situation, you should understand some things need to be changed — like terrorized women, who have nowhere to go."

Charles flicked the reins. Ranger picked up speed. "Neither law, politics nor community expectations kept my mother in that house," he said, his voice gruff. "Her lack of courage did."

"It wasn't only a lack of courage." She laid a gentle hand on his forearm. "She probably had no options."

Her gaze returned to the horse still running around the enclosure. "As a child, did you ever think about running away?"

He nodded. Somewhere along the line this had become about him, not her. "Sure." He exhaled. "But I've learned memories travel with you."

They were both pinned by their pasts. The thought shook him, but he laid it aside to examine later. "Why not learn to ride? On a horse, you can feel that freedom. Feel in control, in tune with the world." He pushed back a wisp of hair that had blown across her cheek. "If you'd like, I can teach you."

She swatted at his hand. "I'll do no such thing."

He shot her a grin. "Too scared?"

"I am not."

"Good. That's what I thought." Then he clicked to Ranger and snapped the reins. He wished he were riding Ranger, with Ad-

226

die tucked close, his arms encircling her and the wind blowing in their faces. "Once you get used to the size and power of a horse, you might find you enjoy riding as much as I do." He knew how to give her a taste of that freedom. "Here, take the reins." She shook her head, hanging on to the side of the buggy. "I won't let anything happen. Come on, you can do it."

She released her grip and scooted closer, reaching for the leather ribbons.

Charles gave her an encouraging smile. "Good, now flick them." Ranger broke into a trot and Addie gave a little gasp. "Isn't this fun? Feel the freedom, Addie?"

"Oh, yes!" She glanced at him briefly and her eyes shone with delight. As the landscape sped by she laughed.

Memories wafted away on the breeze and for a moment, they both were carefree, released from their pasts.

But up ahead, Charles saw their turn and put out a hand for the reins. "I'll take over now."

"Am I doing it wrong?"

"No, we're here." At his gentle tug, Ranger slowed and turned down the lane. "This is the Tulley farm."

And the return to reality.

■ ■ ■ ■

Adelaide took in the limbs of huge elms reaching across the lane like a canopy. An occasional burst of sunshine broke through the shade, throwing mottled, swaying patterns upon Charles's face. He had offered to teach her to ride. Even with the exhilaration of the speeding buggy, Adelaide couldn't imagine climbing on a horse, but she'd do it. Not because it meant spending hours with Charles, but because she wanted to come and go as she pleased. For that, she'd risk her neck.

In the Tulley barnyard, Charles brought the horse to a standstill. A black-and-white Border collie barked hello, then ambled over to greet them.

Charles hopped from the buggy, scratched the dog behind the ears and then crossed to her side. Before Adelaide could climb down, he wrapped his hands around her waist and lowered her to the ground.

She wanted to linger in his strong arms, but she had a mission. Giving wide berth to his horse, she started for the house, hoping Mr. Tulley had something tangible against Ed.

An hour later Adelaide's spirits flagged.

Mr. Tulley had said only positive things, praising Ed for working his fields while Mr. Tulley's hand healed after losing two fingers to a saw. He'd given example after example of Drummond's willingness to help a neighbor — raising a barn after a tornado, pitching in to harvest crops for an elderly widow.

Charles handed Adelaide into the carriage. "I'm sorry you didn't find what you expected, but after Tulley's assurances, you should feel better about William's safety."

"I've seen Ed Drummond in action. He's not the saint Mr. Tulley made him out to be."

"I'm not saying he's a saint, but there's no evidence he's a child beater, either," Charles said, climbing in beside her.

As a newsman, Charles would never trust her instincts on this. She had to find evidence.

As they drove up the lane, possibilities scuttled through Adelaide's mind. "If we did a story on the orphans, we'd have an excuse to gather information on the Drummonds."

Charles flicked the reins and they started down the lane. "You're looking for trouble where none exists. Drop it."

"Because you don't want me involved in the paper?"

He scowled. "A newspaper isn't a tool for your agenda."

She folded her arms across her chest. Charles couldn't see trouble if it were marked with a capital *T*. If she could get out to the Drummond farm, she'd do some investigating of her own. "I'd like to learn to ride or maybe practice driving a buggy."

"Really? What made you change your mind?"

"You did."

Charles beamed. "How about starting tomorrow after Emma leaves for school? I'll have you back before time to open."

Her stomach clenched, but she agreed. She'd no longer allow her fear of horses to control her life. Tomorrow she'd learn the skills that would enable her to check on William and Frances and uncover the truth. She could no more ignore Ed Drummond's treatment of William than she could allow Mr. Sparks to scare her from her goal of improving life for women. Since the banker had threatened to take Emma, she'd prayed daily about her desire to work for suffrage and felt in her bones that God had given her this mission, along with the task of protecting the Grounds children. She couldn't allow intimidation to shape her decisions. If she turned her back on others, she couldn't face herself in the mirror each morning.

Charles's piercing eyes scrutinized her. "You're awfully quiet."

Hoping to ease his inspection, she put a hand on Charles's arm. Such a small thing, she supposed, to feel the hard muscle of a man's forearm beneath the fiber of his shirt. But these small touches enthralled her. She forced her mind away from what she could not have. "How did you get into the newspaper business?"

"It's a long story but I'll give you the condensed version. I left home at fifteen and saw a sign in the window of a small weekly newspaper." He grinned. "No one else applied, so I got a job setting type. I slept in the back on a cot, swept the place, did whatever needed doing. In time, my overworked boss asked me to write a news item. One thing led to another." He chuckled. "You could say I fell in love with the smell of ink."

"I'm sure you love more than that."

"I found the urgency of deadlines and being tapped into the pulse of the community, the entire nation, exciting. Since then, my life has revolved around the newspaper business." He frowned. "I'm talking too much."

"I love hearing about your life." Charles

had been quite young to be on his own. "So why did you leave home at fifteen?"

He shrugged. "My mother died. Sam had already left. No reason to stick around." He said no more, but she knew by the way he bit off the words that saying more would open wounds.

"With all you've experienced as a boy, why can't you understand my concern about William?"

"My past was hardly the little rough wagon ride that upset you. You have no idea what I went through." He let out a bitter laugh. "Sam and I became experts at lying, could make up a reason for a black eye or cracked rib in two seconds flat."

Her throat closed at his words and she swallowed convulsively. If only someone had helped him. If only she could help him now. "Didn't anyone get suspicious?"

"If they did, they never did anything about it. No one helped us, Addie." He took a deep breath and the sound rattled through him like a speeding train on a mile-high trestle. "No one." Charles met her gaze. The pain in his eyes wrenched her heart. "It's not the same as William, not the same at all."

"My heart aches for you, for the defense-less little boy you were. But isn't your childhood proof we don't know what's happening behind closed doors?"

"Isn't it possible Ed's lack of patience is because he's still grieving for his son?"

Grief didn't give a person the right to shove a defenseless child. "Maybe it's less painful for you to put on blinders."

Dark eyes turned on her. "Maybe you're the one wearing blinders. Admit it — you want Emma. The only way to have her is to prove the Drummonds unfit."

His words stung like nettles in her garden. "I'd never make this up, not even to get Emma."

"You heard Tulley. Ed Drummond is an upstanding citizen."

"So was your father — the minute he walked out the door."

Charles didn't respond.

The buggy closed in around her. She turned away, but found the passing scenery had lost its charm. Her gaze dropped to the spot between Ranger's ears. "I think I went to the wrong man for help."

Charles snapped the reins and the buggy lurched forward. He swung his gaze to her, his eyes cold and distant. "Maybe you did."

CHAPTER TWELVE

At breakfast the next morning, Adelaide couldn't get her mind off the way she and Charles had parted yesterday, couldn't forget his cold, distant eyes. Her suspicions about Ed Drummond had reopened a past he wanted to forget. A past filled with fear and violence. Her eyes misted. No one had cared enough to investigate, wounding him almost as much as the abuse he'd endured at his father's hands.

If she ignored Ed's threat to William's safety, she'd be no different than the bystanders in Charles's world.

Beside her, Emma dawdled at the table with a faraway look in her eyes, not eating, aimlessly stirring her oatmeal.

"Emma, you need to eat or you'll be late to school."

A rap at the kitchen door made Emma jump. The child was skittish. Why?

Adelaide found Sally on the landing wearing a bright blue bonnet on her head, and a dishtowel-covered basket on one arm.

"Good morning! I've brought fresh-baked muffins."

Adelaide flipped back the towel and inhaled the enticing aroma. "Mmm, apple cinnamon." She cocked her head. "You drove all the way into town to bring us muffins?"

"I'd have driven to Minneapolis." Sally chuckled. "Another minute looking at the downcast faces of my men and I'd have pelted them with these muffins!" Sally plopped the basket on the table, then chucked Emma under the chin.

The recipient of Sally's treats before, Adelaide knew the symptoms. "Bad day in the woods for your men?"

Nodding, Sally slipped into a seat. "All four went rabbit hunting yesterday and came home empty-handed."

Adelaide chuckled, and then tipped the basket of muffins. "Look what Mrs. Bender brought, Emma. Want one?"

Emma pushed away her bowl, her face glum. "I'm not hungry."

"She should be sitting in my kitchen," Sally said. "She'd fit right in."

"You usually eat every bite. Are you sick?" Adelaide laid a hand on Emma's forehead, relieved to find it cool.

The child hung her head, looking more like a rag doll than her usual perky self. "No."

Adelaide slid into the chair beside her. "What's wrong?"

"Nothing."

Sally tilted Emma's head up with her fingertips. "I bet she doesn't have her homework done. Or maybe she hates recess. Oh, I know, she wants to stay home and clean. That's it. She wants to scrub the floors, all the windows, even the steps out back."

The slightest smile tugged at Emma's lips. "No."

"Well . . . maybe she's upset she didn't catch a rabbit." Sally touched Emma's hand. "Is that what's bothering you?"

A glimmer sparked in her eyes. "I wouldn't hurt a bunny."

"Ah, you city girls don't know what you're missing. Rabbit tastes good, like chicken. If my men ever bag any, I'll bring you some fried crisp."

Emma wrinkled her nose. "No, thank you."

Adelaide smoothed Emma's hair. "Something *is* bothering you, sweetie. Can you tell me about it?"

Sally rose. "Well, I'd better get a move on." She flashed Adelaide a look of concern, then slipped out the back.

Soon as Sally closed the door, Emma dropped the spoon and looked up, her eyes swimming with tears. "William."

A chill crept down Adelaide's spine. She drew Emma's hand into her own. "What about William?"

Tears spilled over her lashes and rolled down her cheeks. "I don't know."

Adelaide let go of Emma's hand and began rubbing her back. "You're worried about William?"

Emma nodded, her face contorted in misery. "Uh-huh."

"Tell me, honey, why?" Adelaide continued massaging Emma's back, and waited, every muscle in her body as tense as the small ones under her fingers.

Emma's mouth tightened. She picked up her spoon and began shoveling the oatmeal into her mouth, avoiding the question.

Adelaide laid a hand on Emma's arm to still her frantic eating. "When life gets me down, instead of worrying, I've learned to count my blessings. Before I know it, I feel better."

Taking Emma's smaller hands in her own, Adelaide showed her how to tick off each blessing on her fingers. But even after enumerating Emma's new hat, Adelaide's cookies and a new best friend, the little girl still looked forlorn.

Emma carried the same fears ticking away in Adelaide's gut. The time had come to take action, not tomorrow, not next week. Today.

An hour later, waiting for Laura, Adelaide paced the shop.

The bell jingled over the shop door. "Morning, Adelaide!" Laura shrugged off her shawl and hung it on a peg.

"Good morning. I hate to leave you alone on your first day back, but I have an errand that needs doing. Is it all right if I'm gone all morning?"

"Don't be silly. I'll be fine. Are you going to the ladies' Bible study?"

"Ah . . . no." Adelaide couldn't lie. "I'll explain later." She gave her friend a quick hug. "Mrs. Brewster is to pick up her alterations today." Adelaide pulled on her gloves, talking fast. "I'll miss a riding lesson with Mr. Graves this morning." Charles might not show up after the way they parted yesterday. "Tell him I'm sorry."

"Are you over your fear of horses?"

"I'm working at it."

"Good for you!" Laura tittered. "Riding

lessons are a perfect way to bring you two together. Don't worry about Mr. Graves."

"See you around noon," Adelaide said and left the shop.

Charles wouldn't approve of her plan, but he couldn't see Ed as a threat to the children. Hopefully, with Ed working in the fields, she could talk to Frances alone.

To get in and out of before Ed came in for the noon meal, she had to hurry. She lengthened her stride, her skirts swirling around her feet. As she neared the café, she passed Mrs. Whitehall tacking up a list of the daily specials.

Mrs. Whitehall's apron was dusted with flour. "Morning, Adelaide."

"Good morning, Geraldine."

"I want to thank you for what you're doing for Fannie. She's practicing her walk, even trying to stifle that giggle of hers."

Reining in her impatience, Adelaide slowed her pace. "Fannie's a lovely girl."

Mrs. Whitehall rosy face broke into a smile. "If you can get away for lunch, I've made apple fritters. The bill's on me. My way of saying thanks."

Adelaide shook her head. "Not today."

At her abrupt reply, Geraldine shot her a probing look.

Adelaide forced a smile. "I'm sorry. Wish

I could."

"Well, another time, then," Mrs. Whitehall said, her tone friendly, her suspicion forgotten.

Adelaide promised, and then hurried off. At the thought of driving a buggy alone, a band of nerves tightened around her throat and her touchy stomach somersaulted.

Now, don't go getting jumpy, Adelaide Crum.

In her mind's eye, she pictured Emma and William's innocent young faces. For them, she'd do anything. In the past, she'd been adept at keeping the peace. Since the orphans arrived in town, she'd learned if she wanted to change things, she had to take a stand. Not that she liked looking for trouble, but to protect the children she must.

Ducking into the office of the livery, she found a young man straddling a bench, working something smelly into the contraption the horses wore between their teeth and over their ears. "Good morning." She'd tried to sound confident, but her voice quavered.

"Ma'am." He got to his feet, dropping the equipment and tipped the bill of his cap. Never in her life had Adelaide seen a face with so many freckles.

"I'm, ah, in need of a . . . conveyance, for the morning."

The young man grinned, displaying a missing tooth. "Well, you're in the right place, ma'am. What do ya need?" He motioned to a hand-chalked sign of the rates hanging on the wall.

She read a list of options. "A buggy will suffice, thank you." Adelaide dug in her purse and paid in advance. They walked into the stable, and the young man left to get the horse.

That had been simple. Now if she could only remember what she knew about driving. She had vivid memories of riding out to the Tulley farm. But most of those memories had nothing to do with driving a buggy.

And everything to do with Charles.

She recalled his strong hands and arms pulling back on the reins to stop the horse, to guide the animal's movements left or right. The memory kicked up her pulse, until she relived his cold demeanor on the ride back into town. She bit her lip. She mustn't think about Charles.

The youth walked toward her, leading a pure white horse.

Fiddlesticks, I might as well advertise my plan in the paper. "Don't you have a less conspicuous one?"

He tugged his cap back off his forehead,

241

revealing a shock of carrot-red hair and scratched his brow. "Conspic, cons . . . I ain't sure what you're saying, ma'am."

She gave her brightest smile. "I thought a black or brown horse would look nicer with the buggy, more like a matched set."

He shrugged and muttered "women" under his breath, but returned the white horse to its stall. Watching him amble along, as if he had all the time in the world, Adelaide tapped her toe. For one so young, he didn't have a speedy bone in his body.

He crossed to another stall and patted the nose of a dark brown horse, a *big* dark brown horse. "Does Shadow suit?"

The name couldn't be more appropriate. "Much nicer."

Not that she needed to be secretive when she visited the Drummonds — this time. Still, she'd prefer avoiding attention.

While she waited, she roamed the livery. Spotting a rag in the hay, she picked it up and draped it over a rail. If Charles had seen her do that, he'd poke fun at her. Not that she'd mind. She enjoyed his teasing nature, which reminded her of their afternoon in the livery. She plucked a strand of hay from the cloth, thinking of Charles's almost kiss. She might be brave enough to drive a buggy, but falling in love —

She shook herself mentally. She didn't want a man so blinded by his past he couldn't see the present, much less the future.

She strolled down the aisle. Over the half door, Ranger stretched out his neck like he recognized her. "You want me to rub your nose, don't you, fellow?" She inched forward, grateful for the barrier separating them, and ran her fingers lightly along his broad muzzle. Ranger was a beautiful animal, almost as beautiful as his owner.

If only she could do this investigating with Charles, but he saw things in black and white — the shades of logic — whereas she saw things in hues, colored with emotion and intuition. They were as different as night and day.

She strolled outside and watched the young man hitch Shadow to the buggy, marveling at the horse's patience despite the lad's absurd slowness. If he worked for her, she'd light a fire under him.

"All set, ma'am."

Approaching the animal, Adelaide looked at the beast's wide back and hoped she could show him who was boss. "Thank you." She motioned toward the horse. "Can he be ridden?"

He scratched his head. "Yes, ma'am, but

generally, when the horse is pullin', folks sit behind in the buggy."

Adelaide pressed her lips together, holding back a giggle. A giggle that would surely sound like Fannie's. "I meant without the buggy."

He looked relieved. "Yes, ma'am, he sure can!"

The young man gave her a hand. She gathered the reins, hoping she held them correctly. "Is there a brake?"

He blinked. "Not on a buggy, ma'am. Just tie up the horse if you stop somewhere."

"Of course, how silly of me."

He stood looking at her. Realizing he waited for her leave, she said a quick prayer and flicked the reins. The horse took off at a lively clip, throwing Adelaide against the seat. Wiggling upright, she pulled slightly on the reins, and, wonder of wonders, Shadow slowed.

Inconspicuous horse or not, she stayed on the back streets. In the country, she flicked the reins again and Shadow picked up speed. Every bit of her smiled, inside and out, at the thought of doing something this bold, this free, taking control of her worries about Emma and William.

Adelaide knew the Drummonds lived on the next farm beyond the Tulley place, a couple miles down the road. She spent her ride thinking about what she'd say to Frances, and time passed in a blur. A red barn came into view with Drummond, 1882, painted in bold white letters. She tugged on the left rein and drove down the lane to the house.

"Whoa!" she said, and Shadow obeyed. Gathering up her skirts, she climbed down and wrapped the leather around the hitching post, then thanked God for giving her safety. If only her investigation went as well.

She marched to the door and rapped. Through the screen, she caught a glimpse of a shadowy figure. "Frances? It's Adelaide Crum. I'm taking care of Emma."

Frances appeared at the door, looking thinner than Adelaide remembered, gaunt even. Pinned in place, a bib-style, rose-sprigged apron covered Frances's house-dress. Her cotton stockings and rundown shoes befitted a hard-working farmer's wife. A mane of dark hair pulled into a tidy knot framed Frances's face, tanned from working in the garden. "Is she all right?"

"She's fine. May I come in?"

Though she moved slowly with a hint of reluctance, Frances opened the door.

"On such a lovely morning I thought I'd drive out for a visit and catch you up on

245

Emma."

The furrow between Frances's brows eased. "I'd heard Emma was staying with you. I'm glad."

"I love having her with me."

"Is she doing well in school?"

"She's doing much better with her reading. Now math, that's another story." Adelaide smiled and Frances smiled back, sharing the knowledge of Emma's Achilles' heel.

"I'm sorry, I, ah, don't get many visitors. Come in." She followed Frances into the kitchen. Adelaide noticed a slight limp, but, otherwise, nothing appeared out of the ordinary.

"If you'd like a cup of tea, the water's hot."

"Tea would be lovely."

While Frances busied herself with cups and saucers, Adelaide sat on one of the battered Windsor chairs surrounding the gateleg table and looked around her. The kitchen might be plain, but Frances kept it meticulously clean. "I haven't had the chance to talk to you since your mother's funeral. The service was a lovely tribute to her life."

"Thank you." Frances approached with the tea, and her defeated expression tore at Adelaide's heart.

Was this the look of a woman who shared a home with a violent man? Or the appearance of a woman who'd lost two precious loved ones?

Adelaide added sugar and took a sip. "This is good."

Frances lifted her gaze. "Is Emma happy? Really happy?"

"Very, but she misses William." If she could get the boy home with her, maybe he'd tell what went on in the Drummond house. Adelaide leaned forward. "I've come with a request."

Stirring cream into her coffee, Frances's hand stilled.

"I'd like William to spend the weekend with Emma."

Frances shook her head. "Ed won't allow it."

"Why not?"

"William has chores."

"Surely, it would be all right for one night. I could pick him up after chores Saturday morning and have him back in time to help Sunday afternoon. I'm sure he misses Emma, too."

Frances shifted in her chair. "Won't do any good, but I'll ask," she said with obvious reluctance.

"Thank you." Adelaide took another sip of tea, wondering how to encourage Frances to talk. "Mr. Graves said you'd been feeling poorly. How are you?"

"About the same."

Relief flooded Adelaide's veins. Maybe Frances didn't plan to have Emma back, at least anytime soon. "I noticed your limp."

"My back's been acting up."

"I'm sorry. Are you lifting too much?"

"Aching backs don't mean less work. Washing and ironing needs doing." She folded callused hands in front of her. "I'm not complaining."

Aching backs were common, but Adelaide suspected a more ominous reason for Frances's limp. Not that Frances would confide in her, even if there were. "I'm very sorry about your mother. I know how close you were." Adelaide laid her hand over her schoolmate's. "Sarah acted strong, not the type to. . . ."

Frances pulled her hand away. As she lifted her palm to her lips, her fingers trembled. "I still can't believe it. Ma *was* a strong woman, a survivor. She knew I needed her —" Frances bit her lip. "When Eddie passed, I looked to Ma for strength."

Adelaide noticed Frances didn't mention her husband. "My mother's health failed about the time Eddie died. I've regretted not being able to do much for you."

Frances shrugged "You sent food."

248

Adelaide laid a hand on Frances's arm, noting its boniness through her sleeve. "I can't imagine that kind of loss."

A long sigh slipped from Frances's lips. "I thought with children in the house, maybe. . . ."

"Maybe what?" Adelaide prodded gently.

"Maybe things would be like they were before."

"But they're not."

Frances shook her head. Tears slipped over her lower lashes. "Losing Eddie nearly killed Ed."

"I can imagine."

But Frances didn't appear to hear, merely looked at a distant spot on the wall. "The morning it happened, I'd gone to Ma's," she said. "Pa had passed a few weeks before, and we were going through his things." She took a breath. "I left Eddie at home with his pa," she said, her voice so hushed Adelaide had to strain to hear. "Eddie's shirttail caught on fire, least-wise, that's what we think. Ed had gone to the outhouse, only for a few minutes, and heard Eddie's screams. He ran to the house, met Eddie coming out, his clothes on fire."

Frances rose from her chair, turning her back to wipe her eyes on the hem of her apron. Tears stung Adelaide's eyes. She couldn't imagine losing a child, especially in such a hideous way. Adelaide stood and gathered her childhood friend in her arms, felt her frailty. How much sorrow could Frances take?

"If only I'd been home." Frances's voice quavered. "And now Ma — I let her down, too."

"You didn't know," Adelaide said gently, holding her tight. "And if she was determined, you couldn't have stopped her."

Frances pulled away, her gaze meeting Adelaide's. "This is a house of death."

Adelaide's pulse skittered. "What are you saying?"

"I can't keep people safe, don't you see?" Frances's voice rose to an eerie pitch.

Adelaide patted Frances's arm, trying to soothe the wild look in her classmate's face. "None of this is your fault. You mustn't blame yourself."

Through the window, a movement caught Adelaide's eye. A man emerged from the woods.

Frances followed Adelaide's gaze, then flinched. "Ed!" Frances swiped at her eyes. "You'd better go."

Adelaide had no intention of going anywhere.

■ ■ ■ ■

Charles entered Adelaide's shop and found an older woman moving a feather duster over the shelves. Alerted by the bell, she headed his way.

"You must be Mrs. Larson."

"And *you* are Mr. Graves. I knew your father. You look just like him."

Charles pasted a tight smile on his face. "So I've heard."

She offered her plump, dimpled hand. "I've meant to stop at the paper long before this and welcome you to Noblesville. It's a pleasure to meet you at last."

He released her hand. "The pleasure is mine. Addie —" Heat climbed his neck. How familiar had she become that he'd call her by a nickname in front of a virtual stranger? "Miss Crum speaks highly of you."

Mrs. Larson beamed. "Aw, you've given Adelaide a nickname."

He could see her mind working. He'd best change the subject. "I understand you're helping out at the shop again."

"Yes, I love doing it. Working here gives my daughter a breather. At times, two women in one house can be one too many."

Only half listening to Mrs. Larson, he

251

glanced toward the workroom. Was Addie in there sewing? Making tea? Planning her next editorial? Not that he owed her an apology. Still, he'd disappointed her and that bothered him. "Is Adelaide here?"

"No, she isn't. She had an errand to run."

"I was to give her a riding lesson this morning."

"Yes, she told me." Mrs. Larson smiled and tiny creases danced around her eyes. "Would you join me in a cup of coffee?"

"Sure, but let me get it." And see if Addie is hiding from me.

Mrs. Larson laid her palm on her bodice. "How nice."

"Do you use cream or sugar?" he asked, heading to the back.

"Sugar."

He returned with a tray holding two coffee-filled cups, two spoons and napkins alongside a sugar bowl.

"You haven't forgotten a thing. I'm astonished."

"How so?"

"My son-in-law never lifts a finger in the kitchen and my Bernard, God rest his soul, never served a beverage in the thirty-four years of our marriage."

Charles placed a cup in front of Mrs. Larson. "As a bachelor, I've learned to handle the necessities." He took a seat across from her, then chuckled. "I suspect Addie got cold feet."

"You could be right. I've never known Adelaide to ride." Mrs. Larson leaned toward him, her eyes bright. "You sat on the orphan placement committee."

Charles took a swig of coffee. "She told you about that?"

"Adelaide confides in me, Mr. Graves." She straightened in her chair. "May I confide in you, too?"

Uneasiness settled in his chest. "If you'd like."

She pinned him with her gaze. "Adelaide is a special, giving young woman. Some might even say she's a fix-it kind of woman. Someone could easily take advantage of her."

Not likely. "Addie is a strong, independent woman. She's not about to be taken advantage of, even if someone wanted to, which, let me assure you, I do not."

She nodded, the lines of concern on her face softening. "If I've spoken out of turn, I apologize."

"No need to apologize. I can see you're a good friend."

She eyed him over her cup brim. "As a good friend, I'm also aware of things Ade-

253

laide enjoys, like the Black-eyed Susies growing along the roads into town."

The hint couldn't be more obvious. Maybe the daisies would mend the rift between them. Or should he even try? But thinking how pleased she'd be if he showed up with those flowers tempted him. "I appreciate the tip. Anything else I should know?"

Mrs. Larson leaned forward. "Adelaide would scold me for telling you this," she said, dropping her voice, "but her birthday is in a couple of months, on the twenty-fifth of July."

Charles shifted in his seat. "Is matchmaking a hobby of yours?"

She laughed. "I'm an incurable romantic. I believe love can overcome all obstacles."

This woman lived in a make-believe world. "I have to disagree with you on that point. I've seen that love can't resolve all obstacles, can even die if problems are severe."

She waggled a finger at him. "Perhaps in that case, there hadn't been true love in the first place."

Charles frowned. Perhaps his parents had married for the wrong reasons. Still, how could a man know if he were truly in love? "Yes, well, you could be right. It's impossible to judge."

"No, it isn't impossible. Nothing is impossible." She glanced down at their cups. "My, goodness, I think a refill is in order. I'll be right back."

Charles stared after Mrs. Larson. If only . . .

He mustn't let this woman override his logic. He knew life held impossible situations, unworkable relationships. Things he wasn't meant to have.

Like Adelaide Crum.

CHAPTER THIRTEEN

Frances's hazel eyes went wide with alarm. She took a firm hold on Adelaide's arm, determined to show her out.

"I'm not leaving. I want to ask him about William coming —"

"No, don't." She let go of Adelaide's arm. "I'll, ah, I'll go ask him."

Frances scurried to meet her husband, with every step her limp grew more pronounced. As Adelaide watched, Frances gestured toward the house. Ed's face went from calm to angry. He pushed past her, leaving his wife to struggle along behind.

Adelaide braced herself, refusing to give in to the icy fingers of terror snatching at her belly. She sent up a prayer for assistance. A blessed sense of calm settled over her.

Ed clomped up the wooden steps onto the porch and burst through the door, his face contorted into a scowl.

Any man who could harm a child had to be stopped. Adelaide believed Ed Drummond to be such a man. Frances came through the door and joined her husband.

"You want the boy, too, is that it?" he demanded.

"No, I —"

"You've got the girl. You aren't getting the boy. No one's getting another boy of mine."

What was he talking about? He made it sound as if she'd taken Emma from them. "I only want William to spend some time with his sister. She misses him."

Ed shook his head. "Get yourself a husband and have your own children. Stop trying to get mine."

She raised her chin. "Then stop treating them badly."

He stomped closer until he stood over her, the odor of sweat clinging to his clothes. "Who said I hurt children?"

"Are you?"

Crimson dotted his cheeks. "Until I lost —" He swallowed and narrowed his gaze. "I'm doing the best I can. Leave my children and my wife alone."

"I'm only asking William to visit his sister one night." Adelaide marveled at the steadiness of her voice.

"If Emma wants to be with William, she'll

come back where she belongs."

"I talked with William's teacher. He's missing school. You're breaking the agreement with the Children's Aid Society."

"Until the crops are in, I need William in the fields." Ed folded his arms across his chest. "I'm teaching him the importance of work and of obedience, like my father taught me." He unfolded his arms and pointed a finger in her direction. "You have no idea who I am. What me and the missus have been through." He tugged Frances close. "I mean to take care of what's mine."

"If any harm comes to William, I'll contact the sheriff."

He shot her a glare, then faced Frances. "You'd better not have asked that meddler here."

Frances shook her head. "She came on her own, Ed. I swear."

"She's not to step foot in this house again."

"I won't let her in. She didn't mean nothing by it."

Ed pushed open the screen door, and then turned to face Adelaide. "Enjoy Emma while you can. I aim to have my family back together." He smiled an odd, secretive smile that didn't reach his eyes, then stalked across the yard.

"You shouldn't have said those things," Frances whispered. "You upset him."

If this visit set the wheels in motion for losing Emma, Adelaide didn't know how she'd bear it. She'd been foolish to run ahead. Why hadn't she prayed about the situation? Adelaide swung around to face Frances. "Tell the sheriff what your husband is like."

Frances looked at her blankly, then sank into a chair, weariness settling on her face. "Give Emma a kiss."

Adelaide bent down beside her and touched her arm. "Come home with me."

She shook her head. "He'd only come after me and blame you for my going. He'll simmer down."

"Please, I can't leave you here."

"Ed needs me. You don't understand what he's been through." She pulled herself to her feet and walked to the sink. First she picked up a knife, then a potato and peeled it. "I've got dinner to fix."

Adelaide couldn't drag Frances out of her home. If Ed was abusing his family, fear or some kind of misguided loyalty would keep her at his side.

"Adelaide."

"Yes."

"You made Ed mad. The more he thinks

about it, the madder he'll get. Don't dawdle. Tell Emma William sends his love."

Not looking up, Frances nodded. Though it pained her to do it, Adelaide hurried out the door, leaving her classmate behind.

Clearly Frances blamed herself for the tragedies in her family — perhaps the main reason she wouldn't leave.

Had Ed Drummond been responsible for the death of his only child? Had his wife and mother-in-law known it and been afraid to tell the sheriff? Or perhaps, after tragically losing those they loved, both the Drummonds had lost their minds.

Adelaide untied the reins and climbed into the buggy. She looked back at the small, faded farmhouse, the wood leeched by the sun. "The house of death" Frances had called it, and it looked that way.

Please, God, protect Frances and William.

No one could make her bring Emma back here after her visit today. She'd find a way to get William out of there, too.

As she took up the reins, her hands trembled. What if Ed insisted on Emma's return? Perspiration beaded her forehead. She would do anything to keep Emma and William safe.

Anything.

Slapping the reins on Shadow's back, she

drove out of the barnyard, a cloud of dust kicking up behind as the horse clipped along. Her mind drifted to the encounter with Ed. A pheasant flew low in front of the buggy, catching the horse unaware. Before Adelaide could react, Shadow shied and bolted, ripping the reins from her hands. The reins flapped against the horse's back, out of reach. Up ahead she saw a sharp turn.

"Whoa!" But the spooked horse didn't hear. Shadow didn't slow. Adelaide held on with both hands.

Rounding the bend too fast, the right back wheel slid off the road. Adelaide screamed. The buggy tipped dangerously, and then righted, only to slam against a rock. Wood cracked and the buggy lurched, almost throwing her from the seat. The weight of the buggy got the horse's attention and Shadow slowed, coming to a winded halt beneath an elm tree.

Heart pounding, Adelaide scampered down to survey the damage. The wheel tilted outward and the buggy sat at a precarious angle. She peered beneath the buggy. "Oh, no."

Something had broken. This buggy was going nowhere and neither was she.

She looked up and down the road, but saw no one. She didn't dare ask the Drummonds for help. She'd walk to the Tulley farm.

At a distant shout, her head snapped up. In the field next to her, Ed Drummond hurried across his acreage. Before she could move, he broke into a run.

"God, help me."

Remembering Frances's warning, Adelaide raced to the horse and with shaky fingers clawed at the buckles of the thick leather straps on Shadow's back and the front of the buggy. They stuck, then gave way with a jerk. She worked to free the poles holding the lathered horse in place. At last, they fell away.

Holding tight to the leather strap on Shadow's head, as the horse pranced nervously beside her, she glanced over her shoulder. Her heart stuttered in her chest. Ed was getting closer, maybe a hundred yards away.

No time to remove all the pieces of leather. She tugged, yanking the reins free, and then looked again. Ed — fifty yards away and closing the distance fast.

Adelaide ran to the side of the buggy, pulling, coaxing the horse nearer, her fear of the man greater than her fear of the animal. Hanging on to the reins, she scrambled aboard the conveyance and thrust out a leg.

The animal sidestepped away from her rustling skirts. "Please, Shadow, let me get on." Ed ran hard, but Adelaide kept her voice soothing.

As if the horse understood her plight, on her second attempt, Shadow stood motionless. She threw a leg over his back and pulled herself upright. She bunched up the long reins in her hands and held tight to the padded belt encircling the horse's back. Praying Shadow wouldn't get tangled up in all the loose straps hanging from him, she clicked to the horse. He started off slowly. *Too slowly.*

She glanced back. Ed stretched out his arms, ready to grab her. She kicked Shadow's flanks. "Move, Shadow! Move!"

The horse sprang to life beneath her. A death grip on the belt, she slid backward, but hung on, and they galloped up the road as Ed jumped the ditch, shouting obscenities. Over her shoulder, she saw him, fist raised toward her, standing amidst the dust stirred up by Shadow's hooves.

Minutes later, with Ed out of sight, Adelaide slowed the horse, sagged against his neck and thanked God for keeping her safe and for Shadow. The horse had accepted his passenger, dragging gear and all, and hadn't caused her one whit of trouble, a blessing because she had no more heroics left.

She slipped into town by the back streets. A few passersby gawked as she rode past. Back straight, she nodded as if riding bareback through town dragging leather occurred every day.

With the livery in sight, she thought she'd made it without discovery, but then Charles exited the wooden building. He gaped and ran to her, taking hold of Shadow's bridle, bringing the animal to a halt. "Addie, are you all right? What happened?"

She couldn't very well say where she'd been. "I had a problem with the buggy I rented. The wheel broke so I rode the horse back to the livery."

"You rode a *horse? Bareback?*" His normally chiseled jaw hung slack. "Dragging that leather, you could have been hurt."

"Well, I wasn't." It gave her satisfaction to see the amazement in Charles's eyes, and maybe a dash of admiration, too.

He gestured. "Climb down. I'll ride the horse in for you."

Adelaide lifted her chin. "I'm doing fine on my own."

He frowned. "Why were you out in a buggy alone?"

"Don't you have things to do at the paper?"

He took a step back. "You're a stubborn woman, Adelaide Crum," he grumbled as she clicked to the horse and rode past. "And adept at avoiding my questions."

Pretending she hadn't heard, Adelaide rode to the stable door. The freckle-faced lad stopped in his tracks, squinting into the noonday sun. "Sakes alive! What happened?"

"If you'll give me a hand down, young man, I'll explain."

Dropping the water buckets he carried, he ran to her side, probably faster than he'd moved in his entire life. Adelaide slid off the horse, right into his arms. By the time her feet hit the ground, his face matched his carrot-red hair.

Needlelike pain shot through her legs, and they almost buckled beneath her, but she remained on her feet. Peeling off her gloves, Adelaide explained what had happened. "I'm sorry about the buggy. It's out on Conner Road." She smoothed her skirts. "I'll pay for the damages, of course."

"Probably an axle. I'll tell the boss."

Adelaide nodded. "I'll be sure and tell Mr. Lemming how considerate you've been."

Except for a small rip in the seam of her

skirt, she looked no worse for her experience. Walking home, every step sent an ache through her backside and up her limbs. Still a tiny thrill of pleasure slid through her. She'd managed to escape Ed Drummond, had ridden a horse — without a saddle, at that — and had even impressed Charles.

When she reached the back of her shop, Adelaide stopped short, her heart pounding in her chest. There on the brick in red capital letters and dripping like blood, someone had painted: YOU'LL PAY FOR THAT MOUTH.

The threat, still damp to the touch, hadn't been there when she left this morning. That meant Ed Drummond could not have penned it. Who had? Who wanted to scare her?

Perhaps someone angry about her stand on suffrage had done this.

Then she remembered Jacob Paul's icy stare when she'd caught him setting that fire a few weeks back. Could it be Jacob, a boy she'd once had in Sunday school?

Inside her shop, Adelaide could barely keep up with Laura's chatter. Normally she loved her friend's chitchat and would want every detail of her visit with Charles, but today she needed time alone, time to think about the meaning of those words in the alley. But most of all on what she should do next about Ed Drummond. What would he have done if he'd caught her? She shivered.

With God's help she'd get William out of that house, maybe Frances, too.

"Adelaide, you look worried to death." Laura's voice cut into her thoughts. "I didn't say *that* much to Mr. Graves."

"What?" Adelaide gave Laura's arm a squeeze. "Oh, I'm sure you didn't. Would you mind staying this afternoon? I forgot some pressing business."

"Is something wrong? You aren't yourself."

"I've let some things slide and now that you're here, I'd like to tend to them. Can you stay?"

"Of course."

"I'll be back in time to pick up Emma from school."

"It's only a few blocks. Why not let her walk alone?"

"No, I couldn't." Adelaide realized too late how sharp her tone had been. "I like to get her myself."

Laura's brow furrowed.

Adelaide patted Laura's arm. "Thanks for looking after things."

Adelaide grabbed her bag and rushed out the front door, turning right toward the sheriff's office. Dodging a group of men quibbling over who owned the best hunting dog, she hurried to her destination.

By the time she reached the jail, she'd formulated a plan. First, she'd ask the sheriff if there'd been anything suspicious about Eddie Drummond's death. Then she'd wire Mr. Fry, the agent for the Children's Aid Society, and insist he send someone to look into William's safety.

The days when Adelaide stood by and let others determine her future, and the futures of those she cared about, were over.

Resolutely, she turned the handle and stepped inside. Her eyes took a moment to adjust to the dim light. When they did, she blinked in surprise.

Charles. Shooting questions at Sheriff Rogers and scribbling furiously on a notepad. At the sight of him, her pulse skittered.

The door banged shut behind her. At the sound, the men turned around. The middle-aged sheriff's belly rolled over his waistband, but his muscular arms and massive shoulders promised he could handle trouble. Thankfully, in Noblesville, that generally wasn't much. If not for his reporter paraphernalia, Charles, all lean lines and broad-shouldered, could easily pass for a lawman.

Through an open doorway, Adelaide could see two cells. She wrinkled her nose.

In the first cell a snoring prisoner, reeking of liquor and vomit, sprawled across a cot. The other cell remained empty, a perfect place for Ed.

Charles greeted her with a frown. "What brings you here?"

She wouldn't tell Charles about her visit to the Drummonds. "I, ah, found something painted on the brick out back of my shop." Adelaide sucked in a breath. "It said, 'You'll pay for that mouth.' "

Charles stepped to her side, his face etched with concern.

The sheriff frowned. "Sounds like someone wants to scare you. Any idea who?"

Adelaide sighed. "I suppose it could be several people. My view on suffrage hasn't been popular."

Charles's mouth tightened as if to stop him from letting out the words, "I told you so."

"Could be the Paul kid getting even with you for reporting his attempt at arson," Sheriff Rogers said.

"I thought of him."

Adelaide glanced at the pad in Charles's hand. The words — Sarah Hartman, murder — leapt off the page. Adelaide swayed on her feet. *Had Ed Drummond killed his mother-in-law?*

Sheriff Rogers pulled out a chair. "Have a seat, Miss Crum, you look peaked."

Adelaide dropped into it.

Charles leaned over her. "Are you all right, Addie?"

Adelaide nodded, but it wasn't true. If Ed had killed Sarah, Frances was alone with a murderer, and William would soon return from school. She had to convince the sheriff and Charles that Ed Drummond had to be the culprit.

"Sheriff, did someone murder Mrs. Hartman?"

"Now what makes you say that?"

"I got a glimpse of Mr. Graves's pad."

Before the sheriff could respond, Charles moved in front of her. "You've had quite the scare today. Why don't you go home and get some rest?"

"Mr. Graves makes a good point." The sheriff patted her hand. "No need to worry your pretty head about such gruesome matters."

Heat climbed Adelaide's neck and she rose to her feet. "Sheriff, my pretty head, as you call it, has a working brain."

"I don't doubt your intelligence, but determining how Mrs. Hartman died is my job."

Before Adelaide could respond, Sheriff

270

Rogers took her elbow and escorted her to the door.

Outside, Adelaide paced in front of the brick structure. They wouldn't listen, yet her future and that of Emma and William depended upon convincing the sheriff who had committed the crime.

She peeked through the front window, could see Charles scribble something on his notepad. If she could only hear —

Slipping around the corner of the building, she headed for the lone barred window. Too high for her to see inside, but she could hear every word and they couldn't see her.

"What made you decide to pursue what you'd originally deemed a suicide, Sheriff?"

Adelaide heard a chair creak. "At the time, I thought it odd to find freshly baked bread in Mrs. Hartman's kitchen. On the table, alongside a cup of tea, was a partially eaten slice. Didn't make sense she'd have a bite to eat, then go out to the barn and hang herself. It looked like someone interrupted her."

"But your search of the premises found nothing to indicate foul play?"

"No — until now. One of the Long boys found this while digging in the drainage ditch running along the front of the Hartman farm. His father brought it in."

Adelaide wished she could grow two feet taller to see what they were talking about.

"After examining this garrote, I found a gray hair," the sheriff continued.

Remembering Mrs. Hartman's neat gray bun, her gentle smile, Adelaide cringed and sagged against the brick. Just last year, Sarah had bought a pink Easter bonnet from Adelaide.

"Any idea who'd want Mrs. Hartman dead?"

"None. I'll ride out this afternoon and talk to her daughter. See if she has any ideas."

Well, Adelaide certainly had an idea. She pulled away from the building, strode around the corner, took a deep breath and opened the door of the sheriff's office, slamming it behind her.

Sheriff Rogers leapt to his feet. Charles spun to face her.

Adelaide met the sheriff's gaze. "I know who did it."

Charles frowned. "Have you been eaves-dropping?"

She pulled herself erect. "What if I have? Didn't you hear what I said? I know who killed Sarah Hartman."

Sheriff Rogers leveled his gaze on her. "All right, you have our attention, Miss Crum. Who killed Sarah Hartman?"

"Ed Drummond. It has to be him."

Sheriff Rogers shoved his chair under the kneehole of the desk and rested his hands on the back. "Why him?"

"I suspect he's been abusing his wife and possibly William, an orphan staying there, and maybe even Emma, William's sister, who's living with me, temporarily."

Sheriff Rogers came around the desk. "Any proof?"

Instead of answering the question, Adelaide asked one of her own. "Did you investigate Eddie Drummond's death?"

Sheriff Rogers rubbed his forehead. "Before you get all fired up, Eddie isn't the first child to die from a stove-related fire. I found nothing suspect about his death. Are you telling me you have information to the contrary?"

"No, but Frances said she wasn't home when it happened and she called her home the 'house of death.' "

Sheriff Rogers grabbed a gun belt from a peg on the wall and strapped it on his hip. "Sounds like the ravings of a highly strung woman who's hiked through hell and back."

"It's more than that. I saw Ed Drummond firsthand. Saw —"

Charles scowled. "You were at the Drum-

mond farm this morning, not running er-
rands."

"What choice did I have? You wouldn't
see danger if it hit you over the head."

"What happened at the Drummond
house?" the sheriff asked.

She pivoted toward him. "Ed got angry
when I asked if William could spend the
night with —"

"Did he hurt you?" Charles interrupted.

"No, but he came after me when my
buggy hit a rock and broke a wheel."

The sheriff frowned. "Could he have been
trying to help?"

"By screaming obscenities? I think not."
Adelaide took a deep breath, struggling to
slow her speech. She sounded panicky, even
to her own ears. "Frances is afraid of him
and afraid for me, too. I pleaded with her to
come into town, but she refused."

Sheriff Rogers ran a finger over his mus-
tache. "If she were in real danger, surely
she'd have done what you suggested."

The sheriff didn't believe her.

Adelaide looked to Charles for help, only
to see his seething gaze.

Adelaide paced the room. "Emma
couldn't even eat breakfast. I think she
knows what's going on, but is afraid to say."

Sheriff Rogers harrumphed as if he didn't

put much credence in the actions of a child.

"By going to the home of a man you consider dangerous, you put yourself at risk." Charles thrust a hand through his hair. "Why are you acting foolishly?"

Adelaide heard the anger in his voice and the underlying worry. "I'll do whatever it takes to protect those children." Did she see a flicker of respect in his eyes, even if begrudging? "I had to get evidence. But all I got was a stronger feeling he's an evil man."

"Lots of folks around here think highly of Ed Drummond," the sheriff said. "Can't see why he'd kill his mother-in-law, unless he wanted to get his hands on her property. I'll talk to his wife. See what I can dig up." He turned to Adelaide. "More than likely a drifter killed her, but if you're right, he's dangerous."

Charles took her hand. "Promise you'll stay away —"

Adelaide shook free from his grasp. "I won't stand by and let anything happen to those children."

Charles stepped closer, and his gaze locked with hers. "If you must go out there, let me go with you."

With Charles so close, Adelaide found it impossible to disagree. "I won't go alone."

The sheriff plucked his Stetson from a hall tree near the door. "I'll make a point of seeing the boy."

The tension in her shoulders eased. "Thank you, Sheriff."

Adelaide laid her hand on Charles's arm. "Is the sheriff's investigation of Ed enough reason to take William out of their home?" Adelaide wanted that so badly she couldn't breathe.

The sheriff plopped the hat on his head. "Don't say anything to the committee yet." He turned a stern eye on Adelaide. "If Drummond isn't involved, I wouldn't want to blow this out of proportion. After I get back to town, I'll look into that message on your brick."

Adelaide nodded. Charles took her hand and tucked it in the crook of his arm. They followed Sheriff Rogers from the office.

As she and Charles walked toward her shop, Adelaide's eyes misted. "I can't understand how anyone could kill a sweet woman like Sarah. She never hurt anyone."

"It's anger, uncontrollable anger."

"I can't understand that kind of anger."

"Consider yourself lucky. A man can do unspeakable things to the very people he should love and protect." He lowered his voice. "I've got the scars to prove it."

Adelaide winced for what Charles had endured as a child, a vivid reminder of what William might be going through at the Drummond farm. "Then why won't you believe me about William?"

"I'm a man of evidence, Addie. Show me proof and —"

"The proof is here." She pressed a hand to his chest right above his heart. "But you never trust your heart, do you?" She pulled her hand away.

"I don't like the idea of finding a man guilty without more hard evidence than we have on Drummond. But whether he killed his wife's mother or not, he's got it in for you, so stay away from him." He exhaled. "With you gallivanting around the country-side, I'll never have a moment's peace."

Adelaide knew one thing for sure. Charles Graves couldn't have it both ways. "You can't tell me how to live my life, Charles, when you're not willing to be a part of it."

With that, she walked away. He made no attempt to stop her.

CHAPTER FOURTEEN

That evening Charles stopped at the back of Adelaide's shop. A section of the brick had been painted with black. Addie had wasted no time concealing the threat against her. His chest swelled with admiration for her plucky attitude, though it might get her into deeper trouble.

Whether she wanted him around or not didn't matter. He might not be able to become part of her life, but he sure didn't intend to stand by and let her lose hers.

On the landing, he rapped on the door. Addie opened it, but didn't invite him in. Her face looked carved out of stone, but even with her righteous anger wrapped around her like a hedge, her goodness showed through.

"What are you doing here?"

Not exactly a warm welcome. "I came to apologize."

"Or to see if I have Ranger tied up out

back, ready to ride to the Drummond farm?"

He had to protect Adelaide, but he needed to do it without getting her riled up. He chuckled. "No bridles and reins tucked away in that kitchen, as clean as it is. Hmm, smells good, too." He gave her a grin. "Any chance you'd take pity on my growling stomach?"

"Your stomach is not my concern."

"I'll clean up the kitchen afterward."

She tried to hide her amusement, but her mouth twisted up at the corners.

"What's cooking?" he asked.

"If you insist on being nosy, ham and sweet potatoes."

His stomach put in its two cents, reminding him he'd only had half a sandwich at noon. He'd probably find the other half buried in a pile of work on his desk. "If I apologize for trying to tell you what to do, will you toss me a few scraps?"

Grinning, she stepped back to let him in. "Maybe."

She shooed him into the parlor so she could put the finishing touches on dinner. He hoped she believed his excuse for coming. After learning Sarah Hartman had been murdered and now someone wanted Addie silenced, he had no intention of letting her out of his sight. The woman wouldn't take orders unless they came directly from God. Addie had tried her best to look annoyed, but he could tell she welcomed his company. No matter how brave she tried to appear, Ed Drummond frightened her. Maybe she'd think twice before confronting Ed again.

Emma passed in the hall and saw him. She dashed to his side. "I didn't know you were here!"

"I've been invited to stay for dinner."

She plopped down beside him. "It's my job to set the table. Wanna help?"

"Sure."

Arriving in the kitchen, he filled glasses while Emma laid out the flatware, chattering about her day. Charles tried to keep out of Addie's way as she hustled about, ignoring him.

Soon they gathered at the table. This time Emma said grace.

"Have you told Emma about your adventure?" Charles asked.

"I've told her I rode a horse. She wants me to teach her."

Charles winked at Addie. "Giving me the boot, Emma?"

Emma's gaze skipped from one to the other, and then a big grin split her face. "I want *both* of you to teach me."

Charles grinned. "You'd make an excellent diplomat."

"What's a diplomat?"

"Someone in government who's a skilled talker, tries to make everyone happy."

"Okay! I like to make people happy. And I like to talk."

Addie touched Emma's cheek. "You make me very happy, sweetheart." She looked at Charles. "It's nice of you to assume Emma might one day hold a position in government. Perhaps my position on suffrage has swayed the editor."

Charles chuckled. When he'd made the comment, he hadn't thought of the implications. He could well imagine Emma getting that choice someday. But, did Addie have to lead the charge?

Toward the end of the meal, the conversation drifted to circulation figures, and Emma caught Charles's eye.

He tapped Addie's hand and pointed at the little girl who had nodded off at the table. "Apparently, we bored her."

Her gaze soft with tenderness, Addie smiled and rose. Charles scooped Emma in his arms, and followed Addie to the child's room. When he laid Emma down, she opened her eyes. "Do I have to go to bed?" she asked with a yawn.

"You're sleepy," Addie said.

While Addie stayed to oversee Emma's bedtime ritual, Charles returned to the kitchen. As he washed and set the plates to drain, the gentle melody of a lullaby drifted to him.

His mother had sung that same tune to him and Sam. The memories it brought back were bittersweet, tinged with pain and loss, but also with his mother's kisses and gentle touches. The sweet sound of Adelaide's voice carried through him, soothing his spirit. For an instant, he wanted to capture the feeling, to stay with Adelaide and Emma, to promise them ever after.

But the moment passed. He had no reason to think he'd be capable of that kind of love. Everyone who'd loved him had let him down. And he'd do the same.

He returned to the task, scrubbing at the pans. He'd best remember what life had taught him and not let a sentimental song give him hope. Nothing had changed. He must take a solitary path.

A touch on his shoulder made him jump.

"Sorry. I didn't mean to startle you." Addie's gaze scanned the spotless kitchen. "Looks like my timing's perfect."

"I told you — if you cook, I'll clean up." He patted his abdomen. "I got the best part of the deal."

She smiled. Charles reveled in the beauty of that smile.

"Care for a cup of coffee?"

"Sounds good." He dried his hands on a towel. "I heard you singing. My mother used to sing that song." He cleared his throat, trying to disguise how much it had meant to him. "Reminded me of the happy times she tried to give Sam and me."

She laid a gentle hand alongside his jaw. "I'm glad."

Her touch healed like a balm, releasing some of the pain of his childhood throbbing anew in him. He covered her hand with his. For an instant, he felt whole, reborn, but then he dropped her hand and moved away from her touch.

Adelaide stepped back, giving Charles wide berth. Once again he'd put up an invisible wall between them, still running away from what they could have together. But he wasn't ready, and she wouldn't push him. She couldn't force love. If it had to be forced, it wasn't love.

Besides, Emma brought enough joy to her life — if Adelaide got to keep her. For that to happen, she had to get to the truth.

Had the sheriff learned anything at the

Drummond farm? She wanted to get Charles's thoughts on the murder. "Why do you suppose Ed Drummond killed his mother-in-law? Do you think he just lost his temper, killed her in a fit of rage?"

"If he killed her," he said, raising a brow, "he planned it. A garrote isn't something you just happen to have. She must have posed a threat, at least in Drummond's mind."

"Mrs. Hartman? I can't see . . ." Her hand flew to her mouth. "Unless she knew Ed beats Frances and threatened to expose him."

He shrugged. "People are murdered for less."

"Your job hasn't made you an admirer of mankind."

"Some would say it's made me callous."

She shook her head. "You may try to be, but you have a kind heart. I see that with Ranger, with Emma, with me." She took another sip of her coffee. "In the short time you've lived here, you've earned the respect of the town fathers."

His brows lifted in surprise. "Why do you say that?"

"Your work with the selection committee, the way the committee agreed with your suggestion to place Emma in my home,

284

Sheriff Rogers's obvious regard."

He smiled. "Placing Emma in your home was an easy decision. I knew you'd take excellent care of any child."

Adelaide reached across the table and put her hand on his arm. "It appears you and I respect one another."

He laid his palm over her hand. "I guess we do."

She pulled out the columns tucked into her purse. "I wrote two columns on women's suffrage."

"Let me see them," he said in a weary tone.

Adelaide handed them over. "I own the paper, too, and I want the first of these to run in the next edition."

Charles glanced at the sheaf in his hand. "Then I don't have much choice, do I?"

"I'd hoped you'd want to support the women in this community, that you'd want to support me."

"I do support you."

In many ways he did, but not in the most vital ones.

He read the pages in his hand and lifted his gaze. "You sound very convincing." He studied her. "You're determined to teach women to be courageous, to expand their sphere of influence, their focus, no matter the cost. Are you sure you're ready to take such a risk?"

That question weighed on her. "Yes, my mind is made up."

"I hope you're prepared for the consequences."

A shrill scream brought them to their feet and sent them racing to Emma's bedroom. Adelaide's heart pounded in her chest. Had Ed gotten into the house?

They found Emma cowering under the covers, quaking. Weak-kneed with relief, Adelaide sank onto the bed and gathered the weeping child in her arms. Charles sat beside them.

"He was here!" Emma wailed.

"Who?" Emma didn't say who lived in her nightmare, but Adelaide never doubted the man's identity. "It's only a dream," she crooned, rocking the little girl on her lap. "You're fine."

Charles put his arms around Adelaide, around them both. Soon Emma quieted and Adelaide sang the lullaby she had earlier. This time Charles joined in, his deep baritone blending with the melody. Emma fell back to sleep.

Nestled in the comfort of Charles's arms, Adelaide let her song trail off to a soft hum, and then looked at Charles. A sense of oneness passed between them. Charles cared for Emma, cared about her, too, or he wouldn't be here this evening.

Filled with contentment, she gently laid the sleeping child on the bed. Pulling up the covers, she kissed Emma's soft cheek. Then she and Charles slipped out of the room.

I can picture us doing that with our own children.

Suddenly, aware he stood behind her, his breath warm against her neck, she turned toward him.

He raised a hand to cradle her chin. The waiting was unbearable, though surely only a few seconds passed while she wondered would he?

And then he lowered his mouth to hers, the feel of his lips gentle and sweet. Her breath caught and she swayed toward him, clinging to his lapels for support. She was taking a huge risk, but her heart refused to listen. His kiss dismissed every coherent thought in her muddled brain. Her eyelids drifted shut, her heart insisting she belonged here.

He pulled away and lifted his palm to her face.

"You pretended to want a meal, but I suspect you came because you were worried. Thank you for watching Emma and me."

"Don't forget to lock up," he said, tucking an arm around her.

They walked downstairs together. At the door he gave her a hug, then slipped out. Leaning against the frame, Adelaide closed her eyes, remembering his scent, the roughness of his jaw under her palm, the timbre of his voice.

Her pulse skipped a beat.

Was it possible? Did Charles love her?

Or was he just as scared as she was by what had happened?

Adelaide woke with a start. Something, some noise had awakened her. Slipping from her bed, she tiptoed to the window and pulled back the curtain. The street was empty. In the moonlight, everything looked peaceful, but a nudge of disquiet sent her to her bedroom door.

She turned the knob, opened it a crack and listened. She didn't hear anything, but she slipped out the door, and padded down the hall. Snuggled under the covers, Emma slept peacefully.

Tension fell from her shoulders as Adelaide headed back to bed. Whatever she'd heard — a tree branch in a strong gust of wind, perhaps — everything looked in order. She drifted off to sleep.

CHAPTER FIFTEEN

The next morning, Adelaide came down the stairs with Emma on her heels, complaining about school.

"You have to go, Emma." Adelaide said automatically. "Did you remember your lunch bucket?"

Emma liked recess and her teacher, but she hadn't yet caught up with her work. Maybe if she —

The thought stuttered to a halt, and so did Adelaide. Emma collided into her back.

"Emma, go back upstairs."

"But —"

"Do as I say."

After making sure Emma obeyed, Adelaide crept down the remainder of the stairway. Seeing no one, she exhaled the breath she'd been holding. Pulse hammering, her gaze darted about the showroom.

Unwound from bolts, pastel ribbons dangled from mirrors and cabinets.

Smashed silk flowers and papier-mâché fruit were hurled around the shop. On the floor, fabric lay in twisted heaps. Hats, with crushed crowns and bent brims, settled where they'd been flung.

She moved from behind the counter and stumbled through the debris, picking up a hat. "Oh, no." The crown had been slit.

The culprit had dumped her desk drawer, along with the bigger drawers holding supplies, but strangely had not tinkered with the cash register. She picked her way to the front of the shop, noting a shattered pane and jagged pieces of glass scattered on the floor. Someone had reached through the opening and unlocked the door. Without thinking, Adelaide turned the lock, though the broken pane made the gesture meaningless.

The noise she'd heard last night must have been breaking glass or perhaps the bell. No, the bell had been torn from its moorings.

A thought slammed into her. A thought so unwelcome she shook her head, trying to shake it loose, but it stuck tighter than flypaper to a shoe.

Only one person could have done this. Ed Drummond.

If I'd come down to investigate, what would have happened then?

He could easily have come up to her living quarters, could have plucked Emma from her bed.

Perspiration broke out on her forehead. Nausea washed over her. She lunged for the back door and deposited her breakfast in the flowerbed, then leaned against the brick, wiping a shaky hand over her mouth.

When her heartbeat slowed, she trudged to the well and primed it, then pumped the handle until water splattered at her feet. She filled her cupped hands with water and rinsed her mouth and face, removing every sign of her weakness.

Dropping to her knees, she turned to the One who controlled the universe. "Thank you, Father, for your protection. Please, let no harm come to Frances, Emma and William. Give me wisdom, Lord, and courage."

Feeling stronger, she rose and dashed inside. She found Emma sitting on her bed, her face pale. "What's wrong, Miss Adelaide?"

"Someone broke the glass in the door last night. Probably boys looking for excitement, but at first it worried me. I'll get it fixed." She patted Emma's knee. "Better hurry or you'll be late."

Avoiding the usual way out, Adelaide led Emma through the kitchen and onto the open-air landing at the top of the back stairs. By keeping up a rush of conversation all the way to school, she avoided any questions from Emma. Before school let out for the day, she'd have order restored.

After settling Emma in her classroom, Adelaide took the teacher aside. Though she doubted Ed would grab Emma in broad daylight in a schoolyard full of children, she asked the teacher to keep a close eye on Emma during recess.

The terror she'd experienced earlier turned to anger. The worst kind of coward, Ed Drummond preyed on women and children. How could Frances stay with him? After the sheriff's visit yesterday, hadn't she suspected Ed of killing her mother?

Adelaide's steps slowed. She hadn't walked in Frances's shoes, hadn't known the fear that could control and subdue the spirit. Like Charles's mother, Frances had few options. She must be terrified for her own life or for the lives of the children.

Down the way, Charles crossed the street, his stride purposeful. On the boardwalk in front of her shop, he stopped.

"What's this?" He pivoted toward her. "Addie, what happened? How did this pane of glass get broken?"

Adelaide pulled the key out of her purse

and unlocked the door. "Ed Drummond broke in last night."

"Ed Drummond was here, in your shop?" He followed her inside. "It looks like a cyclone struck. Are you and Emma all right?"

Before she could answer, he pulled her into his arms. The magnitude of what had happened struck full force and she laid her cheek against the rough fabric of his coat.

"He didn't come upstairs?"

Charles believed Ed Drummond had done this.

"No." Relieved to have him here, to share the burden hanging heavy on her, tension eased from her body. "Last night a noise awakened me, but when I checked around upstairs, nothing looked amiss. I didn't come down here."

"Thank God." He picked up one of the damaged hats, poking a finger through the slit in the crown. "This is a warning, Addie." He dropped the hat onto a chair and laid his hands on her shoulders. "The sheriff needs to see this. Will you be okay while I'm gone?"

"Ed Drummond wouldn't bother me in broad daylight. Cowards prefer the dark."

"If he feels cornered, he might do anything. Now stay put until I get back." He

294

gave a lopsided grin. "No cleaning until after the sheriff has investigated."

He'd tried to lighten the mood by teasing her. Adelaide forced the corners of her mouth up. "You'd better hurry, then. I won't be able to resist the urge for long."

Sheriff Rogers poked around and admitted he couldn't find any evidence of who had vandalized the shop, so she and Charles went after the mess like pigs after slop. Well, at least Adelaide tackled the task in an orderly fashion while Charles roamed about the showroom, accomplishing little.

"Addie, is this something worth keeping?"

Adelaide left the pile of bric-a-brac she sorted to look at Charles's latest treasure. He held two pieces of a papier-mâché apple in an open palm, a question in his eyes.

"No, it's damaged beyond repair."

"This apple doesn't tempt you? With a dab of glue —"

She smiled. "No amount of glue will fix that apple."

He tossed it away. "If only Eve had had your strength."

Adelaide giggled. With Charles here, she didn't get much done, but still, she treasured his presence.

A few minutes later, a tickle along her jaw sent a shiver spiraling down her spine.

Charles stood over where she sat, sporting a lazy grin and trailing the tip of a feather down her neck. "Maybe if you pressed them in a book?" Charles held out a handful of colorful feathers.

"Their spines are broken. Please, put them in the trash."

"I wouldn't want to toss anything important. I don't see anything wrong with this." He grabbed a long-stemmed silk rose from the pile and held it in his strong white teeth.

Adelaide gave him a playful nudge. "You're hopeless."

Removing the bloom, he hauled her to her feet and slipped it into her chignon. "It looks better here."

Cradling her face in his hands, he brushed his lips across one cheek, then to her mouth with a tender and gentle kiss. He tugged her close, pulling her against his chest. "I worry about you."

"I'll be fine." She prayed God would protect them all.

She glanced at the clock. If she had to keep supervising Charles, she'd never get order restored. "What I really need is to have the glass replaced. Could you do that?"

"Are you sure you don't need me here?"

No matter what he'd said, he looked desperate to leave. "I'll try to manage without you."

He flashed a grin. "I'll be back as soon as I can."

Charles strode for the door and on the threshold met Sheriff Rogers, holding Jacob Paul by the shirt.

"I'm taking Jacob in for questioning," Sheriff Rogers said. "Want to talk to him about a nasty cut on his hand."

Air left Adelaide's lungs. Jacob hated her so much for reporting his arson that he'd destroy her shop?

Jacob's dark eyes sparked with defiance. "I didn't do anything. I cut my hand whittling."

Sheriff Rogers ignored the boy's claim and met Adelaide's gaze. "His father is meeting us at the jail. I'd suggest you come, too, Miss Crum."

Later, inside the jail, the sheriff released Jacob. The boy crossed the room, wearing a scowl on his face, and slumped down in a chair, ignoring his father pacing near the door.

Mr. Paul pointed his finger at Adelaide. "You've accused my son to get even with me."

The sheriff cocked his head. "Why would Miss Crum want to get even with you, Thaddeus?"

"For turning down her request for an orphan, that's why."

Adelaide planted her hands on her hips. "That's absurd."

Sheriff Rogers held up a palm. "Miss Crum didn't accuse your son. I thought of Jacob first thing. You have to admit, Thaddeus, the boy's been in trouble more than out."

Mr. Paul's shoulders stiffened. "That doesn't mean he's done this."

"No," Sheriff Rogers said, "but that ugly cut on his right hand puts him under suspicion."

Jacob shifted in his seat. "I told you, I cut my hand whittling."

The sheriff's eyes narrowed. "Are you left-handed, boy?"

"I'm right-handed but the knife slipped." He smirked. "I never said I was good at it."

Adelaide folded her arms across her middle. "So show us what you're working on."

Jacob gave a cocky grin. "After I cut my hand, I hurled the piece of wood in the river. There's nothing to find."

The sheriff's mouth tightened. "Thaddeus, can you vouch for your son's whereabouts last night between midnight and dawn?"

"He was home sleeping."

Adelaide felt like shaking that smirk off Jacob's face. The boy had no respect for authority.

"Did you sit in his room all night?" the sheriff asked.

"Of course not! This is an outrage. You have no proof my son vandalized that shop."

"Not yet, but that cut puts him under suspicion."

"He explained that." Mr. Paul gestured toward his son. "I'm taking him home."

The sheriff stood over Jacob. "You're free to go, but I'll be watching you."

Father and son headed for the door. As Jacob sauntered past, he brushed against Adelaide's skirts, probably trying to frighten her. Well, he did. After the fire-setting episode, she'd prayed for him. It appeared she had a lot more praying to do. She'd thought Ed Drummond had broken into her shop, but now Jacob appeared to be the most likely culprit.

The heavy door rattled shut. Adelaide met Sheriff Rogers's gaze. "How could you let him go? Surely you don't believe that whittling story."

"I have no proof. I can't arrest him on a hunch or for a bad attitude. I didn't find red paint at the Paul house, but I did find an opened can of red paint in the alley behind the general store." He sighed. "Anyone could have painted that threat or ransacked your shop, Miss Crum. Anyone."

Charles closed his toolbox. He'd replaced the pane in the door. Not that new glass would stop anyone from entering Addie's shop. That insight sank like a stone in his stomach.

Addie came up beside him. "Thank you."

His gaze scanned her face, noting the furrow in her usually smooth brow. What he needed to say would only add to her dismay. "You know, I've been thinking. Printing another article on suffrage is apt to stir up more trouble."

Her gaze, sharp as a well-honed blade, probed into him. "I can't believe my political opinions are behind the vandalism or the threat."

"Until we know what's going on, it might be a good idea to keep your name out of the news."

Her hand motioned around the room. "Jacob is a troubled kid. He vandalized my shop to get even. Or . . ." Her mouth went dry. "Ed Drummond wants to scare me so that I'll stop investigating his treatment of William. It's ludicrous to think some ordinary citizen could be irate enough to do this."

"Don't be so sure. Suffrage is a hot issue. You're asking for trouble by —"

"I'm asking for nothing, Charles. Except the right to express my opinion so that women like Frances and your mother and, yes, even me, can have some control over their lives."

"I'm not opposed to your position on suffrage. Can't you understand? I'm concerned about your safety."

"You agreed to print my views. Are you breaking your word?"

Why must she make this about them? Didn't she see the danger? He grabbed the toolbox, his jaw as tight as a vise because this stubborn, opinionated woman wouldn't listen to reason.

"Have it your way, Addie," he said, opening the shop door. "You won't listen to me."

CHAPTER SIXTEEN

Adelaide gathered another armload of her ruined stock and dumped it into the garbage can, relieved she only had a few more piles to clean up.

The bell jingled, thanks to Charles who had reattached it to the door.

Laura peeked in, carrying a napkin-covered plate. "I heard about your vandalism." Her gaze roamed the shop. "Probably boys running wild," she muttered. "Why, in my day, the boys tore down and reassembled a carriage on Old Man Hiatt's roof." She put the plate on the counter and picked up an unwound spool of ribbon and began winding it.

Clearly, Laura had no idea of the seriousness of the situation. "This wasn't a prank."

Laura tucked the rewound spool into the drawer and turned to Adelaide. "It wasn't? Oh, my. Well, then who did it?"

"The sheriff found no evidence of who

did it. I have my suspicions, but for now, I'd better keep them to myself."

Laura's brow furrowed and she looked tempted to pry, but instead she picked up the plate, peeling back the napkin to reveal the spongy cake beneath. "I brought you a wedge of angel food cake. In a crisis, I turn to sweets." Laura giggled. "Actually, I turn to sweets when good things happen and when nothing happens."

Smiling, Adelaide gave Laura a hug. "Thank you for the cake and for coming. Every time I need you, you're here for me."

"And you for me, dear."

Adelaide could put the gift to good use. "This might soften Charles's resistance."

"Resistance to what?" Laura raised her brows, a gleam in her eyes. "You?"

"More like my words. A couple more columns I've written that he's not exactly eager to print."

"For goodness sakes, Adelaide, you already have a business. You don't need more to do. What you need to concentrate on is that man. Take Mr. Graves the cake and sweeten your relationship." She shook her head. "This vandalism is a sign you need a man to take care of you."

"I can take care of myself. You know that."

Laura sighed. "Would it hurt to pretend

you can't?"

Adelaide grabbed a broom and swept the last of the debris into the dustpan. "Why would I do that?"

"A man likes to feel needed." Laura planted her hands on her hips. "All this independence is your mother's fault."

Adelaide straightened. "How?"

"Because of her, you've held in your feelings all those years and now you can't let them go."

Though Adelaide wanted to deny what her friend said, the words resonated inside her. But what did it matter? Letting go of feelings only led to getting them trampled. She dumped the dustpan into the garbage. "I don't let my emotions control me."

"Are those columns about women getting the vote? Lands sake. Don't we ladies have enough to do as it is, without worrying about politics?"

"Don't you want a say in what happens in your life?"

"I'm a widow, I have *all* the say. Even my daughter has started listening to me." She shook her head. "Can you imagine? After all these years, she's decided I might be right about a couple of things." Laura wagged a finger. "You should listen to me, too. Forget politics. Concentrate on finding happiness."

Adelaide's shoulders sagged. Even Laura fought her ideas. "I'd expected the men would need convincing, not the ladies." She laid the broom aside and picked up the plate. "I'll take this to Charles as a thank-you for fixing the broken pane. Will that make you happy?"

Laura nodded. "See, a man can be useful."

"You'd love to see me attached to one, wouldn't you?"

"Yes, dear, I would. Underneath, I think you want it, too."

Adelaide opened her mouth to argue with her, but Laura gave her a hug. "I'm leaving before you start lecturing me on suffrage," Laura said with a wink. "Whether you can vote or take this vandalism in stride, you still need someone to love." Laura sauntered to the door. "Why don't I pick up Emma after school? I'll take her to the café for a glass of lemonade. That will give you more time to . . . do whatever it is you must."

Even though Laura didn't agree with her, she was supportive, a good friend. "Emma would like that. Thank you."

Adelaide closed the door behind her friend. Laura thought marriage solved every problem, but marriage only meant more trouble. Look at her mother's life, at Charles's parents, the Drummonds. She needed a way to protect Emma and William, not a fairy tale.

She removed her apron and hustled upstairs to wash her face and hands. Later, she checked her appearance in the mirror — not to impress Charles, but to be sure her hat tipped at the proper angle. She folded the column and placed it in her purse, then picked up the slice of cake on her way out.

Crossing the street to *The Ledger,* she resolved to have her way. After all, she owned the paper, too. She wouldn't give up this chance to influence the community.

As she arrived, James left the paper, rushing off to whatever assignment Charles had given him. He seemed like a nice young man, very conscientious. But if he got a chance, he'd probably be telling her what to do, too.

She halted on the boardwalk. There, through the window, stood Fannie, her face aglow, her hand on Charles's arm. A surge of something Adelaide refused to name roared to life in her midsection. As she watched, they broke apart and Charles walked her protégée to the door, laughing at something Fannie said.

Demureness apparently had done its work. Only two lessons and Fannie had Charles pinned to the target.

Adelaide flattened her back against the brick. She didn't want to be caught spying.

Out on the boardwalk, Fannie rose on tiptoe and kissed Charles on the cheek. Casually, as if it were a common occurrence, and then giggled before walking up the street, her skirts swishing like a broom at full speed. Some things never changed.

Adelaide's grip tightened on the plate. She had no rights, no claim on Charles. The concern he'd shown her, the kiss they'd shared, meant nothing. For an instant, the back of her eyes stung. She blinked hard. This had been a difficult day. That's why she felt close to tears. Not because of Fannie and Charles.

Charles started back inside the paper, *her* paper. Then he stopped. "Addie, what a pleasant surprise. I didn't expect you'd have that mess cleaned up for hours." He glanced at his pocket watch. "Oh, the afternoon is nearly over."

"Spending time with a friend has a way of making time fly."

"What?" Then his brain connected with her words. "Oh, you mean Fannie." He studied her and then an annoying grin spread across his face. "You saw that kiss?"

As if Adelaide even cared. She lifted her chin. "You're more than welcome to kiss any woman who'll have you."

"I didn't kiss her. She kissed me — on the cheek." His grin got broader. If he kept it up, she'd be able to shove the plate, cake and all, into that cavern. "Are you suggesting I kiss *you* instead?"

"I'm doing nothing of the kind."

He made a tsk-tsk sound. "My, my, aren't we testy?"

"If you'd had the day I've had, you'd be testy, too."

His expression turned grim. "I'm sorry for teasing you. Come in." He took her free hand and led her into the office.

She should march back home and take the cake with her, but something stronger than her resolve sent her forward.

At his desk, he eyed the plate in her hands. "So what's under that cloth?"

She cleared a spot and put it on the desk. "It's for you, as a thank-you for repairing the pane of glass." Though now she wanted to take it back. Let Fannie bake him a cake. She hoped he realized the bottom would be charred.

Charles lifted the napkin and leaned over the plate, inhaling. "Angel food cake, prepared by an angel." He gave her a wink. "Even if at the moment, her halo is off-kilter."

Without thinking, Adelaide gave her hat a tug. Some halo, decked out with feathers. "Laura made the cake, not me."

"Did she ask you to bring me a piece? Or was it your idea?"

"Can't you just say thank you? Not everything is a story for the paper!"

He chuckled. "You *are* grumpy, but you're right. Thank you for the cake." He pulled out the chair. "Have a seat. I'll pour you a cup of coffee."

The coffee smelled strong enough to stand a spoon in, exactly what she needed to summon the starch absent from her spine since the break-in. "I'd enjoy a cup."

Adelaide removed her gloves and laid them in her lap. Charles returned with her coffee, looking confident and in control. She wanted to punch him.

"You're fresh as a daisy. I'd never guess what a hard day you've had."

"Are those the same words you said to Fannie?"

He grinned. "Why, Miss Crum, you're jealous."

She dipped her head to sip. "Jealous? Certainly not."

Beaming now, he resembled a bullfrog all puffed up with pride. "Is that so?"

Adelaide lowered her gaze, not daring to look him in the eye. She *was* jealous. And that surprised her. And, worse yet, he knew it. That put her at a disadvantage. "Not at all. As half owner of the paper, I perceived your behavior as . . . unsuitable for the editor of our newspaper. In public, no less."

She took a second sip of coffee and grimaced. It tasted twice as awful as the first gulp. She jutted out her chin. "I've no interest in who you kiss. Or who kisses you."

His eyes twinkled. "If you're not interested, then I won't tell you why Fannie kissed me."

He played with her like a cat toyed with a mouse. Adelaide let out a gust of frustration. "All right, why? And I'm only asking out of journalistic inquiry, I'll have you know. In case I should decide to write a column on —" she scrambled for something to say "— lip ointments."

He whooped with laughter. "With a tale like that, have you considered writing fiction, Miss Crum?"

"Perhaps I will some day." Here she told one fib after another, trying to pretend Charles meant nothing to her. If she kept this up, God might not think much of her, either.

"I'll give you the scoop. I told Fannie I'm old enough to be her father, figuring that might cool her interest." He grimaced. "I needn't have bothered. James came in and before he left, the two of them were drooling over each other."

Adelaide's coffee splashed up the inside of her mug. *"James and Fannie?"* She'd been wrong, as wrong as she could be.

"Grateful for my introduction to James, Fannie gave me a kiss." Then he chuckled. "I never had a woman drop me so quickly, except maybe for you, just now."

Did that imply they had a relationship?

She reached over and set the mug on Charles's desk. "You might have told me right away why Fannie kissed you."

Charles guffawed. "So it's my fault you're mad at me?"

Her claim lacked logic, but she had no other. "Yes, it is."

"Well, you should've asked instead of skulking in the shadows, spying."

"I did not skulk or spy. I . . . I merely checked my reflection in the glass." She slapped a hand over her mouth to stifle a laugh.

"In that case, will you forgive me?"

"Since you asked nicely, yes, I will."

He took her hand and held it for a long, quiet moment, his large palm, warm and slightly rough against her own. Their gazes locked. Adelaide's breath stopped coming, her heart held its beat. With his other hand, he ran a finger along her jaw, sending shivers down her spine, and then spoiled it by tweaking her nose. No wonder. She probably appeared as desperate as Fannie.

Teddy walked out from the back, carrying an inky piece of equipment. "Boss, can you take a look at this?"

Charles headed over to confer with Teddy. Adelaide rose and crossed to the window. Outside the wide plate glass, the world kept moving. Buggies, wagons, people . . .

But in this office, a different commotion brewed, one inside her. She pressed her palms to her hot cheeks, and then drew in a breath that sank to the bottom of her stomach to war with the other conflicts between her and Charles. Yet even with all that troubled her, she had to face the truth.

She wanted Charles.

How did she get into such a mess? Whenever he came near, he kept her heart drumming double time. Why? Besides driving her crazy with his untidy desk, he didn't want her interference in the paper, even when she had every right. And he was pushy and opinionated and stubborn.

And yet . . . this man helped Mary and her boys. He'd stood up to the committee and had brought her Emma.

In short, though he didn't appear to know it, he gave of himself. And she knew he cared about her. She looked at him, so strong, dependable. He gave her a feeling of comfort, of safety. For a woman used to relying on herself, that was . . . nice.

Well, sometimes. Something she could get used to, though she knew she shouldn't.

And yes, she liked his kisses. But she could do without them. After all, he wanted her to behave as he thought she should, not how she needed to be. He tried to keep her out of his dream, out of everything important. And he couldn't commit to anything but the newspaper, making it his life.

No, she didn't need a man.

And now she must convince him to continue publishing her suffrage articles. To light a spark that would help other women have the power and voice she, and the generations before her, had lacked. And yet . . .

A sigh slipped from her lips. She stepped to Charles's chair and ran a hand over his coat. She fingered his pencils, the things

313

he'd touched; somehow dearer than mere objects should be because they'd been in his hands.

Earlier when Adelaide had seen Fannie out front, the young girl glowed, had a spring to her step. Just being in the reporter's presence had left her changed. Adelaide understood that change, all too well. Caring brought happiness but also recklessness, a tendency to forget what was important.

A moment later, Charles pulled up a chair beside her. He gave her a smile. "You've had a tough day. How about I take you and Emma on a picnic? I want to talk to you about something."

CHAPTER SEVENTEEN

Adelaide watched Emma clamber over the rocks by the river, delighting in every flower, every bug she came across. Scattered clouds moved slowly across the pale blue sky. What an idyllic spot for their picnic.

Adelaide leaned back, letting the sun warm her face. "When have you seen a more beautiful spring?"

Charles moved closer. With gentle fingers, he turned her face toward his. "All I can see is how beautiful you are."

"Thank you." Her heart leapt at his words.

His gaze locked with hers. "You and I are a lot alike. We're both afraid of feeling too much. Of getting hurt."

"That's because we've been hurt by the people who were supposed to love us."

He plucked a blade of grass. "Except for you and Mary, I've known few truly good people in my life."

"Not even your mother?"

He draped an arm over his bent knee, his gaze focused on some distant point. "Ma said and did things to protect us, to keep the peace as best she could. If that meant stretching the truth or bending her principles, well, she did." He turned to her. "I'm not blaming her, you understand. She lived scared."

Adelaide nodded.

"Now Pa, well, he wore his values like a Sunday suit, shrugging them off when he walked in the door." He cleared his throat. "We'd try to please him, but we never could." Sudden moisture filled Charles's eyes and he blinked it away. "Eventually Ma quit trying. That's when things got really ugly." He raised his gaze. "No one in my life has been like you."

"I'm far from perfect, Charles."

"To me you are." His voice grew gruff. "I don't want to bring you any harm."

"How could you harm me?"

He took her hands and studied her face. "In countless ways." His eyes filled with misery, something close to despair.

She shook her head. Charles would never hurt her intentionally. "No matter what you say, I believe in you. It's your relationship with God that divides us. Even our dispute about writing my column pales in comparison."

Charles released her hands. "I believe in God."

She leaned toward him. "Then why won't you attend church?"

His gaze wandered the grassy bank, watching Emma chase a butterfly. He cleared his throat. "Church has been your haven. My father used Scripture as an excuse to beat us. Attending church was a farce, a pretense to dupe the community into believing we were a happy family."

"That doesn't mean you can't worship now."

He waved a hand to indicate the green grass, tall leafed-out trees, the gurgling water winding through the river. "I feel closer to God right here than I would in church."

"When you stay away from church, you separate yourself from the teachings, the chance to serve and praise God."

Charles rose. "God can't want me there, knowing the resentment I harbor. Knowing the man I am."

What did he mean? She reached a hand to him, but Charles moved out of her grasp. "What are you trying to tell me?"

"I'm a man who can't trust." He stepped

farther away, jamming his hands into his pockets. "Even myself."

Adelaide scrambled to her feet. "Why not?"

His head drooped. "I told you. I'm not good like you."

"We're all sinners, Charles. I see the decency in you."

He shook his head. "You see what you want to see."

"You don't have to be perfect before you can come to God. He'll give you the strength to overcome your past."

"I can't. I want to, but I can't." He pulled her close. "I'm sorry." Taking her chin in his free hand, his voice turned rough with emotion. "I know that's not what you want to hear."

It wasn't, but she could see the conflict in his eyes. "Trusting is a choice, a decision. People might disappoint you, but God won't."

"Don't you see? He's already disappointed me." Charles pulled away. "I have to work this out on my own."

"Until you're able to make peace with God, you'll never heal from the past."

Without Adelaide noticing, clouds had gathered. The rising wind warned of an approaching storm.

"I hope —"

He stopped her with a raised palm. "Let's take a walk."

They strolled along the bank. Emma scampered over to show a toad she'd found, then dashed off in search of more discoveries.

Adelaide turned her gaze on the man, who, regardless of her intention, had taken up residence in her heart. Perhaps in time, he'd see how God walked through every day, held the present and every tomorrow in His hands.

As much as Adelaide wanted to convince Charles to come to church, she understood his hesitancy. She'd continue to pray for healing from his past.

They came to a large rock along the riverbank. Charles sat and pulled her down beside him. He drew in a breath and turned to face her, capturing her hands in his. "I have something to ask you, something important." His grip on hers tightened. "Hear me out before you answer. I'm hoping your answer will be yes."

Say yes? She blinked. "Yes or no about what?"

"This has to do with us, with our future. From you, I've learned to speak up about what's important to me."

What did he mean? Her mind ran through the possible questions he could ask and arrived at one.

Did Charles intend to propose?

She'd known him for such a short time. Huge issues between them needed to be resolved. Still, marriage to Charles . . .

Her heart tripped in her chest. "What do you want to ask me?"

His gaze met hers and he drew in a breath. "Will you —" he hesitated "— sell me your half of *The Ledger*?"

The words slammed into Adelaide's head. *Ledger. Sell.* She jerked her hands out of his grasp. Her supper formed a lump in her stomach. "*That's* what you wanted to ask me?"

"You can still write your fashion column —"

"You want *full* ownership?" A strangled laugh escaped her lips and she rose to her feet. "You'll be so generous as to *let* me write a fashion column?"

Charles only cared about regaining control of the paper. He didn't want to share that part of his life with her. Any part of his life, really. "What a fool I've been." Every inch of her hurt. Tears sprang to her eyes but she willed them away. Pride was all she had, pride and Emma and God who strengthened her.

Back straight and shoulders set, she signaled to Emma. "Time to go home!"

"Addie, wait, I'm only trying to protect you. Can't we —"

"No, Charles, we can't. Not now, not later."

A rumble of thunder sounded in the distance. Emma raced over, interrupting Charles's efforts to argue his point.

"Do we have to go?" Emma whined.

"Yes, it's going to storm." Adelaide took Emma's hand and the three of them walked to the area where they'd picnicked. "We'll come again. Just you and me," she promised Emma.

Pain twisted in her heart until Adelaide could barely breathe. Had she been thinking she could trust a man? That she could risk her heart? Whenever she did, she paid the penalty.

Once again a man wanted to silence her. Even knowing its importance to her, Charles wanted full ownership of the paper, asking her to sacrifice the opportunity to express her views. Well, she couldn't make him love her, but she could hang on to ownership of the paper.

She straightened her shoulders. She would survive without Charles, as she had survived when her mother had kept her at arm's length. The days might be drabber, might not hold the promise they once had, but she would not think about that now.

Emma skipped ahead picking a few dandelions along the path home.

Charles touched her arm. "Please, you don't understand why I want to do this."

Wheeling around, she said, "You know what, Charles? I might buy *you* out. As for this . . ." She swept a palm over the blanket. "You made a mess of our picnic. Now you can clean it up."

Her heart heavy with loss of something, someone she'd never really had, Adelaide sat sewing in the workroom, grateful for Emma's sweet voice in the showroom as she played with her doll. Thankfully the little girl was blissfully unaware of the impasse between Adelaide and Charles.

Adelaide heard a crash, breaking glass and then Emma's shrill scream. Barely able to breathe, she scrambled to her feet and ran. She found Emma cowering on the floor with shards of glass only two feet away.

Adelaide scooped up the trembling child, doll and all, into her own trembling arms and darted to the corner, away from the window to check for cuts or bruises. "Are you okay?"

Against her shoulder, Emma nodded. "Someone broke the window. I'm scared."

"Of course you are," Adelaide said, rubbing Emma's small tense back.

Carrying the child, Adelaide picked her way through the glass to the frame of the shop window that now had a gaping hole in jagged edges of glass and peered into the street. She saw no one suspicious.

Edging away from the window, the toe of her shoe hit something solid. A rock. A piece of paper had been tied to it with a knotted string.

Hot fury distorted Adelaide's vision and she swayed on her feet. If that rock had hit Emma in the temple, the impact could have killed her. With Emma clinging to her, Adelaide knelt and picked up the stone, the weight of it heavy in her hand.

"Emma, would you like a cookie?" Adelaide asked, forcing a note of cheer into her voice.

The little girl raised her head and nodded. "Can I have two? One cookie for me and one for my dolly?"

"Two it will be."

Later, while Emma sat across from her, nibbling on the treat, with the sweet scent of vanilla and cinnamon from Emma's cookie filling her nostrils and a sickening wad of fear filling her gut, Adelaide removed the string, and unfolded the slip of paper. Barely discernable, the words appeared to be printed by someone using his left hand. It read: You're going to pay for the trouble you're causing.

Adelaide shivered and tears welled in her eyes. She bit her lip, determined not to frighten Emma more. Had Jacob done this? Or Ed Drummond? Or someone else? Her heart stuttered in her chest. Her actions had put Emma's life at risk.

Weeks before her life had been simple with a future of loneliness spread out before her. She'd taken action, sought change. And now even her home, once a haven, had become a dangerous place. She'd have to go for the sheriff — again.

If only she could turn to Charles . . .

No. Every fiber of her being yearned to lean into the comfort of his arms, but Adelaide would not run to Charles. She might not know who threatened her bodily harm, but she knew without a doubt if she didn't stay away from Charles Graves, her heart would be broken.

Charles might as well give up his job. Instead of doing any of the hundreds of things that needed doing, he'd spent the morning staring out the window. All because of Adelaide Crum.

Days before, she'd marched off, leaving him indeed, with quite a mess. And she hadn't even given him a chance to explain.

By offering to buy her out, he'd been trying to protect her from herself, from the damage her views brought into her life. Against his better judgment, he'd published her third suffrage article. But that hadn't mended the rift between them.

Addie was right across the street, a wide thoroughfare, but nothing compared to the gulf separating them now. He'd seen the broken glass in her store window, and Sheriff Rogers had told him about the rock-throwing incident. His eyes stung. She'd hired a handyman to replace the glass rather than coming to him for help. For comfort. But that didn't matter. He only cared about her safety.

"Afternoon, Charles."

Charles jerked up his head to see Roscoe Sullivan standing near his desk.

"Hello, Roscoe." Charles took in the wide smile on Roscoe's narrow face. "You look like life's treating you well."

"It is, and that's a fact. Even my rheumatism's eased."

"Glad to hear it."

Roscoe plopped down in the opposite chair, the chair Charles now kept tidy thanks to Addie. She wanted to straighten more than his office. She wanted to straighten him out, too — a job, too big even for Addie.

"I miss the energy of this place, even if I almost ran it into the ground." Roscoe glanced out the window. "Say, I've been wondering, who broke the window in the millinery shop?"

Charles shifted in his chair. "I don't like to say this, Roscoe, but your nephew is one of the suspects."

"That's ridiculous! Where did you get such an idea?"

In dangerous territory, Charles knew to tread with care. "I saw Ed in town that day. And he has a beef with Miss Crum."

"So do a lot of people. That suffrage column of hers has the whole town in an uproar. *She's* the cause of any problem my nephew might have with her." Roscoe jumped up and paced in front of the desk. "From what I heard, she wants Emma *and* William and will go to any length to get them. Even as far as breaking Frances's and Ed's hearts to steal those youngsters away."

Roscoe stopped in front of Charles's desk

and leaned on his palms, his face inches away. "She's obviously got you in her clutches. You'd better stop seeing her, Charles. The fact you're courting her gives her status in the community."

Now that Addie wasn't even speaking to him, the irony of Roscoe's words twisted in his chest. "See here, Roscoe, Miss Crum had the respect of the town long before I came."

"That's before she went off her rocker with these obsessions with children and voting."

Charles let out a gust. "She's saner than anyone I know."

"It's your fault. You've given her too much leeway at the paper. Appears to me you're on *her* side."

Even though he questioned the wisdom of her column, he *was* on Addie's side. "Miss Crum is half owner of *The Ledger.* She has a right to run what she wants in the paper."

"I'm going to talk to John Sparks. Emma should be back where she belongs."

Charles's throat tightened. "You need to reconsider that. If Ed did vandalize Miss Crum's shop or threw that rock, he has a serious problem. The children might not be safe wi—"

"What are you saying? That my nephew

327

could hurt a child? Knowing what he went through losing Eddie." He pointed a finger under Charles's nose. "Mark my words. I have considerable influence in this town. If either you or Miss Crum harms my nephew's family, I'll do whatever I can to ruin that shop of hers and this paper. You can bank on it!"

Roscoe pivoted and strode to the door, slamming it behind him, setting the glass dancing in its frame. Charles tugged his fingers through his hair. Roscoe had the clout to ruin their reputations and their businesses.

Since owning the paper, Charles had taken charge of his life, his destiny. Now, thanks to his father's malicious will, he didn't own it outright. Addie's column added fuel to the fire of opposition Roscoe resolved to light. But somehow the paper no longer mattered to him.

He leaned forward, dropped his head in his hands and closed his eyes. And saw the sweet face of Addie. A face filled with joy at receiving Emma, then fear when her shop had been vandalized, and later determination.

His stomach knotted. How far would the evildoer terrorizing Addie go? Where would this end?

■ ■ ■ ■

That night, restless and unable to sleep, Adelaide climbed the stairs to the attic, hoping to take her mind off the rising hostility and the fear it planted in her mind.

In her hand, she held a lantern, and in her heart, a determination to find a clue to her mother's relationship with Charles's father. Crossing the attic floor near the eaves, she stepped on a squeaky plank. She didn't want to risk waking Emma, but first thing tomorrow morning, she'd nail that board into submission. How many nails would she need?

She knelt on the floor and noticed that the board had no nails. Her heart tripped. She sped to the toolbox at the top of the stairs, removed a screwdriver, then knelt and pried off the loose board.

Underneath the plank, she found a packet of envelopes tied with a thin red string. Butterflies fluttered in her stomach. Could this be what she sought?

She slid the first envelope out and opened it. Her gaze flew first to the salutation, then to the date, September 8, 1866, and then down the page to the signature, Calvin Crum. The father she never knew.

As she read, phrases jumped off the page and hooked her heart. ". . . not a man to settle down." ". . . better off without me." ". . . free you to marry the love of your life."

With only this letter, her father had deserted them, without a doubt breaking her mother's heart. No, not breaking — hardening it. She'd only been a few weeks old when her father left. Tears slid down Adelaide's cheeks and plopped onto the page. She suddenly understood her mother's bitterness, her loss of joy, her distrust of men, distrust that she drummed into Adelaide.

She read on to where her father referred to the love of her mother's life — it had to be Adam Graves.

With shaky hands, she pulled out the next letter from a smaller envelope, addressed in a tight, wobbly script. Not from her father. From someone else.

Adelaide scanned the page and the signature at the bottom. "This is from him," she whispered.

For a moment, Adelaide wanted to put it back under the narrow red string, to not know these things about her mother. But the past had intruded into her life and she couldn't turn back. She read the words from thirty years ago.

January 6, 1866

Dearest Constance,
 From childhood on, I expected we would marry. That you could betray me this way, become pregnant with another man's child, is more than I can bear. Though my hand shakes with anger as I write this, I love you still. I will never recover from this blow, but I will attempt to put you out of my mind. I cannot fathom how I will succeed.

Always,
Adam

The paper quivered in her trembling hand, then fell to her lap. This letter must have arrived mere days before her parents' wedding. Had her mother loved Adam? Had she wanted to cancel the nuptials? Or had she married the man she loved?

Adam, with his claim of undying love, hadn't offered marriage. This letter was a rebuke, not a solution to her dilemma. Beneath his declaration of love lay a veiled cruelty.

How had this letter affected her mother? Or her father, if he found it?

Adelaide sighed. Had they argued over Adam? Or worse, had her father left to clear

331

the way for Mama to have the man he thought she loved? Maybe in here . . .

Adelaide opened the last letter.

October 22, 1867

Dearest Love,

I cannot tell you how exhilarated I was to get your letter. And how devastated. To hear you love me as much as I love you brought untold happiness. Your declaration that you'd never stopped loving me and had made a huge mistake heals the wound that your infatuation with Calvin Crum ripped in my soul.

To know you're divorced and free to marry, now that it's too late, is the vilest irony, the worst of nightmares. For you see, I married a woman I met in Cincinnati and she's already expecting my child. My heart will be with you always, but I can't shirk my duty and leave Beulah to raise the child alone.

If only I could. For in every way she is a disappointment. I feel cheated, enraged at this cruel twist of fate. I cannot stop thinking of you, as you once were, the lovely innocent girl of my dreams. No

one will ever fill your place in my heart.
        With undying devotion,
                Adam

And there, in Adam Graves's stifled scrawl, were some of the answers she'd been seeking and even more questions. Imagining the pain these letters must have brought her mother, tears flowed down her face. If Adam wanted to stay with his wife, why had he held on to his feelings for her mother?

She stared again at the yellowed sheet, willing it to provide more answers. But it held the same words as before.

Adelaide wiped her eyes, then folded the letter and laid it in her lap. She couldn't comprehend how her mother and Adam had such a great love for each other, but couldn't love their own flesh and blood.

Whatever Adam had felt, it hadn't been love. Not the kind of love spoken of in the Bible. As they'd read the passage on love, Pastor Foley had explained to the congregation that charity meant the same as love. The words paraded through her mind. Love is patient, love is kind, not easily angered, keeps no record of wrong. Always protects, always trusts, always hopes, always perseveres.

If only she and Charles had grown up in

loving homes.

She choked back a sob. The last shred of hope of finding something that would truly explain her mother's indifference drifted like dust to the attic floor. In her unhappiness, her mother had distanced herself, had wasted years, losing opportunity after opportunity to love her daughter.

Replacing the letters in their envelopes, Adelaide slipped them under the string, and then returned the packet to its resting place.

She remained motionless in the attic thinking about what might have been if her mother had seen past her infatuation and realized Calvin Crum wasn't a staying kind of man.

How ironic that Adam Graves couldn't let go.

Or had her mother been the lucky one? If she'd married Adam, would she have suffered as Beulah had? Or had discontent with the way his life had turned out led to such bitterness that Adam had taken it out on his family?

A mouse darted past, his tail flicking as he scooted under a chair and into the dark depths of a corner. Adelaide roused.

Her days had been filled with one shock after another, first the vandalism, then Charles's request to sell him the paper when she'd thought he wanted to propose, then the rock shattering her window and her peace of mind and now these letters from the two men who had ruined her mother's life.

Life wasn't easy, and as Charles once said, was often unfair, but with God's help, she'd survive. Though tonight, she had no idea how.

Adelaide opened the shop as usual, but so weary she feared her bones might collapse beneath her. She'd been up half the night, thinking about the letters, missing Charles. Unable to sleep, she'd stewed about Ed or Jacob coming after her and the shop's lack of business. She sighed, ashamed when she needed it most, she'd been unable to release her worries to God.

Against her will, she crossed to the window to check for any sign of Charles. Leaning her face against the frame, she ached to have him near. Somehow, she'd find a way to go on without him. Inside she felt hollow, as if a space had been vacated that no one else could fill.

The bell jingled. Forcing a smile to her face, Adelaide crossed to the door to greet her customer. "Mrs. Hawkins, I'm glad you stopped in. I have your alterations done."

Her face pink and moist from the heat of the warm spring day, the buxom matron nodded. "I'd hoped you did."

Adelaide led her to the counter and pulled the wrapped garment from underneath, then handed Mrs. Hawkins the bill. "While you're here, would you like to look for a hat? I've repaired the damaged ones from the break-in. They're a bargain."

Digging in her purse, Mrs. Hawkins shook her head. "If I came home with one of your hats, Leroy would pitch a fit. Roscoe Sullivan told him you and the new editor blame Ed Drummond for the trouble you're having. Leroy's worked up." She slapped the cash to pay her bill on the counter and the coins bounced to the floor. "He and Ed are hunting buddies."

Adelaide bent to retrieve the coins. Did Charles now suspect Ed rather than Jacob or some disgruntled citizen?

Mrs. Hawkins's hands fluttered in front of her like a bird on its first flight. "Where on earth did you get the notion ladies should vote?"

"You don't think women should have the right to express their opinions?"

"Not when it causes me trouble."

"I'm sorry —"

"You should be! I need a new hat and now

336

I have to order it out of the catalogue, without getting to try it on first. Too bad you didn't think of anyone but yourself." Mrs. Hawkins grabbed the bundle and headed for the door.

Adelaide watched her customer's retreating back, biting her lip, squelching a desire to weep. Exhaustion — that must be the reason for her reaction.

Why had she tried to bring about change for herself and the women of Noblesville when all that mattered were Emma and William? And now after her columns, no one respected her suspicions about Ed Drummond's treatment of the children.

She wouldn't write another article on suffrage until she'd gotten William out of that house. Change for women wouldn't come overnight. But harm to the children could. How could she ensure their safety?

Three days had passed since Charles had spoken with Addie, but she never left his thoughts. Determined to protect her, at night he'd watch her window until her light went out, then he'd patrol the streets. When the sun rose in the eastern sky, he'd give up his watch. He didn't bother going home to sleep, but bunked on a cot in the back, tossing and turning until Teddy arrived and the smell of brewing coffee dragged him out of bed.

Across the way, he saw Adelaide and Emma chatting with Mary and his nephews. Obviously, Addie didn't miss him. Nor had she thanked him for printing her third column or criticized him for placing it on the back page. Instead, since their argument, she'd gone on with her life while he'd become a man of stone, unable to function at work, unable to smile, unable to sleep. What had happened to the stoic newsman he'd been? He hardly knew himself.

Remembering the way she laughed, her scent, the essence of Addie, left him longing to talk to her. He left the window and walked to his desk.

Teddy glanced his way. "You're up and down so much, you're making me dizzy. Why don't you go over there?"

"Where?" Charles said feigning ignorance.

Teddy chuckled. "To Miss Crum's hat shop, where else. You've been watching the place all week. Wouldn't it be easier just to go over there?"

Charles dropped into his desk chair. "I'm the last person Miss Crum wants to see."

Teddy took a seat across from him. "You two have a spat?"

Charles leaned back, focusing his gaze on

the ceiling. "You could say that."

"Women have a way of squeezing an apology out of us men sooner or later. Tell her you're sorry. Take her a new apron or something." A rumble sounded from Teddy's stomach. He dropped his foot to the floor and unfolded his body from the chair. "I'm heading home to dinner. My advice is to take her flowers and if you're really in trouble, a nice brooch, too."

But Charles knew flowers and trinkets wouldn't solve this mess. He'd destroyed Addie's feelings for him. He wondered why he cared. She represented everything he'd run from most of his life — family, God, marriage. So why did he feel like he'd lost a part of himself? The good part.

When the door to the paper opened, he scowled. Teddy better not have returned to pester him.

Mary poked her head in the door. "Are you busy?"

"No, come in." Seeing his sister-in-law's happy face took the frown off his. "Where are my nephews?"

"They're out front in the wagon nibbling on some of Adelaide's cookies. I decided I could afford a luxury so I bought one of her hats." Mary spun around in front of him, letting him admire it from all angles. "Do you like it?"

"Very much. It suits you." Charles stared at the hat that had lain in Addie's capable hands. For some unknown reason, he brushed a hand along the silky rose hugging the brim.

"Why thank you, kind sir," Mary said with a laugh.

A lump rose in Charles's throat. "How is she?"

"Pretty good, considering you tossed her out of your life like yesterday's news."

"I did not. She tossed *me* out of *her* life."

"Well, if she did, she must have her reasons. She looks almost as miserable as you."

Addie looked miserable? Not when he'd seen her across the way. Did she miss him? Or was she frightened and unable to sleep? Charles circled the room, his gaze never leaving the millinery shop. He hadn't worried like this since his childhood, when he'd listen for his father's footsteps.

Could he protect Addie any better than he'd been able to protect Ma and Sam?

He stopped beside the window and hit his palm against its frame. "If I could only be sure she'll be safe. It's driving me crazy. I watch her place all night."

"You what?"

"With everything that's happened over

there, I'm keeping an eye out for trouble."

Mary stepped to his side and straightened his collar. "No wonder you look dreadful." Studying him, she tapped a finger against her lower lip. "Sounds to me like you're in love."

He groaned.

"There are easier ways to protect her." She cocked her head. "You could marry her."

And open her to heartache? Never.

She flashed him one of those knowing woman smiles. "Then she'd be safe. *And* probably get to keep Emma." She gave him a hug. "And you'd both own the paper. Marriage would take care of all your problems."

He studied the floor. "I can't do that."

Mary folded her arms. "The trouble with you, Charles Graves, is you're in love and won't admit it, even to yourself."

He jerked his head up. Everyone talked about love as if it were the simplest thing in the world. He knew better. "I'm not even sure I know what the word means."

"What you want is a guarantee. There's no guarantee with love. No guarantees for anything worth having. Like my boys out there." Charles's gaze settled on Michael and Philip perched on the wagon seat. "I'm

341

both mother and father to them — doing the best I can. I suppose they could grow up and break my heart. But maybe, just maybe, they'll make me proud."

Her voice cracked with emotion. She swiped at damp eyes. "Well, I'd best be going." She gave him a kiss on the cheek. "My advice, Charles Graves — don't let a woman like Adelaide Crum slip through your fingers."

CHAPTER EIGHTEEN

On Sunday, Charles stood outside the imposing edifice of the First Christian Church. He tugged at the tie choking his neck, buttoned and then rebuttoned his jacket and adjusted his hat. Through the open windows of the church, a song drifted on the cool morning breeze. A long time ago, he'd sung the familiar tune.

Bowing his head, he let the song "What a Friend We Have in Jesus" flow through him, the words soaking into his parched soul. The song promised peace — if he prayed. But he couldn't. Not since his childhood prayers had gone unanswered, destroying something between him and God. Charles swallowed past the lump in his throat. If only he could find that serenity, serenity that had been missing most of his life. Maybe inside the church he'd find the answer, find his way back to God, to that promise of peace.

He tried to lift his foot, to climb the steps leading into the house of worship, but he couldn't move. Sweat beaded his forehead, and the lump swelled in his throat until he felt he'd suffocate. He bent over and dragged oxygen into his lungs.

A cloud passed between him and the sun, covering him in shadow. A sudden chill streaked down his spine.

He couldn't move. Couldn't pray, couldn't worship.

Too much stood between him and God.

Listening to the sermon and singing praises, a blessed peace stole over Adelaide, along with the conviction that whatever happened in her life, God sat on the throne, controlled the universe and would take care of William and Emma. If only Charles would attend services, he might find a measure of peace.

She and Emma rose for the benediction and afterward followed the parishioners into the aisle. At the door, they shook hands with Pastor Foley then walked down the steps.

"Adelaide, wait up!"

Recognizing that voice, Adelaide led Emma to one side as Fannie emerged with James. The couple moved toward them and Adelaide noticed Fannie walked with grace. Why, she looked like a lady right out of

Godey's. Pleased some of her lessons had taken root, Adelaide smiled.

Fannie tugged James forward. "Adelaide, have you met James Cooper?"

"Yes, I have. We've run into each other a time or two."

James's eyes twinkled. "She means that literally, too. I almost plowed her down one morning."

She wanted to ask James about Charles, but didn't. "No damage done." Adelaide grinned. "This is Emma Grounds."

The couple greeted Emma. Then Fannie smiled. "I read your articles. They were wonderful." Adelaide's face must have revealed her surprise because Fannie giggled. "Since I've met James, I'm reading the paper."

"Unfortunately, not everyone agrees with you," Adelaide said.

"Really? Well, it makes perfect sense to me. We ladies are people, aren't we?"

Emma touched Fannie's hand. "I'm a people, and someday I'm going to be a dip . . . dip . . . lomat. Mr. Graves told me so."

James lightly tugged at the ribbons on Emma's hat. "Well, if women get the vote, and I hope they do, you'd be my first choice for a diplomat, Emma."

Fannie smiled adoringly into James's face and he beamed back, looking equally besotted. "Wasn't the service uplifting? Did you hear James singing? He has the most beautiful voice."

"Fannie thinks I'm a great singer because she can barely carry a tune."

Fannie giggled. "That's true."

James sighed, love softening his normally probing gaze. "Don't you adore her giggle, Miss Crum?"

Before giving an answer, Adelaide gave Emma permission to join a group of children playing nearby. "Fannie is Fannie," she said, hoping that would suffice.

"That's exactly what I like about her. There's no pretense with Fannie."

The young woman leaned close. "I guess I won't need more of your lessons, Adelaide. James likes me just the way I am."

James accepted Fannie, giggle and all. Adelaide's composure faltered. Had she done the same for Charles?

Having lived without her mother's approval, she should have understood the need for true acceptance. Taking Fannie's hands, Adelaide gave them a squeeze. "Thank you."

The young woman's eyes widened. "For what?"

"For teaching the teacher a thing or two,"

she said softly.

A puzzled expression took over Fannie's cheery face, and she giggled again. "Me? Teach you?"

Adelaide nodded, suddenly unable to speak. Why hadn't she seen the truth earlier? "You've taught me more than you know."

Later, as the young couple ambled over to talk to friends, Adelaide pondered the lesson they'd unknowingly taught. When you love someone, you accept them for who they are.

She'd criticized some things about Charles that didn't matter a whit and had judged him for far more than a messy desk.

She, of all people, should understand how a painful childhood could damage a person. Charles had suffered at the hand of a church-going hypocrite. She should have had more compassion for his refusal to attend church. Maybe if they'd read Scriptures and prayed together, or if she'd asked Pastor Foley for suggestions, she could have found a way to help him.

When you love, truly love a person, you help rather than censure. Perhaps her mother had influenced her more than she realized. She hoped it wasn't too late to change.

■ ■ ■ ■

Thursday afternoon, Emma ran across the schoolyard, the pigtails Adelaide had carefully braided that morning flying out behind her and unraveling around her face. Adelaide scooped the little girl into her arms. Hand in hand, they started for home.

Adelaide squeezed Emma's hand. "How was your day?"

"Billy said his papa didn't like what you wrote in the paper. He said you're dumb. What did you write?"

"An essay on why women should be allowed to vote."

"What's dumb about that?"

"Nothing. Some people don't like women to make decisions."

"Like Tad won't let us girls pick teams at recess?"

"Sort of like that."

"Well, it's not fair." Emma thrust out her lower lip.

Adelaide patted the little girl's shoulder, Charles's words, *Life often isn't fair, Addie,* tumbling in her mind.

Adelaide stopped and bent down, hoping to make Emma understand. "I agree, sweetheart. Everyone in this great country should

348

have a say in who makes the rules."

"Can I make some of *our* rules?" Emma asked, her blue eyes shining with mischief, the unfairness of her life forgotten.

Adelaide laughed and tugged Emma toward her for a hug. "We'll have to see about that."

Emma grinned and they walked on. Adelaide had started to say Emma could make some rules if she had the wisdom. But men used a woman's perceived lack of wisdom as their objection for suffrage, putting women on the level of children.

Her mind on suffrage, Adelaide almost bumped into Frances Drummond huddling in front of the pharmacy, her gaze riveted on Emma and filled with longing.

Emma's brow furrowed in concern. "Where's William?"

Frances stroked Emma's cheek. "He's at the mill with Ed."

Before Emma could say more, Adelaide touched her shoulder. "Would you run back to school and get your McGuffey's reader? I'd like you to read from it tonight."

"Sure."

"I'll wait for you here."

Emma gave Frances a smile. "I'm a good reader," she said, then dashed off toward the school.

With Emma out of earshot, Adelaide turned back to Frances, who looked even thinner and paler than the last time she'd seen her. A faded bruise marked her left cheek.

Frances took a shaky breath. "You and Emma love each other. I saw it in both of your eyes." Her voice sounded thick, as if tears ran down the back of her throat. "I want to talk to the committee."

Adelaide's heart thumped in her chest, hope galloping through her. "Why?"

Frances's eyes misted. "To tell them about . . . Ed's abuse. Get William out of harm's way."

Realizing this decision cost Frances dearly, Adelaide clasped her hands together to keep from giving her a hug.

"You're a good mother. I want you to have both children."

Unable to speak, Adelaide covered her mouth, holding back her tears — tears of joy for her, tears of sorrow for Frances.

"Those articles you wrote in the paper are the reason I'm speaking up."

Adelaide could barely comprehend that her words had given Frances such courage. "Would you like me to go with you?"

"I'd be obliged." Frances dashed away the tears sliding down her cheeks. "Could we meet in the early afternoon? Ed doesn't come in from the fields until dark so I should be able to leave without him knowing."

"How about two o'clock tomorrow afternoon in the courthouse?"

Frances nodded.

"I'll take care of it."

"Thank you."

"For what?" a gravelly voice demanded.

Adelaide's heart skipped a beat. She swung around to encounter the glowering face of Ed Drummond. How long had he been listening? How much had he heard?

"For . . . helping Emma with her math," Frances stammered, resting a tentative hand on his arm. "Where's William?"

"He'd better be waiting in the wagon like I told him." Ed shrugged off his wife's touch and pivoted to Adelaide. "You're quite the rabble-rouser, aren't you? Now you're trying to turn husbands and wives against each other with your radical ideas."

Ed lowered his head and placed his mouth close to Adelaide's ear. "You aren't as smart as you think you are, missy," he whispered, his breath warm on her neck, raising the fine hairs at her nape. "Leave us alone, and let me take care of my family like God intended."

How dare he liken his treatment of Frances to God's design?

Ed's lip curled into a snarl. "And stay away from the sheriff, you hear? I won't warn you twice."

Fear slithered down Adelaide's spine and coiled in the pit of her stomach.

Ed took his wife's elbow and stalked off. Adelaide watched the Drummonds enter the law office two doors down, and then expelled the breath she'd been holding.

She scanned the street. Long fingers of terror closed a stranglehold on her throat. *Where's Emma? She should be back by now. Had Ed gotten Emma before he joined them?*

Adelaide set off for the school, holding up her skirts and running fast, begging Heaven for Emma's protection. Soon her breath came in hitches and pain gored her right side. Up ahead, she spotted Emma, swinging along and singing at the top of her lungs. Dropping to her knees, Adelaide thanked God for the precious little girl's safety.

Emma saw her and sprinted to her side. "Miss Weaver asked me to wash the slates." Emma beamed with pride and then held up a tan book. "I got my reader."

Rising to her knees, Adelaide draped an arm around Emma's shoulders and inhaled the scent of soap, chalk, damp skin. She'd never smelled anything sweeter in her life. "That's wonderful, honey. You're a big helper."

"Where's Mrs. Drummond?"

"She had an appointment and couldn't wait. Would you like to help me sew a hem this afternoon?"

"Can I thread my own needle?"

Adelaide smiled at the eagerness in Emma's voice. "Yes, and you can thread mine, too. If you'd like, you can thread every needle in my sewing box."

Emma beamed. "I love you, Miss Adelaide."

Adelaide blinked and tears welled in her eyes. Emma's mouth formed a perfect O and her blue eyes grew round with surprise.

"I love you, too." Adelaide gathered Emma close. "So very much."

Emma squeezed Adelaide with all the might in her small body. For a moment they remained motionless in each other's arms, their declarations settling around them, as satisfying as manna from Heaven.

Adelaide played Emma's words over in her mind. For the first time in her life, someone had declared feelings of love. How had she been granted this most wonderful of gifts? What had she ever done to deserve it?

Nothing. Nothing at all.

God had given her Emma, plain and simple. No one was going to take away that precious gift. *No one.*

Later that afternoon, with Laura taking care of the shop and supervising Emma's homework, Adelaide had gone to the paper to ask Charles to arrange a committee meeting, but he wasn't there. Teddy had pointed her toward the livery.

As she stood outside the stable doors, Adelaide watched Charles brush Ranger's coat. Stepping closer, she noticed lines, usually faint around Charles's eyes, now deep and grooved. Dark smudges beneath his lashes revealed his fatigue.

Well, she was tired, too. Tired of waiting for trouble. Tired of handling that trouble alone. Tired of missing Charles.

If only she could move into his strong arms, have them close around her, and for a while, let him take her burdens. But she had no time for games, not when Ed Drummond held William in his clutches.

She straightened her spine. "Charles."

He jerked up his head. "Addie!"

She steeled herself against the joy she heard in his voice. As much as she loved him, he didn't love her. "I need a favor."

He hurried around the horse, his gaze skimming over her, as if making sure she wasn't a dream. "Anything."

"Better hear me out before you make any promises."

Her words slowed his steps. "I'm listening."

"Frances Drummond wants to meet with the committee. To expose Ed's abuse so she can get William out of there." For a moment, too emotional to continue, Adelaide laid a palm over her trembling lips. "She spoke up because . . . of my columns," she said, her words tinged with wonder.

He nodded. "You're making things happen, bringing change."

"She wants me to have both the children permanently."

"That's wonderful!"

He reached out and drew her into a hug. The scent of his skin, the hard plane of his chest and the heat from his body filled her senses — as familiar as coming home.

She lifted her face and met his gaze, wanting his kiss with a hunger that left her reeling.

But then the smile in his eyes slipped away. He released her and took a step back. "What are the chances the committee will allow you to have them, merely because

Frances says so?"

"What she wants should count for something."

Charles's brow furrowed and he studied the floor, obviously hesitant to speak his mind. "You're still a single woman."

His words held the pain of a slap. Again, a man — or the lack of one — made the decisions in her life. "Being a single woman isn't comparable to abuse. Surely the committee would rather I have those children than Ed. The committee only has to talk to Emma to see she's happy with me."

"Things aren't always that simple, that fair."

"No, but I'm not letting that stop me. You know more than anyone how I feel about Emma."

"You're a great mother." He shook his head. "But I need to warn you — that doesn't mean the committee won't find another home for Emma and William, one with two parents. You need to prepare for the possibility."

Behind them Ranger stamped his foot and Adelaide barely resisted doing the same. "Prepare to lose those children? Never! I'm through with my life — my future — being dictated by men." She stepped toward him. "With or without your support, I intend to fight for Emma and William."

He raised a hand then let it fall. "You could be hurt."

She and Charles had spent their lives captives of their pasts, afraid to take a risk. "I may get hurt but at least I'll be living." She bit her lip to keep from crying and poked his chest with her finger. "Too bad you won't do the same."

"You don't understand. I miss you, but —"

"The problem with you — there's always a 'but' in the way."

He flinched, but she didn't care. Clearly he wasn't going to fight for the two of them.

"When should I schedule the meeting?"

"Two o'clock tomorrow afternoon at the courthouse. Tell them Mrs. Drummond has something important to say."

His gaze locked with hers. "I'll take care of it."

"Thank you." She moved toward the door, her reason for being there finished. But her feet dragged and her mind nagged at her, telling her to go toward Charles, toward the man who stood with his arms at his sides. She paused.

Put them around me, Charles. Take a risk.

But he didn't. Instead he walked back to his horse. Anger churned within her, but remembering the lesson Fannie and James had taught her, she tamped it down. When you love someone, you never give up on that person. This might be her best chance to talk to Charles about trust and forgiveness. About God.

She pivoted to where Charles stood. "God loves you. Do you have any idea how much you matter to Him?"

Head down, he leaned against Ranger, quiet and tall, a silhouette against the open door at the other end of the livery.

At last, he lifted his gaze, his pain-filled eyes bleak. "Then why did He allow me to be beaten, Addie?" he said, his voice cracking. "I prayed and prayed God would stop my father. He didn't."

Tears sprang to her eyes. How did she answer that? Would Charles ever understand on this earth? And what of her own lonely childhood? They'd both paid a price for something they didn't do. But she truly believed God had a plan for their lives.

"Charles, I'm not sure why God allowed you to suffer. Maybe we'll never know. But could it be we're the people we are today because of our childhoods? That you and I survived and are stronger for what we experienced?"

Please God, help me say this right.

358

"Maybe you went through that nightmare so you could help others — if you'd let God use you."

Charles took a step back. "God wouldn't use me. He isn't close to me like He is to you."

What did Charles mean? She wasn't getting through to him. "God hasn't moved. Let Him into your heart."

Then the thought came — lifting a huge weight from her shoulders. Only God had the authority to bring Charles to Him. She'd do all she could, but in the end, saving Charles remained in God's hands.

Still, before she left, something else needed saying. "Open the Bible. All you need is in there."

He grimaced, his face etched with years of hurt and struggle, as easy to read as *The Ledger.* "You make it sound simple." He picked up the brush, running it along Ranger's side.

"It *is* simple. Let Him in."

He turned to her, his gaze forlorn, ripping at Adelaide's heart. "Which door do I open, Addie? All of mine were nailed shut a long time ago."

Her eyes misted. "You said you believe in God."

"Yes, but unlike you, I don't believe He

gets involved with people's lives. If He did, He'd never tolerate my father, or the Ed Drummonds in this world." Charles's mouth thinned. "From what I've seen, evil goes unchecked and the innocent suffer."

How could she get through the wall he'd built? "Your past and the newspaper business have skewed your view of mankind. Good people outnumber the bad."

Down the way, a horse neighed and Ranger nodded his head as if he understood. God had created the animal world with care and purpose. How much more He cherished human beings fashioned in His image. Yet God demanded obedience.

"I can't say what He'll do with your father, with the evildoers of this world, but His Word promises He will judge."

Charles's eyes glittered. Were those tears? "I'm sure that's true," he said softly, returning to his brushing.

She wanted to touch him, to hug him to her like she did Emma, but she kept her distance, afraid she'd be rebuffed. "You're thinking about your father. Well, I've been thinking about him, too. Wondering why he left such a will. Maybe, before he died, he repented."

Charles snorted. "Why would you think that?"

"Couldn't the will be his way of bringing us together? Trying to give us the life he and my mother never had." She took a breath. "Maybe Adam *wasn't* trying to hurt you."

"You have it all figured out, but it's all conjecture. There's no proof he repented. No evidence of that at all."

As usual, Charles wanted tangible evidence, but weren't a man's actions proof of change? "You believe your father gave me half of the paper to hurt you, but think about it," Adelaide said. "If he'd wanted to hurt you, he could have sold the entire paper right out from under you or left it all to Mary." She held his gaze. "With the two-month time frame, he gave us a chance *and* a way out. Isn't it possible he regretted what he'd done to his family?"

"What if he did? It doesn't change anything, except maybe he got to die in peace," he said, his tone bitter.

"Oh, Charles, if your father truly repented, then he'd have enormous remorse." She sighed. "I'm heartsick he used my mother as an excuse to hurt you and your family. I wish I could undo that, but I can't." She took a deep breath. "Any more than I can change the fact my mother couldn't love life, couldn't love me . . . or maybe she just couldn't show it." Trying to make him understand, her voice rose, filled with earnestness. "We aren't responsible for their choices. You'll never forget what your father did, but you can forgive."

"Forgive *him?*" Charles hurled the grooming brush across the livery and it thudded against a post, falling into a pile of straw. "I can't."

"With God's help, you *can* forgive. You can do anything."

"Did it ever occur to you God might not want to help me? God knows me better than you do, Addie. I'm not His man."

Charles had said something like this before. "Why do you say that?"

He turned his back to her. "God can't approve of a man like me. There are things you don't know. Things I can't tell you."

She laid a palm on the back of his head, letting her fingers settle into his thick hair. "You can tell me anything. Anything, Charles."

He didn't speak, didn't even look at her. She'd done her best. She had nothing left to say. Her hand fell away and her throat constricted. She could barely get out, "I'm leaving now."

Charles touched her hand, halting her. "I'll be there tomorrow with the committee.

I want you to have Emma and William. You know that, don't you?"

"I know." She pressed a hand to her chest. "Until you let God in and learn to forgive, you won't be able to move beyond your past."

"Can't we at least —"

"No!" She started for the door. "Nothing has changed between us, Charles. Nothing at all."

CHAPTER NINETEEN

In the uneasy silence the ticking pendulum of the clock echoed off the courtroom walls. Dwarfed by the imposing two-story coffered ceiling, Adelaide struggled to keep her composure. Across from her, Charles leaned against the witness stand. The rest of the committee sat at the prosecutor's table, staring at her, their eyes hard and suspicious.

The courtroom, the only room available for their meeting, had seemed a fitting place to mete out justice to Ed Drummond, but instead, Adelaide appeared to be the one on trial.

Her gaze darted to the cased walnut clock, its hands pointing to half past two. With each tick, her anxiety grew until her breathing grew rapid and shallow, bringing an odd tingling to her limbs.

Where was Frances?

Mr. Paul's pocket watch clicked shut. "Miss Crum, I don't know what game you're playing, but I, for one, am tired of it."

These men were angry, ready to pounce. "It's not a game, Mr. Paul. Mrs. Drummond wants to disclose Ed's abuse of her and William."

Mr. Paul scowled. "So you say, but I don't see her."

"Something must have detained Frances," Adelaide said, trying to delay. "I'm sure she'll arrive shortly."

Despite her words, Adelaide wasn't sure of anything and shot another glance at the timepiece. But clock watching didn't make Frances materialize. Had Frances lost her courage and changed her mind? Had Ed learned of her plan and stopped her?

Adelaide closed her eyes and prayed harder for Frances's arrival, her foot jiggling in rhythm to the ticking clock.

Charles folded his arms over his chest. "Mrs. Drummond isn't that late. We'll wait."

Mr. Sparks scowled at Charles. "Graves, you've let this woman use *The Ledger* to spread her rebellion and disrupt the harmony of our little town. And now she claims the wife of one of our upstanding citizens is going to condemn her own husband." He snorted. "She's using this committee —"

"She's doing nothing of the kind."

Charles's gaze traveled around the group. "Gentlemen, let's not take chances with a child's life. Until we're assured of William's safety, the boy should be removed from the Drummond home."

Grateful to Charles for standing up to the others, Adelaide gave him a wan smile.

Mr. Wylie shook his head. "Without Mrs. Drummond's testimony, there's no reason to disrupt William's life."

"Frances said she would be here," Adelaide spoke up. "Her husband must have caught on —"

"And what, killed her?" Mr. Wylie leaned his chin on fisted hands, hunching his powerful shoulders, his tone scathing. "My, my, Miss Crum, you do have an active imagination."

Bile rose in Adelaide's throat, leaving behind the acrid taste of fear. "Oh, I hope not."

"You'd better hope he *has.* Because, as things stand now, we won't let Emma remain with you, a woman who'd accuse an innocent man to serve her own purposes."

Adelaide felt the blood drain from her face and the room dipped slightly. Take Emma? *Oh, God, help me.*

Charles crossed to the table, crimson coloring his neck. "Miss Crum doesn't lie.

If she says Mrs. Drummond asked her to set up this meeting, then it's true."

Mr. Sparks's eyes narrowed. "Spoken like a suitor, Graves."

Adelaide gasped and clutched her seat for support. "It's not like that."

Mr. Sparks tapped a pencil on the table in front of him like a gavel. "Perhaps not, but from what Roscoe Sullivan has told this committee, and from what I've seen with my own eyes, you two are, shall I say, *very* friendly? One could even say wantonly."

"Mr. Graves has been seen leaving your shop after hours, Miss Crum," Mr. Paul said, rising from the prosecutor's table. He strolled past her, speaking with eloquence as if addressing a jury. "Surely, women's hats aren't the draw."

Charles stepped in front of Mr. Paul. "You owe the lady an apology, Paul. Miss Crum is a woman of virtue. I won't allow you to imply otherwise."

No apology came from Thaddeus Paul's narrowed lips, but he scuttled back to the table.

How could Mr. Paul, who'd known her most of her life, believe her a loose woman? Had the times she'd questioned the committee and her suffrage views fueled this reaction? Or was he retaliating for her reporting Jacob to the sheriff?

Adelaide rose. "I can't believe you'd imply I'm lying and Mr. Graves is in cahoots with me." She took a deep calming breath. "When all you need to do is ask Sheriff Rogers to ride out to the Drummond farm and make sure Frances and William are safe."

"The sheriff doesn't have time to snoop into the lives of decent citizens, any more than we do. We have businesses and farms to run." Mr. Wylie turned to Charles. "Well, unless *you* have time for such foolishness, Graves. From what I hear, the paper is losing subscribers."

Adelaide's gaze flew to Charles and read the truth of Mr. Wylie's words in his face. Hadn't she heard the same from others in town? Her own shop suffered for a lack of business thanks to her attempt to make change in a town that viewed change as anarchy.

Mr. Wylie spoke a few whispered words to Mr. Sparks and Mr. Paul. The men nodded and folded their hands. Mr. Wylie rose. "The committee has decided how to proceed."

Charles frowned. "I wasn't consulted."

Mr. Sparks kept his gaze on Adelaide, ignoring Charles. "We feel Miss Crum isn't the proper influence on a young girl."

Charles threw up his hands. "That's ridiculous!"

"Emma will be returned to the Drummond home today," Mr. Sparks continued.

Adelaide's knees buckled and she dropped into the nearest chair, fighting for control. *God, help me keep Emma safe.* "Emma is afraid of Ed Drummond. Leave her with me until the sheriff investigates."

Mr. Sparks settled onto the edge of the table. "You knew putting Emma in your care was a temporary solution."

Memories of Emma's nightmares stomped through Adelaide's mind. To remove the child from her home would be cruel. These weren't cruel men, not really. They just didn't see the truth.

"Please, don't take Emma to the Drummonds'. Leave her with me until you find her a new home."

"The Drummonds are her guardians," Mr. Paul said. "*If* Mrs. Drummond supports your story, then we'll relocate the children."

Emma would be yanked from her arms and thrust into the terror-filled world of Charles's childhood and she couldn't find the words to stop it. "Frances won't admit her husband's abuse in front of him. She's afraid of Ed."

Charles laid a steadying hand on her shoulder. The others took note of his touch, their faces set in lines of disapproval at the small act of kindness.

"Miss Crum is right. Mrs. Drummond won't speak openly in front of her husband. Don't risk leaving the children there."

Mr. Wylie sighed. "I can't believe Ed would hurt anyone. I've known him for years."

Charles pivoted to Mr. Wylie. "My father was a churchgoer, who battered, bruised and broke the bones of his wife and two sons," he said, his voice hoarse with emotion. "No one realized it, or if they did, they closed their eyes. Please believe me in this. You don't know what goes on behind closed doors."

The pain of the admission plain on his face, Charles stood silent. No one spoke. Adelaide wanted to soothe what his openness had cost him, but she didn't dare, not with the suspicions the committee had already voiced.

"Talk to Sheriff Rogers. But whatever you do, don't take Emma to the Drummonds," Charles said in a pleading tone.

Mr. Paul cleared his throat. "All right, we'll talk to the sheriff and bring the Drummonds in here for a meeting. See what they

370

have to say. But let me make it clear, Miss Crum. Emma will no longer be staying with you."

Adelaide stiffened. "What gives you the right to make that decision?"

"We're the local arm of the Children's Aid Society. Once this is settled, we'll be in contact with Mr. Fry."

"At the distribution, Mr. Fry said the children could refuse to go with anyone they didn't trust. Emma won't go back willingly. If you won't let her stay with me, then put her with Laura Larson's family. Emma will feel safe there."

"We'll take that into consideration," Mr. Wylie said, "though we only have your word that Emma doesn't want to return to the Drummonds and her brother."

"Ask Emma where she wants to go. Ask her!"

"We'll talk to the child, when we pick her up from school."

Tears spilled down her cheeks. "Please, let me get her so I can tell her goodbye. Prepare her," she begged. "I won't cause any trouble."

"Goodbyes will only upset the child." Mr. Sparks thrust his hands into his pockets. "We're acting in Emma's best interest."

Charles scowled. "This is a travesty! You

371

think you know what's best for a little girl you've barely met? Until you've gotten to the bottom of this, leave her with Miss Crum. As a member of the committee, I —"

"You are no longer a member of the committee, Charles."

"What are you saying?"

"You've lost your objectivity where —" Mr. Sparks's gaze moved to Adelaide "— Emma is concerned."

The banker turned to Adelaide. "Don't attempt to see or take Emma out of school. In your emotional state, you'll frighten her."

Mr. Paul leaned toward her, his gaze issuing a sharp warning. "If you refuse to abide by our decision, you will force us to place Emma in another community."

Adelaide gasped. If they did that, she'd never see Emma again. With a shaky hand, Adelaide wiped her eyes.

"The matter is settled," Mr. Wylie said. "Meeting adjourned."

With no hope of changing their minds, Adelaide watched the men walk to the door, each step stomping on her heart until the intensity of the pain all but crushed her.

She looked at the defense table. She and Charles should have sat there. They'd been accused of lying and worse. Three men had proclaimed themselves judge and jury, grabbing the power of the bench, giving no thought on how the verdict would frighten an innocent child. Neither had they acted swiftly to protect a wife and child from abuse.

Through the window, against the overcast sky, tree branches danced in the rising wind. In the distance, she heard the rumble of thunder. A storm brewed, and Emma didn't have an umbrella . . .

A sob pushed against her throat. If these men had their way, she wouldn't see Emma again. Wouldn't hold that precious child in her arms, wouldn't share the love they'd just learned to speak. If these men had their way, she'd never teach Emma a new song on the piano or help her stitch silk flowers on a hat. If these men had their way, she didn't know how she'd survive.

Tears spilled down her face and onto the fabric of her dress, marring the silk with the dark stain of loss.

Charles came up beside where she sat and handed her a handkerchief.

"You warned me, Charles," she said, wiping her eyes. "The suffrage articles cost me Emma. I didn't believe my neighbors would let politics destroy their sense of fairness."

He gave her shoulder a squeeze. "It's not

over yet, Addie." He tugged her to her feet and enfolded her in his arms.

She pulled away from him. "It's ironic when we're no longer seeing each other that gossip is flying through town like tumbleweeds in a windstorm."

The clock tolled the hour. Adelaide's ice-cold hands twisted. "I'm afraid something awful has happened to Frances," she said, her voice trembling. "I've got to check on her."

Charles lifted her chin and his gaze bored into hers. "Addie, no matter what, don't go to the Drummond farm."

She squared her shoulders, ready to disagree.

"Please," he added, softly. "Until we see what Ed is up to, stay with Laura."

Shaking her head, Adelaide walked to the rail. "I won't put Laura's family in the midst of this. I can take care of myself."

He came after her and brushed away a tendril of hair that had escaped her chignon. "Adelaide Crum, you are the most stubborn woman I've ever known." A smile softened his words.

Oh, Charles, I've missed that smile.

But she only said, "I've had to be."

"So you have." He touched her cheek. "I miss you."

Why did he keep touching her? Didn't he know his smallest contact triggered a longing that increased her pain? And she'd reached her limit? "But that doesn't change anything, does it?"

His hand fell away. "Let me see you."

"Knowing there's no point, there's no future for us?" Her heart squeezed in her chest, aware her next words would bring another loss. First Emma and now Charles, the two people she loved most in the world. "No, I won't see you."

Charles's dark eyes clouded, with regret or with yearning? Adelaide didn't know. She was tired of struggling to understand. If God meant them to be together, then He would have to work it out. She had nothing else to give.

He stepped closer and took her gloved hand, then rubbed it with his. "Can we call a truce? Concentrate on keeping you and the children safe without tying anything more to it."

She shrugged, as if she didn't care. She could pretend with the best of them. "I believe Ed Drummond finally has you worried. Now that it's too late, you're trying to put a tiny bandage on a gaping wound."

His brow furrowed. "I don't understand."

"They're taking Emma away from me,

Charles! Why? Because I'm single. Isn't that what it comes down to? And all you can worry about is that Ed Drummond will hurt me, but you've hurt me more than he ever could!"

Before he could respond, Adelaide walked out of the courtroom, away from Charles, from his inability to change. But in her heart, she knew her being single wasn't the only reason they'd taken Emma. The columns she'd written had made matters worse, not only for her and Emma, but for Frances, too.

Adelaide would never forgive herself if Frances had paid a price for her need to speak out.

Alone in the courtroom, Charles stood with his back to the judge's bench. Lightning flashed and rain beat against the windowpanes. Outside a storm raged, but nothing like the storm inside him. He'd let Adelaide and Emma down, when they needed him most. But if Addie truly knew him, she'd never agree to take his name.

Deep in the abyss of his mind, a memory clawed its way to the surface and demanded a hearing. This time Charles couldn't stop it. He didn't even try.

Recalling that night, a lifetime ago, held

him captive; a dark and inexcusable deed kept him in a prison without bars.

He'd come home from his after-school job to find his father beating his mother for the hundredth time. Except this time, Pa wasn't slurring his words or swaying on his feet.

This time, Pa was stone-cold sober.

Ma cowered on the floor, begging him to stop, apologizing for some pitiful infraction of Pa's ever-changing rules.

Inside him something as thin as a twig gave way, something that had held tenuous control over the rage, rage that had been building and building and building for years.

He hurled himself at his pa, swinging fists, grabbing Pa's throat, not seeing, not thinking, only wanting him to stop.

He hadn't heard Ma begging him to release his hold. Hadn't been aware of Pa's hands grasping at his arms, first strong, then . . . weaker and weaker.

He heard nothing but all those years of screams. All those nights he stood by, a helpless child, weeping and wondering when his turn would come.

If Sam hadn't returned and pulled him off in time, Charles knew without a doubt he would have killed his father that night. A sob escaped his throat. What kind of man wouldn't stop even after his father had gone limp under his squeezing hands?

The answer was clear — a man *like* his father, a man with a deadly temper, a man with whom God could have no relationship.

He could never marry Addie. Never be a father to Emma or William. Never enter God's house and taint it with his presence.

He slid to the floor. "Oh, God. Help me."

But once again, Heaven remained silent.

Charles buried his face in his arms and wept.

That evening, Charles trekked from Laura's house toward Addie's shop. The afternoon rain had stopped, leaving a light, clean scent to the air, in sharp contrast to his dismal mood.

Roscoe had all but shut down Addie's business because of what he'd called that spinster's meddling and now, thanks to the committee, Addie had lost Emma. Though all those worries weighed on him, Charles's main concern was keeping Addie safe.

Mercifully, the committee had decided to keep Emma in town — for now — which guaranteed Addie wouldn't ride out to the Drummond house. Tomorrow, Wylie, Sparks and Paul would meet with the Drummonds. If, as he suspected, Frances had been harmed, then the committee would finally be roused out of its complacency.

In some ways, he couldn't blame the others. Until recently, he hadn't seen Ed Drummond as a dangerous man.

With the key Addie had given him earlier, Charles unlocked the door to her shop. She sat at the small table in the center of the showroom facing the door. When he entered, her head snapped up. But then seeing him, she bowed over an open Bible, reading the Scriptures while running a finger along the pink ribbon on a small straw bonnet she held in her hand. Emma's hat.

His gut knotted in anger. The committee had taken Emma, unconcerned about Addie's suffering. He'd hurt her, too, more times than he wanted to remember. But through it all, she prayed, read her Bible, trusted in God.

Addie had once told him God had given her Emma. Well, if He had, He'd also taken the little girl away.

Charles walked to the table. She looked up with dry eyes, crisscrossed with tiny veins of red, evidence she'd been crying. He had news he hoped would bring a smile, though without Emma, he knew Addie's heart had broken.

He cleared his throat. "I checked on Emma."

"How is she?"

"Baking cookies with Laura and looking happy. She asked me to tell you, she's saving you some cookies."

Her eyes glistened. "I want to slip over there to see her, but the committee could be watching the house."

"I wouldn't put it past them." He fingered the brim of his hat. "Late this afternoon, I rode out to the Drummond place. Ed blocked the door and claimed Frances was lying down with a headache. It would have taken a fistfight to get past him. With William there, I couldn't risk that." Before she could ask, he said, "William looked fine. One good thing — we know Ed's at home, at least around five o'clock."

"Did the sheriff go with you?"

"He's been on County business all day, something about tax rolls. Right now, he's over at the Reilly saloon, stopping a fistfight. He'll be watching your place tonight, too."

Her face a mask of misery, Addie fingered the pages of the Bible. He wanted to pull her into his arms, hold her and comfort her.

But she'd made it clear she no longer wanted that from him.

Want it or not, she needed it. He took her hand. "Come here," he said softly and tugged her to her feet. She burrowed into his arms, rocking him back on his heels.

"Emma's fine. I know how you miss her. But until we see what Drummond will do, it's good she's not here."

She pulled back and lifted a questioning gaze.

"I don't want to alarm you, but I don't believe for a minute Frances had a headache, unless Ed gave it to her."

"I'm afraid for Frances and William."

"I know," he crooned, tightening his grip. "Maybe once the committee talks to Frances, they'll let you keep Emma."

Addie pulled away. "You don't really believe that, do you?"

He couldn't meet her gaze.

She kissed his cheek. "Thank you for not agreeing. You're a good man."

His throat tightened. He knew he wasn't a good man, but he treasured her words. "I'll check upstairs."

She nodded, then walked to the counter and picked up a partially finished hat.

Charles climbed the steps for the last time and walked into each room where shadowed memories paraded through his mind. Memories of meals shared in this kitchen. Of Emma plunking at the piano in the parlor while he'd teased Addie about her

Jack-induced willies. Here, in Emma's room, of him and Addie soothing her nightmare with a lullaby.

He stepped to Addie's room, the one room he'd never seen. Neat as a pin, like the rest, his gaze roamed over the ruffled curtains at the window, the brush and comb set on the dresser, the white bowl and pitcher on the washstand. Eyes stinging, he fingered the feathered bird atop the hat that lay on the seat of a rocker, recalling their banter on the first day she'd worn it.

In the hall, he took one last look at the rooms that had made him feel more at home than any place he'd ever been.

Knowing he wouldn't be back slowed his step, but only for a moment. He had a job to do. He headed down the stairs.

Addie sat where he'd left her. With a thimble, she pushed a shiny needle through two layers of heavy felt joining the brim and crown of a hat.

He stopped, frozen by the image of her, absorbing her profile, the tilt of her neck, the sense of her inner strength he admired. But *that* strength would be no match for Ed Drummond.

He thought of losing her, thought of his world without Addie in it, and his heart tripped in his chest. How could he survive?

What kind of place would this town be without Addie?

He reached the bottom, walked to the back and checked the door and window, then returned to the showroom. "Whether you like it or not, I'm standing watch down here tonight."

"I've told you that's not an option. People will talk."

"Let them!"

"Hasn't enough damage been done by gossip?"

Tentacles of guilt clutched at Charles's throat. If he hadn't told Roscoe he suspected Ed had vandalized Addie's shop, would the committee have taken Emma? If he had refused to publish her essays, would she be in this mess?

He kissed her forehead. "You won't answer the door to anyone? Not even me?"

She looked up and gave a feeble grin. "Especially not you."

"Good."

Her brow furrowed. "Why not you?"

"If somehow Drummond overpowered me, he could use me to get to you. Promise, you won't let anyone in, not me, not anyone."

She nodded.

"Really, Addie?"

"Yes, I promise."

Sudden tears welled in his eyes. He made a big production of digging in his pocket for her key and then handed it to her. "Walk me to the door and lock it behind me."

Her face pale and drawn, Addie rose, a woman he couldn't marry but a woman he would protect, at all costs.

At the door, she touched his arm. "Be careful," she said softly, her gaze traveling his features. "I'm praying for you."

Her concern for him ripped at his shaky composure and he could only nod. He slipped out and waited until he heard the click of the lock behind him.

He checked the street and alley. Seeing nothing unusual, he crossed to *The Ledger* and let himself in, tracking mud on the wooden floor. If Addie saw this, she'd scold him for not wiping his feet. If only all they had to concern themselves with was a little dirt.

Earlier, Sheriff Rogers had been called away to the saloon, disrupting their speculation about whether Drummond would come after Addie tonight. Charles hadn't laid eyes on Rogers since.

He'd tried to pray for her safety, but his childhood had taught him he couldn't count on God.

It was up to him and him alone to protect Addie.

In the back room, he squatted before the steel safe, and rotated the dial, four right, two left, six right, counting the clicks with each turn until he heard the lock open. Inside, he found what he sought and pulled away the soft cloth. In the glow from the gaslight, the pistol's barrel gleamed.

He fingered the smooth ivory-inlaid butt, surprisingly beautiful for an instrument of death.

Convinced every man needed a gun to protect what was his, Sam had given it to him for his birthday a few years back. Charles had never fired it at anything more than a target.

Yet, tonight, the next night — some night — that would change. Ed would come after Addie. And Charles would be waiting.

Grabbing a box of ammunition and his gun belt, he picked up the handgun and closed the six-inch-thick door, giving the dial a twirl. He walked to the cot and sat. He opened the chamber of his gun and inserted the first bullet, then another, until he'd filled each slot. Slipping the gun into its holster, he rose and buckled the belt, shoving it down on his hips.

With his right hand hanging loose over

the holster, Charles whipped out the gun, aiming at a spot on the wall about the height of Ed Drummond's heart. If forced to use the gun, he hoped the target practice in Cincinnati wouldn't fail him.

Charles lowered the gaslight, walked out of the room, through the dark office, to the main door. In the doorway, he scanned the deserted street. A horse, tied to a hitching post down the way, nickered, eager to return to a comfortable stall. In front of Addie's shop, a cat promenaded down the walk, then sprang at something Charles couldn't see. Music from the honky-tonk piano drifted on the night air. How odd to find everything looking normal when at any moment this peaceful scene might erupt in violence.

Addie's shop was dark. Overhead he spotted the light in her bedroom. He hoped she could sleep. If only he'd overruled her and stayed below in the shop. But that wasn't Addie's way.

Dear, sweet Addie with her adherence to her impeccable morals and a stubborn streak as wide as the Ohio River in spring. She had spunk, hope and a heart the size of Texas — and wonder of wonders, faith in him.

Tonight he wouldn't let her down. And

tomorrow, well, if they got that far, he'd help her get the children. He needed her back in his life, had missed her every moment of every day since they'd been apart. He hadn't realized what a hollow man he'd been before he'd met her. How much she'd brought to his life, until he'd lost it.

He slipped across the street, moved toward the back of her building, his gaze darting from shadow to shadow, alert to any sound, searching for trouble. Searching for Drummond.

He saw no one, yet he couldn't shake a sense of evil, heavy and thick. He positioned himself between her building and the next. From here, he could see both front and back of her shop.

He waited, his emotions galloping between hot fear and cold dread, yet certain that if he had to, tonight he could kill.

CHAPTER TWENTY

Minutes stretched into hours. The sheriff had yet to appear. Charles ran a hand across his face, the rough stubble scratching against his palm, more tired than he'd ever been in his life. Each eyelid seemed to weigh a pound. With a fist, he rubbed his eyes, gritty from lack of sleep. He was running out of steam. If he didn't get some coffee soon, he would be asleep on his feet. At the paper, a pot of coffee brewed so long ago it could wake the dead, sat on the stove.

He took another look around before heading across the street to *The Ledger.* He'd be gone for two minutes. Nothing could happen to Addie in that length of time.

Adelaide jerked awake. Her heartbeat pounded at her temples, echoed in her ears while she held her breath, listening. An odor smacked her in the stomach.

Pungent, sickly sweet. Kerosene.

Silently, she slipped out of bed, shoved her arms into the sleeves of her wrapper, and then edged toward the door. Easing it ajar, she peered into the dark hall. The smell seared her nostrils, slithered down her throat. Then from below came a noise. Mind-numbing panic seized her limbs and she couldn't move.

Ed's in the shop. God, help me. He's going to burn it down around me.

A faint creak from downstairs caused the tiny hairs on her neck to stand up. Another creak.

He's coming. He's coming up the stairs.
For me.

Adrenaline shot through her body. Ed Drummond wouldn't burn her alive, wouldn't beat her senseless without a fight.

Holding her breath, Adelaide slid through the narrow opening on soundless feet. Then she pressed her back to the wall and glided down the ebony shadowed hall, avoiding the small table ahead, the rug farther down that liked to catch her toes. In the shadows, she could make out the doorway to the parlor. If she could reach the kitchen, she'd escape down the back stairs to the yard. From there she could run to safety. To Charles.

She thanked God for the darkness of the hall, and her navy wrapper that concealed a white nightdress, a sure beacon for Ed.

Down the hall, a door squeaked. Emma's room. Thank God, Emma slept at Laura's.

Heart pounding so loudly in her ears that Ed must surely hear it, Adelaide clamped a hand to her mouth, stifling an urge to scream. She heard heavy breathing now. He was closer. He would be in her room next, and when he saw her empty bed, he'd realize he had no need to move quietly.

And he'd come running.

Yet, Adelaide slipped along the wall, not daring to make any sudden moves that might draw his eye.

At last, she reached the kitchen and felt for the butcher knife she kept near the sink. She grabbed the fat handle. Then the sound of furniture crashing, loud cursing, stilled her hand. Feet pounded through the hall. And then, a second later, she heard "You're dead, missy!"

Move, Adelaide. Move!

Holding the knife, she raced for the back door. Her free hand shot out and grasped the knob. She yanked, but the door didn't budge. With shaking fingers, she fumbled with the bolt and, finally getting it to turn, flung open the door and sprinted onto the back landing.

Fresh air burst into her lungs. Before she

could finish the breath, he jerked it out of her. Her collar was held firmly in Ed's grasp, yanking her back. To him.

"Got ya now!"

Screaming, Adelaide spun, wiggled out of her wrapper and plunged down the stairs. The knife slipped from her hands, clattering down the steps. Heavy work boots clomped down after her. She jumped from the last few steps to the ground and ran. Expletives exploded behind her.

She tore blindly across the yard. Her lungs burned, her muscles shrieked, her heart thundered, each step a prayer.

She slammed into something solid and familiar. *Charles.*

"Addie!" Charles shoved her behind him seconds before Ed threw himself at him. The men tumbled to the ground. Thudding fists and shouted curses pierced the night air.

They rolled, a tangle of arms and legs, pounding flesh against bone. Ed was heavier and filled with the lethal power of hate. Charles would surely die. Their grunts and groans scrambled her mind.

"Lord God in Heaven, save Charles!"

Struggling to think, her heart pumped wildly in her chest. And then she knew. *The knife, find the knife.*

She sprinted to the stairs and scampered up, searching in the faint moonlight. Where? Where had she dropped it? She retraced her steps. "Please, God, please, help me!"

And then, at the bottom of the steps, she spotted a glint of steel. She scuttled down and snatched the knife, then ran across the lawn, slipping on the wet grass, to where the men raged and warred.

On their feet now, they jabbed and ducked, swerved and confronted in some macabre dance while Charles struggled to reach the gun on his hip. Charles had a gun?

Ed's hand whipped out, grabbed Charles's throat, then squeezed, laughing while Charles's fingers clawed at Ed's hands, eyes popping, body jerking, struggling against the monster.

Ed twisted position, tightening his grip. Charles was flailing, Ed rejoicing.

She wouldn't let Charles die.

Adelaide circled them, looking for an opening, a position at Ed's back, praying for accuracy. She took a great gulp of air, trying to ease her breathing. *Steady.* If either of them moved, she'd miss, or worse — hit Charles.

The moon slid from behind a cloud, washing light over the men. Adelaide raised the knife high above her, poised, aiming for Ed's back. Ed swore and threw up an arm. Before she could strike, Charles pivoted, lifted his knee and caught Ed in the groin. Ed crumpled to the ground, rolling, moaning, cursing.

Charles raced to Adelaide's side.

Charles's throat throbbed, his eyes stung. Shoulders heaving, he pulled Addie to him. Each gasping breath burned his lungs, tore at his ribs. He shoved words from his mouth. "Are . . . you . . . all right?"

"Yes! Are you?"

Dragging in air, he nodded. Gently, he pried her fingers from the death grip she had on the knife and then dropped the weapon at their feet. Covering the blade with the heel of a boot, he gathered her into his arms and pulled her close. "Thank God . . . you're . . . safe."

A movement. Drummond crouched, ready to spring. Charles shoved Addie away and in an instant, grabbed Ed's outstretched arm, pulling it up and back behind him with a jerk. Ed screamed in pain and crumpled face-first onto the ground.

Whipping his gun from the holster, Charles stood over him, cocked the gun and raised the barrel until he'd leveled the sights with Ed's head.

Writing on the ground, Ed twisted around and saw the barrel. He threw up his hands. "Don't shoot! Have mercy!"

Charles curled his finger around the trigger. One shot. That's all it would take to rid the town — the world — of this demon. His finger tensed. The slightest pressure and Ed would die.

A bead of sweat slipped down Charles's palm. Blood hammered his temples. Rage distorted his eyesight. A voice pounded in his head. Kill him. Kill him. *Kill him.*

From deep inside, another voice echoed in his skull. *Then you're no different than he is, no different than your father.*

Charles shook his head, clearing his vision. Drummond had shown no mercy to Addie, or Sarah, or Frances.

But Charles wasn't God — he wasn't anyone's personal judge and jury. He relaxed his finger. The gun dropped into place in his holster. He couldn't shoot Drummond, an unarmed man, no matter how much he deserved killing. Unless he had no other choice, Charles didn't have it in him to take a life. But Ed would pay for his crimes. Charles would see to that.

Sheriff Rogers, gun drawn, ran from the shadows. "What happened here?"

Charles grabbed Ed's collar, pulling him

to his feet. "Drummond tried to kill Adelaide, Sheriff."

"He attacked me!" Ed screamed, twisting in Charles's grip.

The click of the sheriff's gun being cocked issued its own warning. "That's enough out of you, Drummond. Raise 'em." In the sights of the sheriff's gun, Ed's hands shot skyward. "Charles, check him for a weapon."

Charles moved behind Drummond. The odor of kerosene filled his nostrils. Like a match under dry kindling, the stench of Drummond's intentions sparked a fury inside him. "You coward! You were going to burn her out."

"She had it coming! Turning a man's wife against him, sticking her nose into my business —"

"Like Sarah?" Sheriff Rogers asked.

"I never killed Sarah." Drummond twisted around to face the sheriff. "You ain't got proof I did."

Charles ran his hands over Drummond's shirt and down to the man's pockets. Inside the right rear pocket his fingers closed around something, something that pulsated in Charles's gut with the force of a sledgehammer.

In the moonlight with a balmy breeze

lending a benign feel to the night air, a ghoulish sight hung from Charles's outstretched hand.

A garrote.

Adelaide gasped. Rogers handed his pistol to Charles and cuffed Drummond's hands behind his back. Charles tossed the cord to the sheriff.

"You're mighty fond of them things, Drummond. Planning on killing Miss Crum with this? Then incinerating the place to make it look like an accident?"

"That busybody wants to take all I have — the orphans, my reputation, my wife. Can't you see? I couldn't let her do that."

"Tell it to a judge and jury." The sheriff pocketed the garrote, muttering under his breath. Then he retrieved his gun and aimed it at Drummond. "Better get this scum to the jail before I'm tempted to wipe my boots with him."

He turned to Charles and Adelaide. "I took a brawler with a broken hand over to the doc's a moment ago." He jerked his head toward Ed. "His missus is there. She's taken quite a beating."

Addie slumped against Charles. "How bad is she?"

"Doc isn't sure she'll make it."

Addie moaned. "What about William?"

"William brought her in. Somehow he got Frances in the wagon. He's fine." Sheriff Rogers jerked up Drummond's head by his hair and shoved his face close. "Real tough guy, aren't you, Drummond, going after children and womenfolk?"

"If Frances had stayed home where she belonged, my boy wouldn't be dead."

Adelaide jerked out of Charles's arms and moved toward Ed. "How dare you blame Frances for Eddie's death. It was an accident." She gasped. "Or was it? Could you have set fire to your own son?"

Ed's staggered. "Kill . . . my boy? Don't you see? My boy's death killed me." Ed's body shook with sobs.

"How could you beat Frances, the woman who bore that child?"

Ed's lip curled. "She was planning to leave. Take my boy and move in with Sarah. I kept my family together . . . the only way I knew how. Frances always fought everything I said, everything I did. And you . . ." He pointed to Addie. "You egged her on."

"I've heard all I can stomach." Pulling Drummond along by the arm, the sheriff strode out of the yard, calling over his shoulder. "I'll need your statements. Tomorrow's soon enough."

Relief flooded Charles, then bone-numbing fatigue. He tugged Addie close. Drummond would be in jail where he belonged. He couldn't harm Addie or Emma or William ever again.

"I could have lost you," he murmured in her ear, his voice raspy. The magnitude of that possibility careened through him like a barbed arrow, hitting bone, marrow and muscle and lodging near his heart.

He breathed in the scent of her hair hanging loose about her shoulders, breathed in her goodness, the goodness he'd been in search of his entire life. Addie cared for him more than he deserved. She fought for what she believed in. And she believed in him.

Adelaide could hear Charles moving around the apartment, methodically opening the windows, releasing the stench of kerosene. Taking charge. On any other day, she would have helped, but her muscles had turned to jelly.

Charles returned to the kitchen, intent on making tea. He fumbled around in the cupboard, muttering under his breath.

"It's in the left door of the cabinet, in front."

"Thanks."

A few minutes later he handed her a steaming cup of tea. "Drink up. It'll help get rid of the shakes."

Adelaide took the cup, grasping its warmth like a lifeline. Her hand trembled and drops of the liquid splashed across her fingers, but she drank deeply, easing the chill that facing death had seeped into her bones.

"Will you be all right for a minute?" he asked.

She nodded.

"I want to open the back door of the shop." He gave her shoulder a squeeze, and then took the stairs at a run.

Adelaide put the cup on the table and leaned against the chair. Icy fingers gripped her heart. If Charles hadn't overpowered Ed, could she have stabbed him? From somewhere deep inside came the certainty that in self-defense or to save Charles, she could have killed — or died trying.

Closing her eyes, she thanked God she'd never have to know. She asked the Almighty to be with Doc Lawrence, to help him ease Frances's pain and save her life, if it wasn't too late.

What a hard life Frances had endured. First losing her only child, then the murder of her mother, now this severe beating.

Charles returned to the kitchen and paused in the doorway. Even battered and bruised, he looked solid, trustworthy, in control. Charles, the man she loved. His smile dazzled her. His voice soothed her. Tension slipped off her shoulders and her breathing slowed — all because Charles stood nearby.

"I found an empty can of kerosene near the back —" He glanced at her and stopped.

Without warning, a deluge of tears flowed down her face. Charles dropped to his knees at her feet and took her hand in his. "What is it?"

"I feel responsible for what happened to Frances." She covered her mouth with a fist. "When she asked to talk to the committee, I should've insisted she stay in town with me." Her voice broke. "Instead, I thought only of myself."

"You weren't thinking of yourself — you were thinking of William." He rose, tugging her with him, drawing her into the comfort of his arms. "Ed would have gotten to Frances, no matter what you did, or what the sheriff tried to do. The man's deranged." He leaned back, cupped her chin with his hand. "Frances did what she did for William, not for you."

With the pads of his thumbs, he gently brushed the tears away and then kissed her cheeks, the tip of her nose and each eyelid. His words and the touch of his lips brought healing, a blessed release from self-blame.

"My brave Addie."

"Brave?" Her voice shook. "Me?"

"You're the bravest woman I know. I saw you with that knife, ready to enter the fray. I've never been so scared."

She shivered. "He was trying to . . . to kill you."

Charles pulled her tight against him. A moan tore from his throat. "Oh, Addie, I could have lost you."

She loved Charles for his courage, for the risks he'd taken to protect her. For being a loving man, though he didn't believe that yet. She started to say she loved him, but then bit back the words. She wouldn't say them just because they'd shared this terrifying night.

Charles stepped back and met her gaze. "We're alive, Addie. We've survived Ed, and we'll survive the trouble in this town. Marry me. I'll see that you get Emma and William. I'll give you everything you ever wanted — a home, a family."

She heard the sweet words and wanted to say yes. He had been in her heart since the first day she'd walked across the street after placing that ad. Her feelings for him had grown until she couldn't imagine life without him. But she couldn't marry him, not without the three little words he did not say.

If she forced his hand, perhaps he would. "What about love?"

A shuttered look came over his face. "I want to, but, I don't know what love is. Something's missing . . . inside. But —"

Her heart plunged. "No buts, Charles." She couldn't marry him and relegate herself to a life half-full. "I won't settle for less than love."

Tears collected in his eyes. "I can't survive being separated from you. Please say that's enough."

"I wish it were." She sighed. "No, Charles, I won't marry you." The finality of her words struck like a bolt of lightning, searing her heart.

"If we're married, we might be able to have Emma and William. That's the only way you'll get the children. Don't you see that?"

His words stung and she moved past him. "That's probably true. But what kind of a marriage would that be for me? For you? For the children?" Her heart lurched into her throat. "You're afraid to love. You can't even speak the word. You can't forgive God for your past, can't worship. You're stuck

402

back there, Charles. Well, I'm looking to the future."

He flinched. "Addie . . . I don't know what to say."

She met his gaze, tried to see what truths were hidden in the depths of those dark pools. "You make your living with words and now you can't speak the words that will open your heart to me."

"I'm not like you."

"People can change. I have. Before I asked for one of the orphans, before I expressed my views in the paper, I didn't speak up on issues that mattered to me. And you know what? I like the new me. You may not realize how much you've helped me change. Whether you meant to or not."

"You've always been strong."

"I get my strength from God, from His word, from worshipping in His house. I can't marry a man who won't trust God and I won't settle for a loveless marriage, even for a child." Her voice broke. "E-even for Emma." She squared her shoulders. "I won't end up like my mother."

"I wouldn't leave like your father did." He took her hand. "If you'll marry me, I'll be committed to our marriage."

"I believe you. You'd stick by me. You'd fill a seat at the table, take care of the hundreds of details a husband would. And day by day I would die in tiny increments, waiting for the words that might never come."

"What do you want from me?"

As if he didn't know. "I want *more* than a commitment. I had that much with my mother." She softened her voice. "I want your *love,* Charles. I've spent a lifetime without it. I know now what it's like to feel it. And you . . . you still don't understand how important love is." She bit her lip, determined not to cry, and pushed him away. "Please — go."

He hesitated, took a step forward.

"You don't have to worry about me any-more."

He stood, looking bereft, but saying none of the things that would have changed her mind.

She lifted a palm to his cheek, seeking one last touch. "You deserve a lot more than you think. One day, I hope you'll believe that and find peace."

Her hand fell away. "You know the way out."

Addie deserved love and Charles didn't have it to give. He left by the back stairs, too tired to move with any speed. Every muscle in his body ached, and his brain was numb with fatigue.

But he still had enough presence of mind to go to *The Ledger* by an indirect route, in case some night owl would see him and spread the story, hurting Addie.

As if he hadn't hurt her enough. She'd asked only one thing of him — to love her.

She had no idea what she asked.

His mother had loved his father and look where that had gotten her — years of demeaning treatment and pain. He'd even loved his father once, always hoping Adam Graves would change, but he never did, and Charles's love had withered and died. Replaced with fiery hot anger at his father and, yes, at himself, for being unable to handle the situation he called his family.

Everyone he'd ever loved had hurt him or let him down, even Sam, getting himself killed in a barroom brawl. He believed Addie was different. But what if he didn't have that kind of giving love in him? What if his capacity to love had been destroyed in the place he'd once called home?

Charles entered *The Ledger's* office. His steps, hesitant, unsure. He walked like an old man, probably from the beating he'd taken and given. The printing press sat silent, the energy gone from the room, along with the appeal of the place.

In the back, he knelt before the safe and removed the bullets in the cylinder, then laid the gun and belt inside, shut the door and twirled the lock.

He might have saved Addie from Drummond, but he'd let her down tonight. Just as the selection committee had let down the Grounds children.

Well, there was one thing he *could* do for Addie, for Emma and William. Tonight. He headed out the door.

CHAPTER
TWENTY-ONE

Within minutes Charles had dragged John Sparks and Thaddeus Paul from their beds. Morris Wylie lived too far out to get tonight, but if he needed to, in the morning Charles would be knocking on his door, too.

Once he explained the evening's events, the two men agreed to accompany him to Frances's bedside.

At Doc Lawrence's they found William looking dazed, sitting in the outer office. Mary sat nearby, calm and competent as always, doing what she could to comfort the boy.

Charles gave her a weak smile.

Mary gasped. "What happened to you?"

He looked at William. "I'll tell you later."

Mary nodded, studying first Charles and then the somber faces of his companions.

"How's Frances?" Charles asked.

"About the same. Daddy wrapped her ribs, set her arm and stitched her up." Mary lowered her voice. "He's not sure about her organs."

"Is she conscious?" Mr. Sparks asked.

"Yes, amazingly, she is." She looked at the boy and smiled. "I've been telling William, Frances is a strong woman."

Sparks and Paul went inside to see Frances. Charles lagged behind. He hoped Frances had the strength to tell the men what they needed to know. He couldn't do anything in there. But maybe, like Addie once said, he could help the boy.

Head down, William drooped in the chair, the slump of his shoulders telling Charles plenty. His hair and clothes were disheveled and stained, probably from Frances's blood. Hands clasped tight in his lap, he didn't look injured, at least not on the outside.

Charles sat on his haunches and laid a hand on the boy's shoulder. William flinched. Charles should have known better than to touch him. "I'm Charles Graves, William, a friend of Emma and Miss Crum."

Frightened eyes turned to him and then darted away. William seemed to shrink into himself, trying to be invisible.

Charles's heart tumbled. He knew the signs. Charles removed his hand, giving the boy some distance. "I've been in a bit of a fight, but I'm fine. And Mr. Drummond is in jail."

William turned solemn eyes on him. "He is?"

"Yes. And that's where he's staying." Charles patted his stomach. "I'm starving. Are you hungry?"

William shook his head.

"How about some milk? I bet Doc even has a cookie or two." Charles put out a hand. "Come on. Let's raid the icebox."

William hesitated, his gaze sliding from Mary, to the closed surgery door and then to Charles. His gaze caught, held there and then he rose and stepped beside Charles.

Mary blinked damp eyes. "I'll check on Frances."

Charles and William walked down the hall to Doc's kitchen. Dishes, glasses, half-full cups of cold coffee covered every surface. Addie would have a heyday in here. Nice to know another bachelor in town would fail Addie's neatness test.

Charles found two clean glasses in a cabinet and filled them with milk. Then pulled out a chair for William at the small drop-leaf table and sat beside him. For the second time today, Charles had no idea what to say.

If only he could find the right words, the

words he would have wanted, needed to hear as a boy. "I'm sorry about Mrs. Drummond. She's a good woman."

Turning his glass in his boy-size hands, William nodded.

"It took courage to get her to the doc's."

William's lips pressed in a tight line, but he kept his eyes averted. Still, Charles could see tears well up in pools, though not a single one dropped onto his tanned cheeks.

Charles pushed his untouched glass aside and leaned his chin on his hands. "I know what it's like, William."

The boy didn't look at him, didn't speak.

"I know the fear, the anger. What it's like to try to keep the peace . . . and fail."

"How?" he said softly, head down, spirit wounded.

"I grew up in a home with a pa like Ed Drummond."

William's head snapped up. Charles waited, letting the words connect them, seeing the moment the boy understood.

"I remember how the hair on my neck would rise, how my gut would knot." Charles swallowed against the old familiar lump in his throat. "How I wanted to run, but knew running would only make it worse. It was the same for you, wasn't it?"

Slowly, William nodded.

Charles lifted William's chin with a palm. "I want you to know something else."

The boy's tear-filled eyes, the color of the sea on a cloudy day, met his.

"It wasn't your doing. *None* of it was your fault, William. You were never the reason for what was said or done. *Never.*"

Charles said *never* again and again until a sob tore from William's throat. The tears spilled over now, slipping down William's cheeks in little rivulets, leaving trails on his dirty face. As he wept, William's breath came in gulping hitches.

Charles rose and knelt before the boy, pausing only a second, and then pulled William tight to his chest. For a moment, William held himself stiff, his heart knocking against Charles's torso, and then he burrowed into Charles's arms.

"I was afraid."

"I know. I know." Charles clutched the boy and swayed to the rhythm of remembered pain that branded the mind and spirit.

"I didn't know how to make him stop," William spoke into Charles's shirt.

Old feelings of inadequacy and helplessness roared through him. "Stopping Ed wasn't a job for a boy. It was a man's job."

"I . . . I always made him angry."

Ah, familiar words from his past. "Ed

411

Drummond's sick. Sick in the head and in the heart. Like my pa. His anger had nothing to do with what you did or didn't do. It was *him*." Charles shifted William in his arms and caught his gaze, then repeated, "It was *him*."

William's gaze tumbled away from Charles. "I hate him."

"I know about hate." All too well. Hate lived in him still, gnawing at him, dumping the past on his every today. As surely as he held William, hate held Charles in its clutches.

Suddenly, he knew what else needed to be said to the boy, to himself, the boy he used to be. "When we can, you and I need to forgive. Hating eats us up inside, keeps us from trusting all the good people." Good people like Addie.

The harsh lines in William's face eased, leaving his expression solemn, but perplexed.

He ran his hand through the boy's silky strands. "Forgiving won't be easy."

Though Addie had told him he should, until that moment, Charles hadn't truly comprehended the importance of forgiving. He had to forgive his mother for staying, and then his father for inflicting wounds that might have mended on the outside, but underneath festered still. Until he could forgive, he'd be stuck, unable to move beyond his past.

And so would William.

"What Ed did was wrong, bad," Charles said, "You'll never forget, but you can forgive him because he's ill." His words an echo of what Addie had tried to tell him about his own father.

William swiped at his eyes. "Why's he sick?"

"That's a tough one. I don't know." Would he ever know? Did it even matter?

"Will I . . . will I be sick like him?"

Charles remembered that first day at the schoolhouse, how William had taken Emma's hand and comforted her. This very night, the boy had rescued Frances instead of running. Everyone started out in life with the capacity for good and evil. Some people, like William, served good, while others, like Ed Drummond, served evil.

"No. You're going to be your own man. You can choose what kind of man that will be."

As William clung to him, tears ran down Charles's cheeks. Together they wept for two innocent boys, for William and for the boy Charles had once been. They'd both faced an enemy far bigger than them.

"You're a good boy," Charles crooned, cradling William in his arms. "A good boy."

The words resonated in Charles's head. *He* had been a good boy, no matter how much he'd heard otherwise. He and William had both done the best they could. And they both could choose a new future.

Not only must he forgive his family, Charles knew he must make things right between him and God. Because he knew without a doubt God had saved him — then and now.

Charles turned his gaze upward.

God, I'm hoping You can forgive me for my anger at You, for questioning Your will.

Forgive me for trying to kill my father, for holding on to bitterness, for not worshipping.

Help me make a fresh start. A fresh start with You.

The dark oppressive load slid from Charles's shoulders and in its place came a long-awaited sense of peace. It filled him with surging hope, warm acceptance, calming certainty. And then, he knew without a doubt. He, Charles Graves, a man who didn't deserve it —

God loved, truly loved him.

God had heard. God had answered. God had forgiven.

■ ■ ■ ■

Charles awakened to someone calling his name. He groaned. His entire body throbbed, his throat burned. Then it hit him.

Last night before stumbling into the closest bed, the sagging cot at *The Ledger,* he'd battled Ed Drummond, proposed marriage to Addie and spoken with God.

No ordinary evening.

The rest struck him full force, like an uppercut to his aching jaw. Addie had turned down his proposal. Was it too late to make up for causing her nothing but pain?

And if so, what would he do without her? No other woman measured up to Addie. The most amazing thing of all — *she* loved *him.*

A spark of understanding exploded in him. His pulse tripped and his heart raced in his chest. With every speck of his being, he grasped the truth. He loved her, too.

I'm in love with Addie.

"Charles?"

Clutching his ribs, Charles rose with a groan from the cot and staggered to the door. Roscoe Sullivan took one look at him and blanched. "Charles? You okay?"

"Yeah." Charles crumpled into his desk

chair and sucked in his breath. That hurt. Everything hurt, as if he'd been run over by a wagon and three teams of horses. "What time is it?"

"Almost nine-thirty."

Addie would be awake, getting ready for church. He'd get cleaned up, then make amends. He started to rise. "I'm sorry I can't talk now, Roscoe."

"Wait!" His gaze took in Charles's face, the bruises on his neck. "Ed did that. Those are *his* fingerprints."

All the fear and anger Charles had stowed during Addie's narrow escape slammed into his lungs. "Yes. Your nephew broke into Addie's home and tried to kill her."

"I know." Roscoe dropped into a chair, his head drooping between his shoulders. His face looked haggard, as if he'd aged ten years. "Is Miss Crum all right?"

Charles pulled back from his anger, realizing Roscoe had also suffered. "Yes, just shook up. Ed splashed kerosene all over the shop. He planned to set it on fire after he'd . . ." Charles couldn't finish, couldn't bear to consider what would've happened if he hadn't gotten back.

"Thank God she wasn't harmed. I should have seen . . . what Ed had become. I should have known Frances couldn't be that clumsy." Roscoe's voice quavered and his eyes filled with tears. He swiped them away with the back of his hand and took a shaky breath. "I've been over at Doc's. Frances made it through the night, but she's got a lot of healing to do."

"I hope she makes it." Frances had shown a passel of courage and, thanks to her husband, had endured more pain than a human being should. "I can imagine how tough this is for you, Roscoe. I'm sorry."

"No, I'm the one who's sorry. If only I'd listened to you, somehow I could have stopped this madness." A faraway look came into Roscoe's eyes. His lip trembled. "Ed was the cutest little tyke. I used to take him fishing. We'd sit on the bank along White River and he'd chatter like a magpie. I'd say, 'Little less talking and a little more fishing, boy.' " As he spoke, Roscoe mopped at his tears with his bandanna. "Eddie's death must've made him snap."

Roscoe stuffed his handkerchief into his pocket. "I came to tell you something else. Frances asked the committee to give custody of William and Emma to Miss Crum. The committee agreed." He gave a wan smile. "Those poor kids have been through enough. Staying with Miss Crum will give them stability. I figured you'd like to tell her."

Charles could well imagine the look of pure joy the news would put on Addie's face. Soon as he could get Roscoe out of here, he intended to put another look of joy on her face. That is, if she'd have him.

"I'll try to undo the damage I did to the paper and her reputation." Roscoe hauled himself to his feet. "I'm headed over to the jail to see Ed. I despise what he's done, but I'm all he has."

Charles walked Roscoe to the door. He clamped a hand on the older man's shoulder. "I'm sorry." The words sounded hollow, but he couldn't find better ones.

Roscoe left and Charles's gaze swept over the printing press, the narrow drawers of type and reams of newsprint. Because of his father, he'd come to this town, fulfilled his dream of ownership. How strange Adam Graves had done that for him after all those years of misery.

Stranger still, by making Addie a co-owner of the paper, Adam had put Charles and Addie together. Addie had been right. His father had reached out to him from the grave. And this time he had thought of someone besides himself.

Charles checked the clock. Nine forty-five.

If he hoped to win Addie, he'd have to make sure she didn't doubt his love. She might even make him eat a little crow. He grinned. If so, he deserved a huge helping. And he knew just where he'd find her this bright Sunday morning.

He hadn't shaved, had fought and slept in his rumpled clothes, but he had to do this. Now.

He half ran, half stumbled the three blocks down Ninth Street and skidded to a stop outside the First Christian Church. Worshippers, shocked looks on their faces, parted like the Red Sea to let him pass. Snatches of conversation told him people had heard about last night.

A man Charles didn't know but recognized clapped him on the back. Another hollered, "Good work, Graves!" A third shook his hand. "I'll be taking the paper again, especially if you keep Miss Crum's column."

But he paid no attention. Instead he searched the crowd. Then, he spotted her at the top of the steps, talking to the pastor. Addie. A vision in a blue dress and hat — no birds on this one, he thought with a chuckle, just a simple rose festooned ribbon encircling the crown. Hands resting on Emma's and William's shoulders, her face radiated serenity. His heart lurched in his chest.

"Mr. Graves!" Emma yelled, catching sight of him.

He waved at her, searching for another welcome.

Addie's gaze traveled the assemblage, a puzzled expression on her face. He hurried closer, until he stood at the bottom of the steps. He held his breath, waiting . . . and then her lips curved in a smile, filling him with a sense of rightness.

Oh, how he loved this woman. Her goodness, the hope she'd steadfastly clung to, her strength. He would spend his life trying to live up to her faith in him.

"Miss Adelaide Crum!" Charles called up to her, quieting the crowd. "I'd like the honor of attending church with you and Emma and William."

She extended a hand toward him but he held up his palm. "Before we go in, I have something to say."

Adelaide took in Charles's battered, smiling face and her insides went liquid with hope. Around her, puffy white clouds drifted across the sky, and a flash of red disappeared into a nearby evergreen. A gentle breeze tickled her nape as the cardinal added his song to the song in her heart.

Charles laid a palm on his chest. "I'm in love with you!" he shouted up at her.

Adelaide's heart leapt at the words she'd been waiting for all her life, the words she needed to hear from Charles.

"I want to share our dreams, bring up these children and grow old together." He released a shaking breath. "I've been able to forgive. I've asked God to forgive me. And though I have no idea why, He has! I'll be thanking Him this morning — in church — for His love and for yours, that is, if it's still available."

Tears sprang in Adelaide's eyes. At last, Charles realized God loved him. He wanted to worship in church. He loved her.

She wished for the words that would change her life, yet waited to see if the editor in him could string together words strong enough to rope her in. Not that it would take much, she decided with an inward grin.

"Oh, and one more thing." He paused. Her heart beat a hundred times in that moment. "Will you marry me?"

She folded her arms across her middle, a tease on her lips. "Not unless you ask me proper."

Charles took the steps two at a time. At her feet, he went down on one knee, raising

421

an arm in a beseeching manner, triggering a few chuckles from the men and dreamy sighs from the ladies.

Adelaide had to hold herself tight to keep from throwing her arms around his neck. Waiting, every moment slowed to a crawl.

"Adelaide Crum, will you do me the great honor of becoming my wife?"

"Yes!" she cried, the word bursting from her lips. "Yes, Charles, I'll marry you!"

A cheer rose up from the congregation and Emma danced around Adelaide's skirts as the reality sank in — she and Charles would spend the rest of their lives together. After years of loneliness, God had given her the desires of her heart.

When the hubbub subsided, Charles's gaze sought the children's. "Emma, William, is it all right with you?"

At Adelaide's side, William's face lit up like a Roman candle. Emma threw her arms around Charles's neck and hugged him with all her might, until she squeaked.

Over the little girl's head, Charles gaze sought Adelaide's with an intensity that promised he'd be there today, tomorrow and always, that they'd be a family, a real family. Slowly, he rose, scooping up Emma, never taking his eyes off Adelaide.

He pulled William close, then took her

hand, his grip firm, and faced the minister. "I've been away a long time, Pastor. Do you suppose God will remember my name?"

Pastor Foley smiled, his hazel eyes crinkling. "Not only your name, but the exact number of hairs on your head."

Charles nodded. "He's probably been tempted plenty of times to pull out a hank."

The pastor chuckled. "Good thing God doesn't work that way or we'd all be bald."

Smiling, Charles tugged Addie close. "It looks like we're going to need your services."

Pastor Foley gave an approving nod. "Whenever you say."

"I hear July twenty-fifth is a special woman's birthday."

"How did you know?" Adelaide asked.

"I told him!" Laura threw her arms around Adelaide and then lowered her voice. "Thank God you're both all right! My knees ache from praying!"

Pastor Foley pulled out his pocket watch, and flipped it open. "Well, I'd better get this service underway." He smiled. "See you inside."

Parishioners flowed past, heading into the church, stopping long enough to give them congratulations. The men slapped Charles on the back and the women hugged Adelaide, some with tears welling in their eyes.

Mr. Paul came up beside them, the tufts of hair on his head swaying in the breeze. "With a strong woman like Miss Crum, you're going to have your hands full, Graves."

"I wouldn't have it any other way."

"A woman like that keeps a man from making some serious mistakes." His gaze met Adelaide's. "Like the ones I've made. I'm sorry, Miss Crum."

This whole town needed a lesson in forgiveness, starting here. Adelaide laid a hand on his arm. "You're forgiven," she said then watched him enter the building.

Everyone in town, well, at least, the membership of the First Christian Church, appeared happy for them.

Roscoe Sullivan climbed the steps last, slowly, as if he didn't have the strength to go on. He stopped before Adelaide, his gaze downcast. "I'm sorry for the trouble I caused you."

Mr. Sullivan had tried to turn the town against her, but if she couldn't forgive him, would she be any different than her mother? He had been taken in by his nephew, as had most of the town. Adelaide gave him a smile. "I accept your apology and hope you'll visit William and Emma. They could use a grandfather."

For a moment Roscoe stood speechless. "I — I'm grateful for your clemency."

"It took me a while to learn to forgive, Mr. Sullivan," Adelaide admitted, glancing in the direction of the cemetery. "But forgiving feels awfully good."

As the bell tolled, announcing the start of the service, everyone had entered the church. "Alone at last," Charles said, bending down and giving her a tender kiss. "Despite the bird in your hat, I love you, Adelaide Crum."

Adelaide gave him a playful punch on the arm. "Despite the mess on your desk, I love you, Charles Graves."

The first hymn drowned out their laughter.

Charles's expression grew serious and he hauled her to him. "I love you," he said, his voice husky with emotion.

She'd never tire of hearing those words from his lips.

She would hear his voice today, tomorrow and all the tomorrows after that, confident she had found the person God intended for her, for them both.

"You know, Charles, it's like my heart was an orphan . . . and it's found a home. In you."

"Oh, Addie, I'm going to spend the rest

of my life showing you how wonderful home can be."

His words were a promise for all the days to come.

Dear Reader,
After coming across a newspaper article about trains that took orphaned and half-orphaned children from New York City to homes in the Midwest and beyond, I knew I had to put this fascinating slice of history in a book. Between the years 1853 and 1929, approximately 250,000 children rode to new homes. But that phenomenon didn't find its way into our history books for years. Although I've taken creative liberties with the facts, I set the story in Noblesville, Indiana, where an orphan train stopped in 1859.

Thank you for choosing *Courting Miss Adelaide,* my debut novel. I hope you enjoyed Adelaide and Charles's story as much as I enjoyed writing it. And I hope that their struggle to overcome painful pasts and to forgive others touched your heart. If you're dealing with similar issues, I hope God will enable you to find the peace that comes from forgiving someone who wounded you.

I love to hear from readers. Visit me at www.JanetDean.net or JanetDean.blogspot.com. Write to me at Janet@JanetDean.net.

God bless you,
Janet Dean

QUESTIONS FOR DISCUSSION

1. Charles and Adelaide had difficult childhoods. How did their pasts impact their behavior? Their outlook? Can you identify with their struggles?

2. How did Charles's father affect Charles's relationship with God? Have you had relationships that impacted your faith, either positively or negatively?

3. How does Emma help Adelaide grow and change?

4. Charles's father leaves half the newspaper to Charles and half to Adelaide. How does his will affect Charles and Adelaide's relationship, both short-term and in the long run?

5. Writing the columns on suffrage helps Adelaide find her voice as a woman,

something few women had in the 1890s.
How do the consequences of her stand
shape her as a woman and as a Christian?

6. Why can't Charles see the possibility of
William's abuse at first?

7. How does Charles's talk with William
help to heal the pain of Charles's past and
lead him to God?

8. What secret is Charles hiding? How does
that affect his relationship with Adelaide?
With God? What finally puts Charles's fear
to rest?

9. Neither Charles's mother nor Frances
Drummond leave their abusive husbands.
Is this difficult for you to understand? Why
or why not?

10. How does the town influence the decisions of Adelaide and Charles? And how
do Adelaide's and Charles's decisions
impact the town? What can we learn from
this?

11. Do you have any sympathy for Ed
Drummond? Why or why not?

12. How do you think the orphaned children felt when they were traveling across the country to unknown families?

ABOUT THE AUTHOR

Janet Dean grew up in a family that cherished the past and had a strong creative streak. Her father recounted wonderful stories, like his father before him. The tales they told instilled in Janet a love of history and the desire to write. She married her college sweetheart and taught first grade before leaving to rear two daughters. As her daughters grew, they watched *Little House on the Prairie,* reawakening Janet's love of American history and the stories of strong men and women of faith who built this country. Janet eagerly turned to inspirational historical romance and loves spinning stories for Love Inspired Historical. When she isn't writing, Janet stamps greeting cards, plays golf and bridge, and is never without a book to read. The Deans love to travel and to spend time with family.

The employees of Thorndike Press hope you have enjoyed this Large Print book. All our Thorndike, Wheeler, and Kennebec Large Print titles are designed for easy reading, and all our books are made to last. Other Thorndike Press Large Print books are available at your library, through selected bookstores, or directly from us.

For information about titles, please call:
  (800) 223-1244

or visit our Web site at:
  http://gale.cengage.com/thorndike

To share your comments, please write:
  Publisher
  Thorndike Press
  295 Kennedy Memorial Drive
  Waterville, ME 04901